THE SAINTS' AND ANGELS' SONG

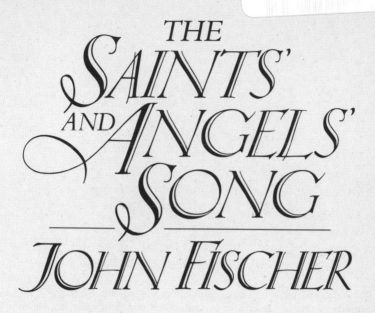

JOHN FISCHER

BETHANY HOUSE PUBLISHERS
MINNEAPOLIS, MINNESOTA 55438

Cover by Dan Thornberg,
Bethany House Publishers staff artist.

Published by Bethany House Publishers
A Ministry of Bethany Fellowship, Inc.
11300 Hampshire Avenue South
Minneapolis, Minnesota 55438

Printed in the United States of America.

Library of Congress Cataloging-in-Publication Data

Fischer, John, 1947–
    The saints' and angels' song / John Fischer.
       p.   cm.
    Sequel to: Saint Ben.

    I. Title.
PS3556.I762S255   1994
813'.54—dc20   94–25132
ISBN 1–55661–474–8   CIP

What people are saying about *Saint Ben*

"Absolutely loved *Saint Ben* . . . was moved to tears several times. Your characters are beautifully constructed, the anecdotes real, and the honoring of each person's soul-search-for-integrity brilliant . . . comparable in impact but more emotionally powerful than John Irving's *A Prayer for Owen Meany* . . . a well-paced, continually engaging and captivating piece of business."

Noel Paul Stookey

"John Fischer has created a cast of lovable characters, a plot that twists and turns, and poignant commentary on legalistic Christianity in his first novel, *Saint Ben*."

Moody Monthly

"Combines a realistic setting, little-boy delight, humor, and the gift of surprise."

Terry Whalin, *Bookstore Journal*

"I just finished recording *Saint Ben* for release on our twenty-station network. As I recorded the last episode, I struggled. I would read for a few minutes . . . stop and cry . . . turn on the recorder . . . read for a few minutes more. I had to stop several times   [John] is a great storyteller."

Wayne Pederson,
Executive Director
Skylight Satellite Network

"Delightful!"

Phyllis Tickle, *Publishers Weekly*

"*Saint Ben* will leave you laughing, choking back tears, and best of all, thirsting for the real faith of a nine-year-old. Fischer's style, wit, and wisdom are a welcome addition to Christian fiction."

Phil Callaway, *Servant* magazine,
Prairie Bible Institute

Books by John Fischer

Making Real What I Already Believe
Real Christians Don't Dance
Saint Ben
The Saints' and Angels' Song
True Believers Don't Ask Why

See that you do not look down on one of these little ones. For I tell you that their angels in heaven always see the face of my Father in heaven.

—The Gospel of Matthew

Our Jane has climbed the golden stair
    And passed the jasper gates;
Henceforth she will have wings to wear,
    Instead of roller skates.

—*Harper's Weekly*, 1890

Contents

Summer 1959

The roof went easily; it was not properly braced. The walls were surprisingly strong under my foot, however. It seemed, for a second, that I could almost stand on them. But the balsa wood two-by-fours were simply not strong enough for my eleven-year-old weight and they quickly gave in with a loud "Crunch!" I stepped back and surveyed the path of destruction that cut a swath through the entryway, half the kitchen, and most of the living room. And then, my cheeks hot with rage, I jumped and stomped on the rest of my cherished model house with both feet. There was a loud protest of crackling and popping and flying beams, but the tiny timbers were no match for my anger. In an instant it was leveled—a year of painstaking and loving attention to every detail, gone in seconds. I jumped and jumped until the pounding of my tennis shoes returned no sound but empty thuds.

The car was next. I knew it would be harder because it was made of metal, but at least the wheels would break off and perhaps the doors would bend so they would no longer work. I was just about to jump when my mother ran into the room.

"Jonathan! What are you doing? Oh my!" She whisked the car up off the floor, setting the wheels spinning in the air.

"Enough!" she said. "This has got to stop. You can't get rid of your memories of Ben this way."

I wanted to cry but no tears would come.

She reached out to try and hold me, but I turned and left the room without speaking.

1

The Bunker

The house where I grew up in Eagle Rock, California, was only a forty-five minute drive from Huntington Beach. I know that now, but to a thirteen-year-old in 1961 it might as well have been Naples, Florida, or the French Riviera we went to in the summer, because that was how far away Huntington Beach seemed to me then. It was a world away from the small neighborhood streets of Eagle Rock with their curbs and sidewalks and driveways that bumped under the wheels of my bike with methodic regularity.

My life at that time consisted of repeatedly traversing three well-worn paths. I walked up and down the block to and from my eighth grade classroom at Washington Elementary; I zigzagged my bike daily over the 3.3 mile maze that was my paper route; and at least a half dozen times a week I rode along on the ten-minute drive to our church in Pasadena in the family car. The only variation on that last theme was whether my father would take San Marino Avenue or Santa Anita Boulevard to get to church. "Let's take Santa Anita today!" he would say with an air of excitement that made you think we were about to embark on a hot-air balloon trip around the world. "That sounds like a good idea, dear!" my mother would say.

I was convinced that our '57 Ford had probably worn a

groove in the pavement between our house and the Colorado Avenue Standard Christian Church in Pasadena where my father was the choir director. In fact, the blue and white Fairlane could probably drive to church and back on its own.

That's why I could hardly contain myself as I sat in the backseat of the Wendorfs' silver Thunderbird watching the orange groves slowly give way to the encroaching motels, gas stations, and hamburger stands of Beach Boulevard as we inched our way in heavy summer-vacation traffic toward the Pacific Ocean. This was one week in my year that seemed like a whole year in and of itself.

For the last two years, Huntington Beach had become a symbol of freedom and adventure, beyond the bounds of my neighborhood streets and the control of parents and church. Two summers ago, Matt Wendorf had chosen me to be his guest for a week at Huntington Beach, where his parents rented the same apartment for two weeks every summer and Matt was allowed to invite a friend for the first seven days. I don't know why he chose me in particular—we were not the best of friends, except for this week together—but he did. This was the third summer he had invited me.

"Doggone this traffic!" said Mr. Wendorf. But I didn't mind. There was too much to see. As far as I was concerned, we couldn't drive slowly enough to take it all in. It seemed to me that every wood-paneled Ford ever made between 1950 and 1952 had found its way to Beach Boulevard with a surfboard or two on top or one sticking out the rear window. Occasionally a greaser on a big Harley Davidson would rumble in between lanes of traffic, invoking a similar "doggoning" from Mr. Wendorf.

If I received a punch in my side from Matt, it was because there was probably a pretty girl somewhere in sight. And thus inspired, Matt would break into a strain of "Itsy Bitsy, Teenie Weenie, Yellow Polka-Dot Bikini" as Mrs. Wendorf kept objecting from the front seat: "Matthew! That's not an appropriate song for a Christian young man to be singing!"

"Aw, leave him alone, Bernice," Mr. Wendorf would say. "Let the kid have some fun." Proving, of course, that Mr. Wendorf truly wished he was the one who could have some fun, something it appeared he hadn't had in a long time, if ever.

Mr. and Mrs. Wendorf were always disagreeing about how much fun Matt should or should not be allowed to have, along with mostly everything else that had to do with raising him. This made for an environment where Matt could pretty much get away with anything, as he had become a master at pitting his parents against each other.

Matt's father was a gruff man who seemed to belong to my grandfather's generation. His rather large nose resembled a road map of broken veins that had lost their sense of direction. He had a mean face and a demeanor to go with it that could occasionally sparkle with wit. But his deadpan humor made it hard to tell whether he was serious or joking; he had the same look on his face either way. Consequently, I never knew when to laugh or shut up, so I generally kept my mouth closed when he spoke.

Mrs. Wendorf had a personality about the consistency of Jell-O. Shake it and it would wiggle; push on it and it would cave in entirely.

Matt was adopted and made no bones about it. He spoke of his parents in a rather distant way, often calling them by their first names. In their presence he gave them the courtesy of "Mom" and "Dad," but when we were away from them, it was always "Leonard" and "Bernice." It seemed odd hearing someone refer to his parents by their first names. I had never heard anyone else do that before. Also, Matt spoke of them the way I might speak about my grandparents, although that became understandable when I realized they were old enough to be just that.

As we got closer to the beach, my excitement was tempered by a growing apprehension. Of all the adventures I had experienced in the last two summers at Huntington Beach, the most prominent in my memory was being kissed by a girl named Margaret on the last day of my visit the previous year. Matt didn't know about it. I knew if I told him, I would never hear the end of it, and whatever was right about it—and I wasn't sure at the time if there was anything, but at least whatever *might* have been right about it—would undoubtedly have been ruined by Matthew Wendorf. Matt seemed to think about nothing but girls and how close you could get to them, which for him was never very close at all.

So there was no one to tell about the kiss, which probably made it a bigger deal in my mind than it was. I knew this, and I tried not to think about it so much, but the more I tried not to, the more I thought about it, until the kiss filled up all I could remember about being in Huntington Beach the year before, even though it had happened in the last few hours before I left. And the closer we got to the beach, the more it grew in my mind.

Questions kept flooding my mind. *Will she be there again this year? Will she remember kissing me?* And, most importantly: *What will I do when I see her?*

I had actually come surprisingly close to not even coming with the Wendorfs because of this, except that I started thinking about bodysurfing and getting a tan and hanging out with Matt and being able to do whatever I wanted, and my good sense had finally won over.

"Hit the road, Jack, and don't you come back no more, no more, no more, no more—" Matt had grown tired of being harassed over teenie weenie bikinis and changed the song. You hardly needed a radio around him. He was a walking jukebox, always up on the latest Top Ten. He said he wanted to be a DJ some day. Happy for a distraction from my apprehension, I joined him, and we started singing and bouncing in rhythm in the backseat, "Hit the road, Jack, and don't you come back no more. . . ."

That song, and repeated versions of it, took us the rest of the way to the apartment only two blocks from the beach. As soon as Mr. Wendorf had pulled into the alley behind the apartment and stopped the car, Matt and I climbed out of the backseat and headed straight for the sand.

"Not so fast, you two," shouted Mr. Wendorf. "You've got a whole week for that. Help us unload this stuff."

A whole week! I thought as I wrestled a big Wendorf suitcase up the pink stairs to the second-floor apartment. Right then, the whole week seemed pretty much like the rest of my life.

Matt and I ran around the apartment checking all the rooms to make sure they were just as we had left them the year before and ended up out on the upper deck. From there you could see the coastline all the way from the Huntington pier, south, to the weird World War II bunker that rose out of the sand to the north like an ancient ruin.

Mr. Wendorf told us that lots of these bunkers had been built along the coastline during the war to protect California from a Japanese attack. The war was over before this particular one was ever completed, and all that remained was an empty shell—the relic of a fear that never materialized. It made for an ideal place to play, though at times it felt eerie being there and imagining guns and ammunition piled up around you and bombs falling overhead. The whole idea of a California beach being a target of war meant nothing to me. The only thing I knew about World War II was that the "Japs" were the bad guys, featured mostly in jokes about Kamikaze pilots. What did mean something, however, was the fact that the bunker was where Margaret had kissed me.

We had been playing hide-and-seek when it happened. Matt was "it," and Margaret and I had both ended up hiding in the bunker. Then, without any warning at all, she just up and kissed me, right on the lips. It came out of nowhere and was over just as quickly.

Now, as I stood on the deck, the smell of sea breezes and sight of the coastline freshened my memories of Margaret. She wasn't what I would call pretty, but she had a cute smile and a sassy way about her that was kind of attractive. That sassy part could be a little bossy sometimes, like my older sister. But Margaret was fun, too. She was a tomboy and had played with Matt and me most every day the past two summers. She and her family were always there for the whole summer, so she knew all the great places—like the bunker, the abandoned lighthouse, the old pier that was half washed away, and where to buy the best snow cones in town. She even taught us how to bodysurf and how to play gin rummy. I never would have learned how to play gin from any of my Christian friends, since Christians weren't supposed to play cards. I wasn't sure why. Something evil about the pictures I think.

That's what had bothered me about kissing Margaret, though, apart from the fact that I had never been kissed before except by my mother and my sister (on the forehead, of course). Margaret wasn't a Christian, at least I didn't think she was, and I was always told never to be unequally yoked with unbelievers. I wasn't sure exactly what "unequally yoked" meant, but I had an idea kissing might have something to do with it. Suddenly I realized that I didn't really like Margaret. I *liked* her, but not in a kissing sort of way. It's just that a whole year to think about that one kiss had thrown everything about her into a different light. Now, closer to all these memories, it seemed clearer to me, and I decided, right then and there, that any more kissing ideas were definitely out. I wasn't even very excited about seeing her anymore. Matt broke in on my thoughts.

"Let's hit the beach!" he said, and we spent the rest of the afternoon diving in the surf like seals set free from captivity, remembering how to ride the waves and roll on our bellies and backs in the sun. For a while, I forgot all about Margaret.

"You boys did it again!" said Bernice after we had our showers late in the afternoon. "No suntan lotion on your first day out. You should have your heads examined."

She was right, but neither one of us would admit it. It was

great to get out of the shower and feel clean and hot all over. I looked at my red chest in the mirror and imagined it the color of bronze.

"Mom, we need some money for soda pop."

"There's plenty of pop in the refrigerator, dear."

"But it's not the kind we want. May I just have some money?"

Matt got a handful of change from his mother, and we made our way out the alley to Ocean Avenue. There was a liquor store two blocks down from the apartment where we always got a six-pack of Vernor's ginger ale and a bag of pretzels. Matt was the one who introduced me to Vernor's, and because of that I always associate it with the beach. Vernor's had at least twice the ginger flavor of other ginger ales, and because of that we always imagined we were drinking something stronger than mere soda pop. I'm sure we could have found Vernor's at the local supermarket near my home, but I never even asked for it. That would have spoiled everything. Vernor's was for the deck of Matt's Huntington Beach apartment, where we sat drinking and eating pretzels and playing gin rummy as the sun set over the Pacific. It's the way we spent every night at the beach.

Getting ginger ale at a liquor store added to the mystique and adventure. I never would have entered a liquor store at home. As far as my parents were concerned, a liquor store qualified as a den of iniquity. Once when my family was on vacation, my father had to go into a liquor store to make a phone call because our car had broken down and it was the only pay phone in town. He complained for the next day and a half about how dirty he felt in there. I have to admit, I felt a little dirty in there with Matt, but that merely added to the feeling of recklessness that was an important part of this whole vacation experience—drinking Vernor's and played cards and carousing on the beach.

And talking about girls, which Matt could do to excess.

"Wow, look at the beauties out tonight," he said on the

way back to the apartment, sporting his one-track mind. "Two weeks to enjoy the view." Upon saying that, he rushed up behind three high school girls ahead of us and began swinging his hips, mimicking their walk, until I wanted to find a hole to hide in.

"Hey, come on. Have a little fun," he said, walking back to me and noticing my displeasure. "I know, let's see if we can find any teenie weenie bikinis."

There actually were not many bikinis to be seen. The song was out and the magazines were full of models wearing them, but not many girls had the nerve to wear one in public.

"No, let's go back to your deck and play cards," I countered.

"I wonder if Margaret will be wearing a bikini this year."

I chose to completely ignore that comment.

"Come on," said Matt, "you can't tell me you never thought about Margaret in a bikini."

Now if I had spoken the first thought that came into my head, I would have said something about Margaret not having anything to put in a bikini yet, but I kept that comment to myself and told Matt that the thought had never crossed my mind, which of course was a lie.

"We didn't see her at the beach today," he went on. "Maybe she's not here. She's always at the beach."

"I saw someone that looked a little like her," I said, "but she was much older and she was hanging out with a bunch of high school guys. It almost made me wonder if she had an older sister."

"Well, she *is* older than us," Matt said, and with that I realized I didn't know how old Margaret was. I didn't even know her last name.

"How do you know she's older?"

"I just know."

"How much older do you think she is?"

"She'd be fifteen now."

"Fifteen? How do you know that?"

"She told me she was fourteen last year."

A knot formed in my throat. I had no idea she was that old. *Fifteen?* My *sister* was fifteen! Suddenly I thought of the changes that had recently rendered Becky a different person. My mother explained it by saying that her daughter had jumped from twelve to eighteen in the course of a year and never stopped once along the way. If anything close to this had happened to Margaret in her fifteenth year, it would render new meaning to the thought of her in a bikini. This must have been what Matt was thinking of. But the more I thought about this the more scared I became, especially about being kissed by someone as old as my sister. Maybe Matt was right. Maybe Margaret wasn't here at all, or if she was, she probably wouldn't want to have anything to do with us anymore. That's the way Becky would be if she were here. I began hoping that Margaret wasn't in Huntington Beach, and as I fell asleep later that night, I couldn't get a certain thought out of my mind. *What if the older girl I had seen was actually her?*

——————

The next two days went by at a lazy pace. The first half of the week always seemed to go on forever as we surfed and sunned and played in the bunker, then settled back each evening at twilight with a six-pack of Vernor's and playing cards on the deck of the beach house apartment. We were creatures of habit, Matt and I, and I loved this habit.

By the third day I had decided that Margaret must not be hanging around Huntington Beach at all this year. I hadn't even seen the older girl who looked like her. So by the fourth day I had pretty much dismissed both my hopes and fears about our meeting. That's why it was a huge surprise when, on the fifth day of summer vacation, I came in wet from the water and found a beautiful girl sitting on my towel. When she saw me coming, she stood up and looked nervously around her.

"Hi, Jonathan," she said, biting her lip. "I'm sorry to have been ignoring you. Look . . . I can't talk right now, but . . . here."

She handed me a folded piece of paper, and for an instant we both held on to it. I knew the exact distance between our fingertips without looking. Then her face broke into a quick smile and she turned and walked up the beach.

Matt came up behind me, dripping and panting. "Who was *that?*" he said as we both watched her gracefully navigate the uneven sand. At that moment she turned and gave a cute little wave with a cupped hand.

I couldn't speak. She was not wearing a bikini, but she could have if she had wanted to.

"You were *talking* to her?"

I only nodded. *She knew me. She knew my name. She sounded like Margaret; she didn't look like Margaret.*

"Wow," Matt managed, his mouth hanging open and his eyes as big as saucers.

"Wow," I echoed. We both stared as she joined up with a group of high school kids and disappeared up the beach.

"What did she give you? Is it a note? What does it say?"

We sat down and I unfolded the piece of paper and read it out loud: "Meet me at noon tomorrow in the bunker. Signed, Margaret."

Matt fell over backwards, flat out on his towel.

"Pinch me. I'm dreaming."

"It can't be," I said. "That wasn't Margaret. That was someone posing as Margaret."

"Of course it was Margaret," said Matt. "She gave you the note. Did she say anything?"

"Something about being sorry about ignoring us . . . but I can't believe it was her."

"It was her," said Matt, "and we're gonna meet her to-morrow! Think of that! Wow, what a babe she turned into!"

"I'm not going," I said matter-of-factly.

"What?" he said, sitting back up suddenly like a surfboard stuck in the sand.

"I'm not going," I repeated.

"Why? What's wrong with you? Are you crazy or something?"

"What do you suppose she wants to meet us in the bunker for? She's so much older now. Didn't you see those guys she's running around with?"

"Yeah, but she ran around with us for the last two years. She probably just wants to see us again. Come on, Jonathan. I'm going, even if you're not. I wouldn't miss this for anything."

"Well, okay," I said. The prospect of Matt and Margaret alone in the bunker didn't set well with me. Especially *this* Margaret, whoever she was.

"Now you're talking," said Matt.

It didn't take long for all my fantasies about that kiss to return. The anticipation of meeting this new Margaret had given them substance. Matt was right; we had been an inseparable threesome the last two years. But I was the one she had kissed. At least I didn't think she'd kissed Matt. No, he would have told me. Probably would have stopped everyone on the street and told them too!

After my shower that night I noticed my chest. All the red had already turned bronze, and my hair was lighter and more shiny—bleached from the saltwater and the sun. We had our usual date with Vernor's and pretzels, and the colors of the sunset seemed exceptionally deep that evening as they reflected off the walls and objects on the deck—even Matt's round face, though it was hard to find anything deep about that. All talk, of course, had to do with Margaret.

"Why do you suppose she wants to meet us?" Matt kept repeating.

You mean meet *me*, I kept thinking.

Though I wanted to talk about Margaret—she was all I could think about—I realized, as I washed a pretzel down with a swig of ginger ale, that it wasn't Matt I wanted to talk to. Somebody, but not Matt. The more Matt and I talked about Margaret, the more I found myself wanting to keep my feelings to myself. Matt had a way of turning everything about girls into something ugly.

"Hey, come on, Matt," I finally said, "it's just Margaret. We played with her all last year, remember? You're talking like she's suddenly some kind of sex goddess or something."

"Yeah," said Matt, chugging a lug of ginger ale and wiping his lips. "That's just the point. She's turned into one, but she's still just Margaret to us. Imagine what we could get away with."

"Matt, cut it out! Don't talk like that! I like Margaret and I don't just want to get away with something."

"Hey," said Matt, "don't get so sensitive. Can't you take a joke?"

"This is nothing to joke about."

I started wishing that I wasn't meeting Margaret with Matt, but then I remembered that he was all talk and no action when it came to girls. It was probably a good thing, since I was still scared about meeting her to begin with, and would be even more scared about meeting her alone.

Those fears came out in my dreams that night. I dreamed that my sister, Becky, was telling me to look out for older girls, and then I saw Margaret, bigger than life, squeezing a bug-eyed Matthew in her huge hands. He was wiggling and screaming for help. That's when I woke up.

The next morning Matt and I were at the bunker by 11:30. It was an exceptionally hot day, but the bunker was always ten to fifteen degrees cooler than the outside. They called them the Bolsa Chica bunkers (there are actually two of them, but the other, smaller one was farther up the coast), and I always thought that was an odd name. It reminded me of the balsa wood model of a house I made once with a friend and how I regretted smashing it later after he died.

The bunker consisted of a long, wide central hallway that ran parallel to the coastline, with entrances from the north and the south. Off the hallway were the barracks and rooms for storing ammunition and supplies. The hallway was long enough to seem like a tunnel, especially if you were in the middle of it. From there, a small rectangle of light was barely visible at either end. It was such a strange and private place, with rooms that we imagined were living quarters for the soldiers and places to store ammunition. The walls must have been at least six feet thick and the ceiling was more than twice that.

"Boy, you could live through anything in here," Matt said, his voice much quieter than usual. It was the same thing he said almost every time we walked into the bunker.

We always got quiet when we first walked in—almost like walking into church. The bunker shut out the sounds of the people on the beach. All you could hear was the faint crashing of the surf.

Talking in the bunker was a little like talking in a tube. Our voices echoed, and Matt and I liked to get on either end of the long hallway and whisper to each other. The dark calm of this place reminded me of a bell tower in our church where I used to sneak away from everybody, especially adults. It was a special place I shared once with a friend, but I had not been up there for a long time.

All similarities with church stopped with the walls. They were covered with writing, pictures, sayings of every kind, and people's names, like "Ralph was here," or "Tom loves Sally." Matt especially liked the more colorful entries, and reading the wall together became a contest each year to see who could find the grossest thing. I always looked for dates because people often put the date next to their name.

"Here's one from 1952," my voice echoed down the tube.

"What's it say?"

" 'Go Ike.' "

"Now *that's* exciting," exaggerated Matt. "Boy, you should see this picture over here." He turned his head sideways. "This guy can draw! What I want to know is: How do you even get your body to do that?"

I didn't want to know. That was the part I didn't like about the bunkers. There were things on the walls that made me want to see them, and then wish I hadn't once I had. Things I found out that I would rather not have known.

"Sooner or later we're gonna have to know about this stuff," Matt would say. "Might as well know about it now. Sure not going to hear about it from Leonard and Bernice."

He was right about that. I knew I wouldn't hear anything about sex from my parents either. We never talked about it at home. I had actually received the bulk of my sex education from the walls of the bunker in the last two years. I figured a lot out from the pictures. I once had a friend I could talk to about these things, but not Matt. He turned anything about sex into a bad joke, like the writings on the wall.

Each summer Matt, Margaret, and I had followed the progress of this graffiti, like time-traveling archaeologists studying what would be the future "cave art" of a lost generation. Each year the writing toward the ends of the tunnel grew more dense as people filled up every available space. Those who wanted more room to spread out their messages and works of art used the area farther in, where there were more open spaces, probably because the light was so dim.

Margaret had even figured out how much the writing moved every year. She measured it from each end with her steps, and based on the average movement over the years she had been there, she calculated that the whole tunnel would be filled up by 1965.

To make her calculations, she had to take into account a small area in the dark, dead center of the tunnel that was filling up much more slowly, but gradually working its way out from the center. These people must have taken the trouble to bring a flashlight in order to put their messages in the belly of the bunker, for whatever reason.

"They probably didn't want anybody to read what they wrote," Matt had said last year.

"But these are the ones that are the most worth reading," I said.

"I know," said Margaret. "These are the people who have something important to say, and they don't want just anybody looking at it. They want you to have to put out some effort to get to it."

We all had agreed that her explanation was the most reasonable. This graffiti was less likely to be seen, so these were probably the more private people. There were hardly any dirty pictures in the middle. People with those interests seemed to be the type who wanted to be sure they had more of an audience.

This time, Matt and I got to the bunker early, partly to be sure and not miss Margaret, and partly to check out the new entries in the center of the hallway. Matt had the flashlight.

"Shine it over here," I said.

There was considerably more writing than I remembered from the year before. A good deal of it was political, having to do with President Kennedy's election and his first year in office.

"What was the Bay of Pigs, anyway?" I said as we surveyed the wall by flashlight.

"It was a whole bunch of people having a big party on the beach and 'pigging out' on lots of food!" said Matt.

I should have expected something like that from him.

"Wait a minute. What was that? Shine the light back over here." I had seen something as Matt panned the flashlight.

When the light came back, I saw it again. There, right in the middle of the middle, were the words: "Ben was here."

"Hold it right there," I said.

"What are you looking at?"

" 'Ben was here.' "

"So? So was Ralph and Tom and Marvin and Susan . . . come on over here, I saw something really boss—"

"No-no, wait! Let me look at this a little more."

"What is it, Jonathan? What's the big deal? There have

probably been a whole bunch of Bens who have been here in the last fifteen years. What's so special about this one?"

"It's just that there's something about the handwriting. If I didn't know he was dead, I'd say that was Ben Beamering's writing for sure. He always made his *B*'s like that. Look how the middle line that cuts it in half doesn't come all the way in to the vertical one."

"Yeah. Looks like a nice set of—"

"Matt! Can't you ever think of anything else? . . . And look at the *N*. It's backwards. The diagonal line goes from bottom to top instead of top to bottom. It was always strange to me that he would make *N*'s like that when he was so smart. He made that same *N* in front of the whole church once. Remember?"

"Jonathan, if Ben Beamering was here, he would have had to have written this at least three summers ago. How come you haven't seen it until now? It's just a coincidence . . . some other Ben with the same way of writing his name."

"Maybe, but I don't think so. I'd know this writing anywhere. This is the writing of Ben Beamering. Maybe Margaret will know something about this."

"Speaking of Margaret, it's after twelve. We'd better head back to the entrance."

We went to the south entrance of the bunker and waited in the shade just inside the opening. Ironic, how in finding the writing on the wall, I had run into the one thing capable of getting my mind off Margaret, the one thing that would put this meeting in perspective. I began to imagine what Ben would say if he were here. Then I realized he probably wouldn't even be here in the first place. He would think this was pretty ridiculous: two thirteen-year-old boys waiting to meet a fifteen-going-on-eighteen-year-old girl in a place they used to play. What were we expecting? That she would play war with us in the bunker?

I started to feel kind of stupid. And when Matt pointed

out that it was 12:30 and we'd probably been stood up, I felt even more stupid.

"Look," Matt said right then, "someone's coming!"

Sure enough, someone was walking briskly toward the bunker. Someone in a sundress. Someone, who, as she got closer, made me wonder if my pounding heart could be heard outside my chest. There was something about the way she walked that made me wish Margaret would never get here. I'd be content just to watch her walk.

"Hi, you guys, I'm glad you're still here."

"Hi," we both said, in a kind of daze.

"What are you doing?"

"Nothing much," I said. It was obvious that Matt and I had not given one thought to what we would do when Margaret arrived. We just stood there awkwardly, not knowing what to do with ourselves.

Margaret did a twirl and sidestepped into the bunker, looking at the writing on the walls.

"There's a lot more this year, isn't there?" she said brightly.

"Yeah," said Matt.

"There's hardly any more room left right here at the entrance," I said, surprised that my voice sounded so high. It had been much lower for the last few months, but right then, when I needed it the most, my future, grown-up voice eluded me completely. It made me not want to speak at all, but I did anyway. "They're going to have to start writing on top of each other." *Did that make sense?* I wondered.

"They're already doing that at the other end," Margaret said, confirming, to my relief, that it did.

"Have you guys been to the middle yet?"

"No. I . . . I mean, yes," I said nervously. My new voice was trying to make a comeback, but the old one would not let go, making them both bounce uncontrollably between each other. I did not remember ever being more completely and thoroughly embarrassed in my life.

"Well, let's go see," she said, grabbing us both by the hand. This was nothing new. The three of us had held hands before inside the bunker because of the dark. But this was different. My hand felt wet and clammy inside hers as she led the way.

Somehow I had the presence of mind to remember Ben. "I want you to see something," I said when we got near the middle. My voice was finally starting to settle down. "Matt, can you find the one about Ben?"

"Do you remember seeing this before?" I asked Margaret as Matt trained the light on the spot.

"I don't think so," she said. "And I'd remember it, with that backwards *N*."

I prayed that Matt would keep his mouth shut about the cleavage on the *B*. He did. In fact his mouth hardly opened the whole time we were with Margaret. Or maybe it never closed. I would never know because we were in the dark most of the time.

"Here, hand me the flashlight," she said, and she walked closer to the inscription, studying it with great care. "This is strange. I can't figure out what was used to write this. It doesn't seem to be paint or chalk. It looks like some kind of stain. Why are you so interested in this?"

"I—we—had a friend named Ben who wrote his name just like this, but it would have to be almost three years old or more if he wrote it, and yet we've never seen it here before."

"What happened to your friend? Did he move?"

"No, he—" and I couldn't finish. The question caught me by surprise, even though I was starting to be able to talk about Ben more freely. It had been two and a half years since he died, and for much of that time I could not speak of it out loud to anyone. Now, suddenly, it felt like I had swallowed my tongue.

"He died," Matt finished the answer for me.

"Oh!" Margaret sounded as if someone had knocked the

wind out of her. "I'm so sorry!" Suddenly I felt her arms around me, and I forgot all about how beautiful she was and how old she was and even how much I was in love with her. All I wanted to do was cry. Something about the warmth of her arms filled me with peace. It was a secure peace—a sense that it was all right to cry—a sense of being completely understood, and though I fought it for a moment, I finally gave in and cried. I cried what seemed like two and a half years' worth of tears. I was out of control, but I felt safe. All the while, Margaret just held on to me.

And then, for some strange reason, I started to laugh. Just a little at first, and then more, until Margaret and Matt joined me. There we were, sitting in a triangle in the center of the Bolsa Chica bunker, laughing. Laughing about crying.

Margaret had turned off the flashlight, and I was glad. Now I could know and remember what it was like really being with her, without being confused by all the changes she had gone through. There in the dark, hearing only our voices and seeing the occasional silhouette of a face in the rectangle of light at the end of the tunnel, we talked. We talked mostly about the things we had done the last two summers and how much fun we'd had. I managed to talk a little bit about Ben, and Margaret talked about what it was like to be in high school.

Finally she got a more serious tone in her voice, and we knew something was coming.

"This will probably be the last time I'll see you both. I'm going to be moving to New York at the beginning of next summer. It's been hard because I've wanted to see you more this summer, but, well . . . things are a lot different now."

"We understand," Matt jumped right in, surprising me.

"It's just that I have a whole year ahead of me with these new friends and I want to make the most of it. It's probably weak of me not to stand up to them, but I just don't think they would understand—" Now she was the one who couldn't finish.

It was Matt again who tried to make a bridge. "You don't think they would understand you running around with a couple of pip-squeaks like us, right?" And the way his voice jumped when he said "pip" made us all laugh again.

"It's okay," Matt said, and his voice suddenly had a quality I had never heard there before. "We will always remember you."

I felt soft thin fingers feel for my hand and hold on tight once they found it.

"And I'll always remember you. Both of you."

Suddenly the rectangle of light behind Margaret's face disappeared as she kissed me. Then I heard another kiss, and we stood up and headed back toward the entrance. As soon as we reached the edge of the darkness, she let go of our hands and disappeared into the burning light of day, never looking back.

2

Shore Break

Matt and I stood there for the longest time squinting into the blinding light. I don't know what he was feeling, but I felt terribly empty, as if someone had just given me a gift only to rip it from my hands like some cruel joke. I wanted to be older in the worst way. I wanted to run after Margaret. I wanted her to come back.

"Let's hit the surf," Matt said, finally, and as soon as he said it, I knew that was what I really wanted to do right then.

"Yeah," I said, "Hit the surf."

We swam for hours, bodysurfing in the best waves of the week. They were short, fast, exhilarating breaks, the kind that were easy to catch and easy to stay in front of, once you caught them. The only problem was, they were breaking right on the shore. You could catch a perfect wave and then suddenly wish you hadn't. Looking down from the top of a five-foot swell that is about to slam you down into inches of water is what I call an "uh-oh" experience.

We soon learned how to pull out of the really nasty waves at the last minute and ride in a little behind the curl, using the churning foam as a cushion. Matt found some success somersaulting down under the waves as they broke, though once he started his somersault a little too late and scraped his back on the ocean floor. By the end of the day we were calling them Kamikaze waves.

We were gluttons for punishment. Though battered around, we kept going back for more. It seemed as if the waves were pounding on my emotions until there was no feeling left. The surf was treacherous, and yet we could handle ourselves in it. Dangerous, but predictable, unlike girls.

Matt was the first to notice the sun getting low in the sky, but we decided to stay until we couldn't see each other anymore in the darkness. We always did that at least one night during vacation, and tonight seemed like the perfect time. Besides, we were running out of nights.

I love bodysurfing at sunset. Most people have left the water by then, and you feel like you have the whole ocean to yourself. The waves start to soften as they pick up the tint of the golden sky, and the cooler air makes the water seem warmer.

Mrs. Wendorf joined Mr. Wendorf on the sand just as the round edge of the sun dropped below the horizon. It was Leonard who loved the beach, not Bernice. He was almost always out there in a Hawaiian shirt and a stringy straw hat, sitting in his favorite beach chair and doing crossword puzzles from a book. As we swam into the evening, they were the only people on the beach. They looked so odd sitting there: Mrs. Wendorf, all black and white, the black from her swimsuit and the dye in her hair in stark contrast to the pearly white skin over the bumpy fatty tissue on her legs; and Mr. Wendorf, all brown with sun-beaten, rhinoceros-like skin hanging from his bony legs.

At dusk they waved us in and Matt shouted, "We're coming," which meant we would be swimming for another half hour, at least. You could tell the two of them were arguing about something as they shook the sand from their towels and folded up their chairs and made their way off the beach. I imagined it was probably Leonard overruling Bernice's objections to leaving us out in the water at such an hour.

Matt was just a faint shadow in the darkness now, and the only part of the water I could see was the white foam. I had to guess when the waves were breaking, since there was no foam until after the curl. Twice I got a mouthful of saltwater, looking back for a wave that broke in my face before I could see it. I was tired and wanted to go in, but I was determined not to be the first to say it. We were tough guys out there, Matt and I, and it made me feel strong to be winning a battle against the surf and the night.

After the two mouthfuls of saltwater, I finally learned to recognize an approaching wave from the pattern of sounds. There were a few slaps inside a wave as it rose, but the telling sign was a second or two of deathly calm right before it broke. That little discovery gave me new energy.

"This is a blast, isn't it?" I called to Matt just before I ducked under a swell.

I was good for a few more rides, especially since the rides themselves were improving, as an uncharacteristically large set of waves moved in. I could tell because of the growing amounts of white water after each break and the fact that we were being pulled farther out into deeper, wider water. I was feeling more for the bottom now as we had to go farther out to get in the throw of the wave. Though they were menacing, these waves were the best of the day. We were finally getting away from the shore break.

"I got a swell ride on that one!" I shouted as I dove back in from a long, sustained ride. "These are boss!" No way was I going to quit now. In my excitement, it had not yet occurred to me that Matt was not acknowledging any of my comments.

The waves picked up their intensity. There was a slap, a whoosh, then an awful dead silence, and I realized I was a sitting duck for a wipeout. Time only to grab a breath before a huge wave cracked on top of me, sending my arms and legs tumbling inside its churning fury. When I finally righted myself and opened my eyes, there was white foam everywhere, reflecting what was left of the dim light in the sky. Round circles, where the foam was melting back into the dark water, gave the appearance of a huge blanket of floating Swiss cheese. Hundreds of thousands of tiny bubbles kept bursting, making a high-pitched sizzling sound as the ocean sucked itself back to crash again.

"Boy, did I get wiped out on that one," I said. "Matt?" I suddenly realized it had been three or four waves since I'd heard anything from him.

"Matt?" I repeated.

When I got no response, panic slammed into my chest as I tightened with fear. Where was he?

"Matt!" I shouted, and the anger in my voice let him know this was no time for joking, if that's what he had in mind.

The only sound I heard was a slap, then the silent seconds before another wall of water rose high over my head and clapped in on itself with a huge cracking sound. I came up from under that wave screaming Matt's name and thrashing about in the foamy translucent fizz.

The ocean seemed impossibly vast. If he was under the water, he could be anywhere. Or maybe he'd already gone back to shore. I looked toward the land and could see only the lights of Huntington Beach. Another wave hit me from behind, knocking me over and under. I came up frustrated and crying.

"Matt! Matt!" My voice was in shreds. Suddenly I thought I heard a voice say, "*Behind you,*" and I turned and moved as fast as I could in a straight line directly behind me.

"Matt, is that you?" I yelled.

Just then my leg struck something under the foamy water. It was Matt. I grabbed and got his hair first. I had to grope for any handhold I could find because the surf was sucking him back out. Next I got a hand under one armpit and held on as another wave snapped and crackled overhead, and then, in the dead spot before the crash, the swell of the wave lifted him back toward me and I got a good lock around his waist as we went churning under. At least we were being driven closer to shore. Coming up, I had a better footing and quickly dragged him out of the water and onto the dry sand.

Out of helplessness and utter panic I started shaking him and pounding on his chest. "Come on, Matt . . . wake up!" I even slapped him in the face, but when my knee accidentally jabbed him in the stomach, water flew out of his mouth and he wheezed, coughed, rolled over, and threw up. Something vile was hanging out of his nose, so I got him a towel and fell back in the sand, exhausted but relieved. Matt wiped his face and fell back as well, and for a while we both lay there gasping and panting.

"Not a word of this to Leonard or Bernice," was the first thing he said. "Not a word to anybody, okay?"

"Sure," I said halfheartedly. I had just saved his life and he didn't want to tell anybody? I wanted to tell the whole world. Besides, my mind was full of questions. How did it happen? What was the last thing he remembered? What was the voice? Was it him?

"What happened anyway?" I asked.

"Forget it," he said, and that was the end of it. Matt didn't want to talk at all.

"Come on, let's get back before they come looking for us." He stood up and started walking, wobbling on his legs. He took two steps and then he bent over and threw up again, followed by what sounded like a sneeze and a cough at the same time.

"Are you okay?"

"I'll be fine," he said.

When we got back to the apartment, Matt made a beeline to the shower before Leonard or Bernice could see him. I went to the shower in the second bathroom and let the hot water run in my face. There in the shower I realized how alone I felt, how lonely. I wanted to talk to someone—I wanted a friend. Was this what it meant to grow up and be tough? Almost drown and not talk about it?

Matt was still in the shower when I entered the kitchen in dry shorts with a towel over my shoulder and started munching on some potato chips Mrs. Wendorf had set out for us.

"Hasn't that boy been in the water long enough already today?" asked Leonard as Matt's shower ran on and on.

"The warm water feels great," I said.

"I'll bet it does," said Mrs. Wendorf. "Was it cold out there?"

"Actually it was colder when we got out. Look at my hands—they're like prunes." The skin on the inside of my fingers was white and wrinkled. We had been in the water for hours.

It took every ounce of control in me not to tell Mr. and Mrs. Wendorf what had happened out there, but I realized that if I did, it would probably be the end of Matt's vacation in the water.

"Oh, my gracious sakes alive, what happened to my little dumplin'?" exclaimed Mrs. Wendorf, running over to Matt when he finally came into the kitchen. He was sporting a scrape and a huge bump on his forehead that I had not seen in the darkness. "Are you all right, dear?"

"Oh, come on, Ma, don't drool on me. I'm fine. I just bumped my head on the bottom, that's all."

"Maybe it'll knock some sense into him," said Mr. Wendorf.

"Now, now, Leonard," said Mrs. Wendorf, wrapping her arms around Matt. "He's a very sensible, smart boy." Matt looked like he was being squeezed by an octopus. He rolled his eyes and waited it out.

"Here," she said in her thickest baby-talk voice, "let me take a look at our precious little forehead."

"It's *my* forehead, and it's fine, Ma. Don't worry about it."

"Nonsense, this is what mothers are for. Goodness me! Shouldn't we do something about this?" she said.

"I know just the trick," said Leonard, talking to his book.

"What's that, dear?"

"Take it off at the neck."

"Leonard! This is no time for jokes."

"Who's joking?"

"Look, Ma, I just want to go sit outside, okay?"

"Well, you be careful. You're the only son I've got."

Matt grabbed the chips and a couple of Cokes, and we sat out on the deck with wet hair that we kept shaking because of the water in our ears. The saltwater's blurring effect on my eyes turned the lights on the coastline into tiny stars. It was a warm, still night, and I suddenly felt strong and proud. What a day it had been! I had been kissed by Margaret and had been a hero all in one day. I felt a new kind of camaraderie with Matt in spite of the silence between us. The silence was starting to feel different to me—sort of grown-up and manly. We didn't need to talk about this. We had faced the elements and won. What I did for Matt, he would do for me in the same situation. That went without saying.

"We can get Vernor's and pretzels one more time tomorrow night," said Matt, covering for his exhaustion. The bump on his head made him look like a cyclops. I picked up the deck of cards and shuffled them, wishing he hadn't brought up the "one more time" remark. I did not want there to be only one more day to my visit.

My thoughts turned to Margaret and the loss of my first love on the same day I found out I even had one. *This is just great*, I thought. *I got to find out that Margaret really did care for me just in time to see her go.* I couldn't decide whether to feel good or bad about this. At least I had been important to her— important enough for her to leave her friends and come meet us in the bunker. Important enough to kiss.

"I wonder what Margaret's doing right now," I said, looking out at the crescent of starry lights that followed the coastline north, interrupted only by the dark outline of the Bolsa Chica bunker.

"Probably out with some high school guy."

"You would have to say that."

"Did she kiss you too?" Matt asked. Why did he have to keep bursting my bubble? In my memories of Margaret, there was no one there but the two of us.

"Yeah, just a peck on the cheek," I lied. It had been on the lips, or as close as she could get to them in the dark. Of course, since it was dark, a case could have been made for the accidental nature of her finding them at all—that she had, in fact, only intended to kiss me on the cheek—but I never entertained that possibility except as a cover in front of Matt.

"Me too," Matt said, and I wondered if he was lying as well. I hoped not. If I couldn't see Margaret again, I wanted my memories of her to remain special only to me. I didn't like the idea of sharing them with anyone, especially Matt with his "wonder what we could get away with" kind of girl-talk.

In that regard, however, I had to admit that there was something different about Matt since our meeting with Margaret. The fact that she had kissed him should have kept him foaming at the mouth all afternoon, when, in fact, it seemed to have the opposite effect. It had quieted him down, almost as though he, too, was guarding those moments.

We played only a couple games of gin rummy on the deck that night. We ate the TV dinners that Bernice brought out for us and decided to go to bed early. I was glad Matt brought it up, because I was tired. I couldn't imagine how he must feel. I would think it would take a lot out of you to almost die, and yet he didn't seem to show it. Even the bump on his head would have brought more than a few complaints if it had happened to me. But, then, Matt never did show how he really felt about things.

It was such a nice night that we decided to sleep out on the deck. Lying there in my sleeping bag, staring up at the stars and hearing the constant pounding of the waves made me relive the fresh memories of our experiences in the water.

I started thinking about how it had all happened—the impossibility of my even finding Matt in the water, and then how I somehow got him breathing again. It made me shudder just to think of it. And the voice . . . where had *that* come from?

Matt must have been thinking the same thing.

"Jonathan?" he said, checking to see if I was awake.

"Yes?"

"I was scared."

That was it. That was all he ever said about it. I tried to say I was scared too, but I had swallowed my tongue again.

My last day at the beach got off to an early start when Matt woke me up a few minutes before eight. It was still early enough for the air to be crisp out on the deck, but the sun was already reaching through it to touch my face. For beach bums like us, eight o'clock was early. We usually rolled out of the sack around nine or ten. Matt seemed somewhat agitated, though, so I forced myself to sit up, letting the sleeping bag fall off my shoulders. The deck around us was still wet with dew, and I felt like the dry fleece Gideon put out to try and avoid facing the Midian army.

"Guess what I just realized," Matt said.

"What?" I said sleepily, nodding at the cyclops.

"We left Leonard's flashlight in the bunker."

"Oh no."

"Yeah. And it would have to be the good one with five batteries. He'll kill me. Come on. If no one found it last night, we can get there before anyone else does this morning."

I wondered if Matt had seen himself in the mirror yet. He looked worse than the night before. The bump had swollen, and one eye was black and blue. I followed him upstairs to get a pair of trunks and came back down stepping into them along the way. That was all we ever wore at the beach—swim trunks and T-shirts—and often, especially toward the end of the week when our tans were showing, we did away with the T-shirts. I had two pairs of trunks so I could switch, when necessary, into dry ones.

Mr. and Mrs. Wendorf were having breakfast in the little nook off the kitchen, and Leonard's face was buried in the newspaper.

"My, we're up early this morning, aren't we?"

"Yes, we aaaare," Matt echoed his mother's singsongy voice. Sometimes I couldn't believe what they let him get away with. If I had mocked my mother like that, I would have had a mouthful of soap and the four walls of my room to stare at for the rest of the morning.

"Oh, poor baby, look at your face! Does it hurt, dumplin'?"

"Only when I laugh."

Matt went straight to the drawer in the kitchen where his father put the household tools that he brought to the apartment.

"What are you doing in my tool drawer?" Mr. Wendorf said without lowering the paper.

"I need the flashlight again."

"You mean you put it back where it belonged? Things are looking up with this boy, Bernice."

"Aren't you going to have something to eat before you go out?" asked his mother, looking concerned.

"We'll be right back."

Matt didn't have to worry about his father noticing he had a different flashlight. Mr. Wendorf's face, as usual, never showed itself.

Being on the beach early in the morning made me wish we had gotten up earlier more often. It was a lot like the beach at sunset, with deep colors and hardly anyone around. The ocean was glassy and the sand looked like it had never been walked on. The only people visible were a few surfers taking long, slow rides on the even waves.

"I bet we could do that," I said as we headed toward the

bunker. It felt strange to have the sand feel cold to my feet.

"It's a lot harder than it looks," said Matt.

"How do you know? Have you tried it?"

"Last year, after you left."

So that's what Matt did the second week of his vacation.

"Are you going to try again this year?"

"I don't know. I didn't like it very much. I could never stand up."

"What are you going to do if the flashlight's not there?" I said when the opening to the bunker was only a few yards away.

"I'll have to tell Leonard before he finds out. Then Bernice will persuade him to go easy on me for telling the truth. That's usually the way it works."

Inside the bunker, we went to what we thought was the middle and searched the floor with the second flashlight, but found nothing.

"Are you sure we're in the right spot?" I said.

"Sure we are, the writing about Ben was right over—" Matt trained the flashlight beam where he was expecting to see "Ben was here" and illuminated a typical smattering of graffiti. The spot of light jumped rapidly around, searching for the writing that had been so obvious the day before. "Hey, wait a minute. Where did it go?"

"Maybe we're at another part of the wall," I suggested.

"No, this is the center. It starts over here," he found one end of the writing with the flashlight beam and swung it across to the other, "and ends over there."

"Could this be a patch of writing that we missed and it really isn't the middle?" We both stared down the length of the tunnel each way and found the small rectangles of light at the openings to be about the same size.

"Let's walk the whole way just to be sure," said Matt, starting down the corridor with his flashlight.

"Wait a minute," I said after going only a few steps. "What was that? I just kicked something."

Matt trained his beam down at my feet and caught a long silver cylinder in the light.

"It's the flashlight!" he said thankfully, picking it up and testing it. "And it still works!"

"Now that we have two flashlights," I said, still preoccupied with the missing writing, "we should be able to find that writing about Ben."

We decided to split up. Starting at each end, we worked our way inside, checking the wall every inch of the way. By the time we met at the middle, it was obvious that whatever we had seen the day before was no longer there.

"You remember seeing it, don't you?" I said, checking out my sanity.

Matt didn't seem too concerned. "Of course. We all saw it. But look at that 'Go U.C.L.A.' over there. Those brush strokes are big enough to have covered it up. Do you remember seeing that yesterday?"

"No."

"Neither do I," said Matt. "I bet that's what happened. Someone covered it up. We know someone was here because of where we found the flashlight. That wasn't where I left it."

It did seem like a plausible explanation, but I was saddened that it was gone. The writing had been like encountering Ben again—something I hadn't allowed my mind to do in over a year. It had brought out my tears, and I had been looking forward to seeing "Ben was here" again to see if the resemblance to Ben's writing was just a crazy idea or something that would confirm itself by another look.

"I can't believe that someone found Leonard's flashlight and didn't take it," said Matt as we sat leaning against the wall very near the spot where we had sat with Margaret the day before. "This is an expensive flashlight. Five batteries and a beam like a searchlight."

"I know. Somebody was pretty honest. Would you have taken it?"

"Finders, keepers," said Matt, imitating Bernice's sing-songy voice.

"Hey, look at that," he said, training his flashlight on the wall opposite us, where it said "Jesus saves."

"I've seen that a whole bunch of times," I said, unimpressed.

"But look what someone wrote under it."

" 'He must make more than I do,' " I read out loud, and we both laughed.

That sacrilegious comment made me think of Ben again.

"I just know that was Ben's handwriting."

"But why didn't we see it last year?"

Matt was right. We had studied these walls carefully every summer. Margaret had measured the growth of graffiti. We had even written down our favorite sayings. We had covered every inch of these walls.

"You're right," I said with a sigh. Still, it puzzled me.

"Come on, let's go get some breakfast and hit the water," Matt said. "This is your last day here."

"Are you okay to swim?" I asked.

"Sure. Just no more somersaults for a while."

3

Sticky Business

The Beamerings lived on a quiet, tree-lined street in an older part of Pasadena. There the streets were wider, the trees bigger, and the curbs higher than where I lived in Eagle Rock. The trees were so big that the whole street was in the shade.

We used to have trees like that on our street, but they had all been cut down early that year to stop the spread of what was called Dutch elm disease, which I never understood, because they were Chinese elm trees. All those great, climbable trees had been replaced by little spineless saplings that had to be wired to green stakes in the ground in order to stay up. It was the saddest thing to ride up and down our street and feel the sky where once there had been a cool, green canopy. Riding up the Beamerings' street reminded me of what my street once was.

In the last three years the Beamering home had turned into a haven for me, a sort of home away from home. I liked to be there because I was comfortable there. With two high school boys in the house there was always something going on. Mr. Beamering (the Reverend Jeffery T.) was the pastor of our church, so there always seemed to be all kinds of traffic in and out the door. I could do anything I wanted at the Beamering home. I could join in and be a part of what was happening, I could just hang around, or I could crawl off somewhere by myself. Whichever I chose, no one would ask any questions.

Once, not long after Ben died, I stayed in his room so long I missed dinner and fell asleep on his bed. The next morning when I showed up for breakfast, everyone treated me as if I were a normal part of the family.

Occasionally Mr. Beamering would start into a speech on my behalf, but Mrs. Beamering would give him a certain look or walk by and lay a hand on his shoulder and he'd stop. But that's to be expected from someone who is used to making speeches, being a pastor and all.

The "somewhere" I would crawl away to was usually Ben's room. I'd spent a lot of time in that room with Ben, so it felt like it was almost my room too. Ben was the Beamerings' youngest son who had died nearly three years earlier, and he and I had been best friends, spending lots of time at each other's houses. I wondered if the Beamerings liked having me around because I reminded them of him.

They had kept his room pretty much the way it was before he died, except they did put away the physics/chemistry set he loved to do experiments on, and they gave away some of his books to the church library. But they kept his files. I know it's unusual for a ten-year-old to keep any files, but there was little that was usual about Ben. I never tired of going over his files. It was like being with him again.

He kept a file full of floor plans for homes cut out of various *Better Homes and Gardens* magazines. These we had used to develop the model houses he and I built in scale with our model cars. He kept a file on the Tournament of Roses parade in Pasadena, one on the Mayor of Pasadena who was Seth Wilson at the time, one on the Ford Motor Company, and the largest file of all was on the Edsel car. All these files were related to his save-the-Edsel campaign.

Ben had had an obsession with the Edsel that proved to be right. He got the crazy idea that if the Edsel died, so would he. He may have preceded the car by a few months, but the Edsel, as an idea, was already dead and gone by the time Ben got fatally ill. Nobody knew that better than he. This connection was so strong in my mind that even to this day I make the Edsel responsible for Ben's death. The last Edsel came off the line on November 23, 1959. I even clipped the article about it out of *Newsweek* and put it as the final entry in Ben's file, just to complete the story. I needed to complete the story myself, though Ben would never be gone from me.

There was also a medical file where he kept the results of his research on the particular heart condition that he'd had from birth: a septal defect, which is the medical term for a hole in the membrane of the heart.

There was a period of time when I didn't go into Ben's room at all. That was when I was mad. I was still angry, but nothing like that first year. I was mad that God got Ben and I didn't. I was mad that Ben handled dying so well but nobody seemed to think about me. According to Ben himself, he had gone to fill up a "Ben-shaped vacuum in the heart of God," or so he wrote in his final message that he slipped into my hand in the hospital. Well, that was probably fine for him. It was the fact that he had to leave a Ben-shaped hole in my heart to do it that I didn't like. He might have made God happy, but he didn't make me happy at all. That's when I got so mad I smashed my model house that we had built together. If I could have gotten to Ben's house then, I would have smashed it too, but Mrs. Beamering hid it from me, and I am glad that she did. I have his house now at home in my attic.

Seeing the writing on the wall of the bunker, though, had been like hearing again from that vacuum in my heart. I had actually gotten to where I was fairly indifferent about Ben, trying to forget him and doing a pretty good job of it. I was becoming more and more popular with the youth group at church, something Ben and I had never considered important since we kept mostly to ourselves. In school, I played after-school sports the last semester and I was looking forward to going out for flag football in the fall. The eighth grade of grammar school was like the senior class of high school—top dog. Never before had I been anybody at school. Then there was summer vacation, and a week at the beach with Matt, and Margaret to occupy my mind.

Then, suddenly, "Ben was here" had come as a less-than-subtle reminder of my past. Yes, Ben was here in a big way, and no matter how much I tried to ignore it, I would never get away from his influence in my life.

I had not been to the Beamerings' house for almost a month. A week of that was due to my vacation with Matt, but the other three weeks were indicative of the avoidance I was trying to engineer—a getting on with my life that many, especially my mother, had encouraged me to do. But after reading the writing on the wall, I had to find out if there was any connection between Ben and Huntington Beach. Had it only been my imagination?

It wouldn't be the first time I was fooled by writing on the wall. Once, even before I knew he was ill, I had imagined I saw Ben's name on an empty tombstone in a neighborhood display of Charles Dickens' immortal *Christmas Carol*. It was right where the "BEN" in "EBENEZER" would have been had the name not been erased at Mr. Scrooge's request by the Ghost of Christmas Future. No one in my family saw anything on the stone, but to me the word had glowed with a strange light of its own, similar to the writing in the bunker.

I was hard-pressed to excuse this new sighting as only a figment of my imagination. Ben was the farthest thing from my mind with Margaret around. At any rate, I was hoping a visit to Ben's house just might turn up something.

As usual, I came flying down their driveway and skidded to a halt with my bike ending up on its side by the back door. Mrs. Beamering heard me right away through the screen door and welcomed me as if she were expecting me.

"Jonathan, you're just in time!" She was at the back door by the time I got there, trying unsuccessfully to open it with

her elbows. The back wheel on my Schwinn was still spinning
and ticking.

"Come on in," she said, and I turned the knob easily from
the outside and stepped in. Her hands were both out in front
of her, covered with cookie dough, so I got a bony elbow
hug.

"As you can see, I'm in the middle of baking," she said
and went back to spooning balls of chocolate chip cookie
dough out of a huge yellow bowl and pushing them off the
spoon onto a cookie sheet with her fingers. "My two helpers
have characteristically vanished as soon as there were jobs to
be done."

"May I help?"

"Sure. In a minute that buzzer is going to go off and I will
have to stop what I'm doing and take a tray out of the oven,
so you can take over for me at this job. It's sticky business,
but it's fun because"—she lifted a dough-caked finger to her
mouth and took a long, slow lick, raising her eyebrows as she
did—"you get to do that!"

Eager to partake of the fringe benefits, I went to the sink
and started washing my hands. The buzzer went off just then
and Mrs. Beamering stole my spot under the water and
washed off her doughy hands, leaving the water running for
me to finish. She put on an oven mitt, pulled out a hot tray
of plump, steaming cookies, and flicked off the buzzer with
her elbow, while at the same time closing the oven door with
her hip.

"Not the best day to be baking," she said, wiping her forehead and setting the hot tray down on the counter, "but I
couldn't resist getting ahead. With this new freezer, I can bake
enough cookies to last until Thanksgiving."

From the looks of it, I thought she might have a shot at
Christmas.

"Freezers are such a great invention. Now I can get all my
baking for weeks over with in one day. And I like that because
I hate to bake!"

I stood there not quite sure what to do. I'd seen my mother do this hundreds of times, but I was never invited to participate, except, of course, for licking the bowl and the beaters on the Mix Master.

"Just drop a dab at a time on that cookie sheet over there—a couple inches apart to give them room to flatten."

I started spooning out cookie dough and was soon absorbed in trying to control the sticky stuff. This was a lot harder than it looked. I kept transferring little wads of dough from finger to finger, unable to get them to fall off, and when they finally did, I could never make them land where I wanted them to. Mrs. Beamering's trays looked like the stars on the American flag, all lined up in rows. My tray looked like the flag was waving in the wind and all the stars were falling off, but she didn't seem to mind.

"So how's your summer going?" she said, not to break the silence, but to truly find out. That was another thing about being at the Beamerings': you didn't fear the silence there. When you talked, it wasn't because there was dead air to fill up, but because you had something to say.

"Great," I said. "I just got back from a week at the beach."

"How nice. But your father wasn't on vacation this week, was he?"

"No. It was just me. I got invited to spend a week with Matt Wendorf. His parents rent an apartment in Huntington Beach every year."

Mrs. Beamering slid her spatula under a hot cookie and stared off somewhere for a moment. Then she laughed privately at whatever it was she saw there.

"Oh . . . I'm sorry," she said, "I was just remembering a funny story about Ben at Huntington Beach."

Ben was at Huntington Beach?

"He never told me about going to the beach," I said, trying to be casual about my surprise at discovering this connection so quickly. "When was that?"

Ben and I had been inseparable during the summer of

'58—Ben's only summer in southern California. I wondered how this could have slipped past me.

"We were there for a weekend with one of the families at the church. Actually, I think you were out of town at the time. I remember because Ben was so disappointed that you couldn't go with us."

My initial reaction was to be a little put out that Ben never told me anything about this.

"Did he like the beach?" I asked, hoping to find out some other piece of pertinent information.

"Not really," she said, and I wasn't surprised. Ben was not a physical person. "He was pretty bored actually. The sun burned him and the water was too cold, so he spent most of his time indoors reading. A couple of times he went exploring along the beach."

"Exploring? What did he explore?"

"That's what I was laughing about. He found some old bomb shelter and spent most of his time in the Huntington Beach Public Library studying up on World War II, trying to find out about it, I suppose. Doesn't that sound like Ben? We go to the beach for vacation so Ben can research the last major war!"

"Yes," I said. "That sounds exactly like Ben."

Mrs. Beamering and I didn't talk about Ben much, but when we did, it was a little like bodysurfing on a shore break. You'd get excited about catching a wave and then suddenly worry about the crash.

"So what did you do at the beach?" she said quickly.

"Well, we spent most of the time in the water."

"You certainly look like it. That's a handsome tan you've got there, young man. Have I told you how good-looking you are? I bet you have to fight the girls off with a stick."

I knew I was blushing but I didn't mind. Mrs. Beamering often talked like this to me and it made me feel great. I did mind it, though, when Peter and Joshua barged in the kitchen from the living room and started cracking jokes about my being Captain Kangaroo putting on a cooking demonstration in the kitchen.

"And in just a minute we're going to get to see Beanie and Cecil here put on a cleaning-up demonstration in the kitchen," said Mrs. Beamering, evening the score. "And slow down on those cookies. You two are eating them faster than I can bake them."

Joshua was only two years older than me, Peter, four years older, but they both seemed like they had arrived at manhood. Their voices were low, their shoulders were broad, and they walked with an air of confidence that made me feel as if I had a lot of catching up to do.

Peter, though older, was more slight of build. He was the musician and the charmer, like his father. Joshua was the athlete, and his bulk made him look as old as his brother. He had already made the JV football team at Pasadena High. He was the trickster and reminded me more of Ben.

"Here, Jonathan, hand me that tray," said Mrs. Beamering, popping it into the oven and setting the timer. "There. That's the last one," she said as she removed her apron. "We'll leave this mess to these two smart gentlemen and go sit in the next room for a minute."

I washed up quickly and walked by the brothers with my shoulders back. "See ya, Beanie. Bye, Cecil," I said.

"So long, Captain," said Joshua.

"I want to show you something," Mrs. Beamering said as soon as we got on the other side of the swinging door that separated the kitchen from the rest of the house. I followed her into Ben's room, where she set down a plate of the freshly baked cookies and a glass of milk, then pulled out his file drawer and began thumbing through the worn tabs.

"Have you seen this one?" she said, pulling out a file labeled "World War II."

"No," I said. Somehow, in all the times I had gone through Ben's files, I had managed to miss this one.

She thumbed through the papers looking for something.

Most of the files had clippings from newspapers and magazines. This one was mostly all notes, probably taken from the library that weekend. Finally she found what she was looking for. It was a clipping from a newspaper that Ben had pasted onto a regular sheet of paper.

"How about this?" she said, handing me the article.

"Nope. Never saw that," I said, because I would have immediately recognized it. It was a picture of the entrance to the main Bolsa Chica bunker—our bunker. Mrs. Beamering left to answer the phone that was ringing, and I sat down slowly on Ben's bed, picked up a cookie, and started to read.

"Built in 1944 by the Army Corps of Engineers, the 600-foot by 175-foot bunker—along with a smaller one nearby—was part of an elaborate defense system planned to protect the California coast from a Japanese attack during World War II. The bunker, designed to hold large gun emplacements at either end, contained huge storage areas for live ammunition as well as a latrine and sleeping quarters for its intended crew.

"Before the facility could be armed and the finishing touches put in place, however, the war ended. For the last few years, the huge empty bunkers have stood as almost irresistible challenges to hordes of local teenagers bent on defying the rules of their elders to enter a place of privacy, darkness, and calm." That last part Ben had underlined.

The article went on to talk about the graffiti on the walls of the bunker and compared it to the drawings in the ancient pyramids or American Indian cave art. "Generations from now archaeologists will probably study these walls in much the same way as they study primitive cave art today."

The title of the article was "Modern Hieroglyphics."

I put the clipping back in the folder and put the folder away. Mrs. Beamering was still on the phone when I passed back through the kitchen on the way out. I told her, in and around her side of the phone conversation, that I had to leave in order to get home in time for my paper route. She waved good-bye and I went out the back door to the accompaniment of the Captain Kangaroo song, courtesy of Joshua and Peter.

Now I knew that Ben *was* there. But what did it mean?

I rode home from the Beamerings feeling a little like cookie dough. That was partly due to the fact that a good deal of it was sitting uncomfortably in my stomach, but mostly because I felt as if I were going through a Mix Master myself. I missed Ben so much that I wanted to find out all I could about him—things that had managed to escape my attention when he was alive. But the more I found out, the more it demanded of me.

I had been doing just fine until I saw that writing in the bunker. Now, in my memory, Ben was doing the same thing to me that he had done in life. He was confusing me—messing everything up. I started wishing I had never seen the writing on the wall, because now I had to figure out what it meant. I started wishing everything about Ben would go away. He had always demanded something difficult from me—something I had never done before—and now he was worming his way back in and doing it again. Then I felt awful for ever even thinking that I was glad to be rid of him. It was all so sticky and unmanageable, like cookie dough you couldn't shake off your fingers.

"Ben was here," said the writing, and for me that could only mean that Ben was back.

4

American Flyer

The Sunday after Matt came back from the beach, Pastor Beamering spoke on angels, and I got a crazy idea in my head. What if an angel left the message in the bunker? What if it wasn't Ben at all, but Ben's angel? One of the verses Mr. Beamering quoted was about how children have their own angels in heaven who are continually beholding the face of God. Well, who's to say that a child who has gone to heaven couldn't, in the same manner, have a few angels down here, on their behalf, beholding *our faces*? It would be just like Ben to send a few of his angels down here just to keep me guessing.

That's what he was always doing when he was here. He kept the whole church guessing for a summer when we were ten. It's hard to even imagine now how we got away with it, but every Sunday Ben and I (it was his idea) had illustrated the Scripture reading with some kind of display. From the little window in the defunct bell tower in the back of the church I would signal Ben, who would be hiding behind the organ pipes, ready to launch some kind of visual volley on the congregation at the appropriate time in the Scripture reading.

I still can't read Scripture without imagining what Ben would do with it. Even that morning as Mr. Beamering was reading verses on angels, I saw Ben's devilish grin cooking up something.

" 'Are they not all ministering spirits, sent forth to minister for them who shall be heirs of salvation?' " Pastor Beamering read from Hebrews 1:14.

"This is great, Jonathan," I imagined him saying. "We could set up something like a storefront window—a wig store. And we could hang a black wig under the sign 'Hairs of Sin' and a blond one under 'Hairs of Salvation.' "

Maybe that's why I lit on the angel theory for the writing in the bunker. Ben got my imagination going in the first place, and it hasn't stopped since. Besides, the angel theory at least explained why we hadn't noticed the message on previous summers. It would also explain how it could be new writing but still look like Ben's. One of Ben's angels would no doubt be perfectly capable of duplicating Ben's particular handwriting style.

"I bet it was hard for a perfect angel to make that *N* backwards, though," said Matt when I shared my idea with him after church. He was back from his holiday and not at all bothered by my suggestion of angelic activity in the bunker. On the contrary, he took it one step further.

"If there was any angel in that bunker, it was Margaret," he said as we talked in the church parking lot.

"Yeah," I remembered wistfully, thinking about her beautiful face and figure. "She was an angel, all right. Just like Bobby Vinton sang: 'Teen angel, teen angel, will you be mine—' "

"No, that's not what I mean," he cut off my solo. "And besides, it was Mark Dinning, not Bobby Vinton." Then he looked around to make sure no one could overhear his next statement, which came out in an embarrassed sort of half-whisper. "I mean . . . what if *Margaret* was the angel—a real one?"

That question hung in the air, and I could only give him a puzzled look. Tough guy Matt talking about being with a real angel was almost laughable.

"Look, I know this seems screwy, but I honestly can't figure it out any other way."

"Figure out what?" I said.

"Jonathan . . . I saw Margaret the day after you left."

"So?"

"What I mean is, I think I saw the *real* Margaret. She was nothing like the girl who was with us in the bunker. She was running around with a couple junior high twerps, just like Margaret would do, and she ignored me completely." His eyes were getting wider as he explained this to me, like he still couldn't believe it.

"Wait a minute! Are you trying to say that the Margaret we saw in the bunker wasn't Margaret?"

"That's what I'm saying."

"How do you know this other girl was Margaret?"

"I just know. If you would have been there, you would have known too. When you know somebody as well as we know Margaret, you know who they are when you see them."

I couldn't argue with him on that, especially after being so confused by whoever it was we met at the beach. Plus, Matt spent one more week with her than I did every summer. He should know.

"Look, the girl I saw and talked to after you left was Margaret, and she hasn't changed that much. Nothing like the beautiful babe we met in the bunker. She made that girl seem like . . ." and we both said it together, "an angel." And then he leaned in even closer to shield this last piece of evidence. "I know it was Margaret because she was like she always was—flat as a pancake!"

Now this was a shock. I was supposed to believe that an angel—a well-formed angel, at that—had appeared to me in a bunker in the guise of a girl I thought I knew . . . and kissed me in the dark?

I started shaking my head and turning away in disbelief,

when Matt put his hand on my shoulder and said, "Wait. There's more."

I couldn't imagine how there could be. This was enough to keep me going for weeks.

"Can you picture Margaret—or whoever it was we saw in the bunker—can you picture her face?"

"Sure," I said. How many times since then had I thought about that face?

"So can I. Can you remember what she looked like when she threw her head back and laughed?"

"Yes," I said, and laughter bubbled inside me just thinking about it. "I can remember everything."

"And you remember the expressions on her face?"

"Yeah."

"The dimples?"

"Well, now that you mention it, yes. She had dimples— long ones off the edges of her mouth, right?"

Matt nodded his head.

"Jonathan . . . do you ever remember noticing any of these things about Margaret?"

"Well, no, but . . . I see what you mean. I just thought she grew up and we didn't. Couldn't that still be it?"

"That's what I thought too—until I saw the real Margaret and realized one more thing. It took me so long to think of this. And you haven't thought about it yet, or else you'd be as freaked-out about it as I am."

"Come on, Matt, get to it. What's the 64,000-dollar question?"

"It's worth a lot more than that." He leaned in so we were almost nose to nose. "How do you suppose we know all this stuff about the girl we saw in the bunker when we were *in the dark the whole time*?"

I felt like I had been hit by a brick. I slowly sat down on the low cement wall that separated the sidewalk from the parking lot. All I could do for a while was stare off at the traffic on Colorado Avenue. Even as I sat there on the wall,

I could see her eyes dancing before me as vividly as the cars that were passing by. I could see light flying from her hair. I could see her dimpled smile as she talked to us.

"We saw her face in the light when she first showed up," I said, searching for explanations. "We could just be remembering that, couldn't we?"

"Yeah, for two seconds!" Matt obviously had had time to consider all the initial rationalizations. "Enough to remember all this stuff? Jonathan, I can see her talking to me in the bunker right now, but I didn't see her then. It's like something that only happened in my memory. It's weird!"

I could see her too. It was just as he said. Somehow we were seeing Margaret some other way than we normally saw people—or perhaps some other way than we saw *normal* people—if, in fact, the Margaret we'd seen in the bunker wasn't normal.

"Wow," I finally managed to say.

"You can say that again."

"Wow!" I said it again. "So you think she really was an angel?"

"How else can you explain all this?"

"But wait a minute. If you saw Margaret—the real Margaret—after I left, where was she for the whole week I was there?"

"She was avoiding us for the same reason that the other Margaret said she was. It's just that she was nasty about it. She grew up, got new friends . . . all that kind of thing."

"How was she nasty about it?"

"Well, I wouldn't have even seen her if I hadn't almost bumped into her in the water. 'Margaret?' I said, and she turned around and looked at me and I'm sure she recognized me, but she was with two other older girls who asked her who I was, and she said she didn't know and told me to bug off. Those were her exact words: 'Bug off, you little twerp.' Can you believe that? After all the time we've spent together?"

"Why that little creep," I said. "That is like something she would do, though."

"I know," said Matt. "That's why I think I'm right about this. It's more like Margaret to insult us than to be nice to us. Jonathan, I think we've been with an angel."

Instinctively I put my hand up to the corner of my lip. "More than that . . . we've been kissed by an angel."

"Yeah," Matt said, his eyes about to pop out of his head. "Mark Dinning move over, we got the *real* teen angel!"

"You know, Jonathan," Matt said after a few moments of stunned silence, "I bet your screwy friend Ben had something to do with this."

"Ben?"

"If you and I have got angels in heaven, why couldn't he have a few down here?"

"This is creepy," I said, "but I've been thinking the exact same thing. That would explain the writing too. Ben would never miss an opportunity to leave his mark."

"What is with you guys?" It was my sister coming to get me. "You look like you've just seen a ghost or something."

I gave Matt a knowing glance and said, "Well, we have, kind of."

"What?" she said.

"Never mind."

"Come on, Jonathan. Dad's waiting."

"I'll see you tonight, Matt, okay?"

"Oh—I won't be here tonight. Gotta go with my parents somewhere."

"Okay. Well, I'll see you around. Say hello to Leonard and Bernice for me," I said to him as Becky and I walked away.

"Are you guys getting to be good buds or something?" Becky asked as we headed to the car. I didn't really think of Matt as a buddy, but now, suddenly, we shared a pretty big secret. I wanted to talk to someone else about this but I wasn't sure who.

As Becky and I hopped in the backseat, I couldn't help

but picture Ben in heaven orchestrating angels the way he had orchestrated our pranks at church. It suited him perfectly. The only difference being, now he was behind a cloud instead of behind the organ pipes, and he had much more powerful helpers to do his dirty work than he'd ever had with me.

"Aw, come on, St. Peter," I imagined Ben's current angel saying in heaven, "do I have to get Ben Beamering again? Can't I have somebody normal and boring for a while? Did you hear what he pulled the other day? The last angel had to be a fifteen-year-old dream girl in a bathing suit for one of his friends, for heaven's sake. Are you sure this kid's been checked out properly? I mean . . . does the Boss know about this?"

"What's so funny?" asked my sister.

"Oh nothing," I said. "Just thinking about angels."

"That was quite a fascinating sermon this morning, wasn't it?" my mother said.

"It's a touchy subject," said my father. "I admire Jeffery for tackling it."

"Are there really angels all around us right now?" my sister asked.

"I'm not sure they are around us all the time, dear," said my mother, "but the Scriptures say they are real."

"I liked his point about the fact that Jesus talked about angels much more than we do," said my father. "That says a lot right there. I mean, He should know!"

"I wonder if they're around our car right now," said Becky, "one on each fender?"

Just then my father had to swerve slightly to avoid a pickup truck turning into traffic.

"Way to go, right front fender angel!" he said, chuckling.

"I don't think you should joke about this, Walter," my mother said. "What do you think, Jonathan?" She must have noticed my smug silence.

"Angels are real," I said with a confidence that surprised everyone.

"There, see?" said my mother, looking disapprovingly at my father, who wiped the remaining trace of a smile off his face as he felt her eyes on him.

"I wasn't saying they weren't real, Ann. I was just having a little fun. There probably *are* angels on each fender. Maybe even an extra one on the hood when *you* drive."

"Walter!"

"How about when I get my learner's permit next month?" said Becky.

"A host!" said my father.

"A heavenly host!" said my mother, giving up and joining in the fun.

"And a personal appearance by Gabriel himself," I said, leaning over to my sister, who pushed me away playfully.

"When *are* you going to take me out driving, Daddy? You promised."

"Soon."

"Why not this afternoon, dear," said my mother. "Take her out to the racetrack. There's lots of room in the parking lot."

"She'll need all the room she can get," I said.

"Oh, shut up . . . can we, Daddy?"

"I suppose . . . but after my nap."

Sunday afternoons were lazy times around our house, especially if we didn't have company, which was the case that day. There was a flurry of activity centered around dinner and clean-up afterwards, but then everyone usually settled in with a section of the Sunday paper and an eventual snooze. I would often fall prey to the heaviness of a generous meal in the middle of the day and the natural tendency of my body to make up for waking itself at 5:00 A.M. to deliver the paper.

This particular Sunday, however, my sister kept the house animated, not wanting anyone to sleep through her opportunity to take the wheel of our Ford Fairlane. At the prodding of my mother, my father reluctantly arose from his big comfortable chair in the living room and took Becky to the racetrack for her first driving lesson. I could have gone with them, but I thought my chances for survival were better at home. Besides, I wanted to spend time with my electric train project upstairs.

Actually, "upstairs" is misleading. It really was "upladder." Like most middle-class homes in California in the '60s, ours was a simple single-level house. It was small, with two bedrooms and what amounted to a third—mine—in an enclosed back porch. "Upstairs," for my purposes, was an attic with enough crawl space to maneuver a permanent setup for my electric trains.

The only access to the attic was through my sister's closet—an inconvenience for me and a severe invasion of her privacy, in her estimation. Most difficult were the times when I was already up there and she came home with a friend and I would drop in on them, literally, unannounced. Though at the time I lacked any real sympathy for her, I admit that it might have been somewhat difficult for my sister to have to explain the sudden appearance of her little brother coming out of her closet door. When I had friends over, the conflict compounded.

"Why don't you cut a hole through his own ceiling, Daddy?" she said, more than once.

"Becky, I've told you a hundred times," my father would say, "you can't get to the attic through the ceiling in Jonathan's room. You only end up on the roof."

"Well, then, put his stupid train on the roof!"

Our family was famous for indirect reasoning. Anything but straight to the point, especially when straight to the point went by way of a conflict—and what we had here was a bona fide conflict. I had to pass through my sister's space to get to my own.

We were probably the first generation of children with the physical luxury that could lead to this kind of problem, which probably led to my father's inability to help us face it. His general method of dealing with such a situation was to shoot down all possible solutions and leave us to somehow grapple with it ourselves.

My sister and I actually did a pretty good job resolving this particular problem on our own. We started with a few ground rules. If her door was closed, I had to knock to obtain permission to pass, and I always had to call down before I descended to make sure she was prepared for my sudden appearance in her closet. If she wasn't home, I had free passage up and down. We also had a card that hung on a hook on the side of the ladder to tell her whether I was up there when she came in. It was green on one side and red on the other. Whenever I went up, I would flip the card to red, and turn it back to green when I descended.

The ladder ran straight up the wall of the closet into the attic through a three-foot-square opening. A wooden cover sealed the hole and had to be pushed up and slid over to the side like a manhole cover in the middle of a street. The opening was right in the center of the floored area that became my layout, so when you came up the ladder, your head popped up right in the midst of another world.

It was a world that had become very important to me since Ben's death—a place where I could be away and be alone and use my constructive talents to build something that didn't remind me of him. Since Ben and I had been interested in cars and model houses, never trains, trains had suddenly become my new passion.

I had received the train set for Christmas when I was seven. It wasn't new—my parents could never have afforded such a gift—it came from my uncle who had accumulated a rather extensive American Flyer set over a number of years and then lost interest. It's the one Christmas gift from my childhood that I can still remember vividly. The train layout took up the whole living room with two switches, a huge steam engine that puffed smoke, and what seemed like a mile of freight cars trailing behind. And I can remember hearing strange noises in my sleep that Christmas Eve and wanting to believe that Santa was really out there bringing me something. It was my father, up the whole night setting it up.

It would be four more years, however, before I would put any real interest into the train. After the initial Christmas excitement, the set was boxed and put in the attic, where it remained until I discovered it again after Ben's death. It's not that I forgot about it entirely; it was just an inconvenience. My father and I tried setting it up a couple of times that first year, but it was too much trouble for the short time the family was able to tolerate having it up and running in and around the living room.

It was a large "S" gauge train, much larger than the standard "HO" trains whose sophisticated layouts can be accommodated on nothing larger than a Ping-Pong table. This train needed a whole room for even the simplest of runs, and after a few weeks everyone in the family, myself included, grew tired of stepping over it.

Then, last year, while I was rummaging through stuff in the attic where I found a box filled with memories of the hobby I had pursued with Ben—garage doors for our model houses; bundles of tiny shingles for the roof, tapered and stacked and tied together with string; scale model trees made of twigs dipped in shellac and then covered with bits of colored yarn for autumn leaves—leftovers from an imaginary world only Ben and I understood, I had also discovered the train box that sent the wheels of my rusty imagination rolling again. Sitting up there in the attic, holding the big eighteen-wheel locomotive in my lap, I suddenly saw the possibility of making a permanent layout right there under the rafters. There was enough room, where the roof peaked, to floor a fifteen-by-fifteen-foot area with at least four feet of sitting space.

My parents had jumped at the idea. They were probably happy to see me interested in a hobby again. The only opposition came, of course, from my sister, whose arguments were quickly overcome by my parents' enjoyment of the happy proposition that the train set could be up and used without being a permanent disruption in the house.

My dad had put the flooring down, and I started designing the layout from ideas I got from a model train magazine. I found out how to build a mountain range out of plywood supports, chicken wire, and paper-mache. I made two tracks go on a grade up the side of the mountain and one go right through it, in and out of a long tunnel.

What I loved best was the prospect of nailing down the track. No more uneven lumps over carpet; no more having to check for open track that had been kicked by careless feet. Now there was actually a place in my house where I could make my own world come true, free from the encroachment of the real one. I could leave it and come back to it whenever I wished and know it would never be in anyone else's way.

This was the way I wanted it. This was the way I had always wanted it with Ben, too, but he never let me get away with it. I wanted an imaginary world out of everyone's way, but Ben wanted a world that clashed with everyone else's. He wasn't satisfied with just his imagination; he had to play it out all the way. To him, it was *all* real. There was no imagining; there was only living out your ideas. He thrived on the confrontation. He would have gotten bored with my train set because it made no impact on the world outside my attic.

Ben was the one who had been unwilling to keep his jokes to himself. He had to share them with the whole congregation. And Ben's obsession with the Edsel car couldn't rest as his own personal hobby. It had to take us all the way to the mayor's office of the city of Pasadena and the front page of the local paper. Small waves were even felt as far away as the Ford Motor Company in Detroit.

Life without Ben was much safer than it had been with him, and I tried to tell myself it was better, though something inside me told me it was not.

"Hi, Sis!" I said after sneaking down the ladder and jumping out of her closet. I had just finished spray-painting the mountains and sprinkling the wet paint with spongy imitation grass when I heard the car pull in the driveway. "How'd it go?"

"Jonathan! You scared me again. You've got to stop doing that!"

"I had the card turned to red. You just didn't look."

"Oh, so I'm supposed to stop and check the ladder in my closet every time I come into *my* room so I'll know if *you* might be *dropping in* on me? I'm sure I'm going to do that!"

"Touchy, aren't we? What happened? Did you run into someone at the racetrack?"

"Of course not. I drove the car perfectly. Ask your father."

"Wait a minute. Just because you can drive doesn't mean you can start talking like Mom."

"You'll have to come next time."

"Well, okay," I said. "I guess it's safe."

"Of course it's safe. Safer than I am in my own room, with you barging in on me at any time!"

We always went to church twice on Sundays. Sunday morning, of course, was more formal. I had to wear a suit, which I didn't like doing, but I had to admit I was starting to look good in one. Sunday night, though, I usually wore a sport shirt and corduroy pants. My favorite shirt for Sunday nights was a green checkered short-sleeved one that had a flap in front that folded under the collar and buttoned down the side instead of the middle. I liked the way I looked and felt in it.

How I looked had only started to be important to me in the last couple of months, and it had nothing to do with Margaret. Margaret was never someone I thought of as a potential girlfriend. She was only associated with Huntington Beach, one week out of the year. She may have been my first kiss, but it was a distant kiss, made even more distant now by the news I'd gotten from the sermon and from Matt that morning.

On the other hand, there was the daughter of the assistant pastor—I could see her almost every time I went to church, which was at least four or five times a week. She was the one I had skated with during every Couples Skate at the last all-church roller-skating party in June—every one except one. My mother had insisted I skate once with my sister.

Couples skating was the only time you could hold someone's hand without it becoming a big deal. Well, it was a big deal, but it would be even bigger if you were just holding someone's hand for no other reason than you liked them.

I knew she liked me, because after the first skate she waited for me in the same place every time they announced "couples only," and she would smile and blush when she saw me skating toward her. I also noticed her hands were always cold and sweaty when we skated together, but then again, so were mine.

It was hard not to be nervous during a Couples Skate. The lights would dim and turn soft colors, the mirrored ball in the center of the ceiling would send stars of light whirling everywhere, and the music would be something romantic like "Theme from a Summer Place." It was the closest I ever got to dancing at that age—the closest the church and my parents would let me get all the way through high school, in fact.

"I had a girl, Donna was her name. . . ." It was no coincidence that this song by Richie Valens was my favorite at the time, because Donna *was* her name, and she was the best-looking girl in the eighth grade.

I wasn't supposed to be listening to pop music, of course. It was forbidden in our house, but not necessarily outside our house—a strange rule, but for some reason Becky and I never questioned it. So my diet of rock 'n' roll came from the hour or so it took me to deliver the papers on my newspaper route. I had inherited my sister's big red transistor radio when she got a new, smaller turquoise one for Christmas, small enough to fit in her purse. I strapped the big red thing on the handlebars of my bike and cruised my route, music blaring. I thought I was pretty cool with V-necked handlebars almost as high as my head, print-stained newspaper bags hanging down from the rubber handlebar grips like saddlebags, and the radio nestled in the bottom of the V just like a radio in a car.

"I had a girl, Donna was her name. . . ." Ben wouldn't have liked the fact that I skated every couples skate with Donna Ivory. He wouldn't have liked it a bit. Not that he would have had anything against Donna. It was her father. I didn't like her father either, but time has a way of making you forget.

Three years ago, Ben and I had revealed to the whole church that Pastor Ivory had secrets with junior high girls. In our spying around the church, we had both seen and heard evidence to that effect. Ben had insisted we do something about it, since we were convinced that my sister was next on his list, so we used our Scripture-illustrating platform for this arresting piece of information. Needless to say, that little message had put an end to our activities altogether. The ensuing investigation turned up nothing. The pastor was exonerated, and we were banished from behind the organ pipes for good.

But Ben never forgot. He never trusted Virgil Ivory, so I knew he would not be happy with my interest in his daughter. I would even carry on imaginary conversations with Ben over this issue. In many ways, the Ben I had known at ten became my conscience at thirteen.

"Come on, Ben, give her a chance," I would say, even out loud, as I was pulling papers out of my saddlebags and skimming them down driveways. "She's not Virgil, you know; she's his daughter. Besides, she's the cutest girl in the eighth grade. You even used to think she was cute three years ago."

The problem with these one-way conversations in my head, however, was that they did not always stay one-way. I had come to know Ben so well that my knowledge of him sometimes came back by way of a response. It was almost like I had a double conscience: my own, and what I knew Ben's would be. For instance, to the little piece of rationale about Donna Ivory, I could almost hear Ben say, *She may be cute, but she's dangerous. She's Virgil's daughter for heaven's sake. There's no way you can get around that!*

I was thinking about Virgil's daughter as I applied the butch wax to my short hair and tried to comb it into a flattop, but with a cowlick on each temple, it ended up looking more like the picture of Stonehenge in my Western Civ book with its pillars leaning up against each other. The green shirt was ironed and ready, and all I could think about was seeing Donna and when the next all-church roller-skating night was going to be.

At church that night they announced it. There was going to be a Back-to-School skate the first week of September. They'd had such a good turnout for the last skate that tickets would be going fast. "Better get yours soon," Pastor Ivory said.

Donna was sitting two rows in front of me, and when her father announced the skate, she glanced back at me and turned red. Her friend, Marcie Baker, elbowed her and they both giggled. I felt a rush of importance. I knew they were talking about me.

"Hi," I said when I found her afterward in the narthex.

"Hi." She smiled as the two girls who were with her vanished on cue.

I stood there for a moment feeling awkward.

"Going to the skate?" I said. *Oh great! Be obvious, Liebermann.*

"Sure. How about you?"

"Yeah. I'll be there."

There was another awkward moment, and then I said, "Well, better be going. See you later."

"Bye," she said.

I walked away feeling stupid. Actually, though, most of our conversations were about like this. I liked thinking about Donna while I got ready for church. I liked skating with her on Couples Skate when the rink wasn't so crowded and I could look at her smiling next to me as the wind created by our rolling wheels pulled the hair back from her pretty face and showed her glowing temples. I fell in love every time I heard "Oh, Donna" on my red transistor radio. But I could never talk to the real Donna very well.

That's because there's nothing going on in her head worth talking about.

Shut up, Ben, I can handle this.

There was still time to spare before my parents were ready to go—they were always among the last to leave church—so I went searching through the lower level of the sanctuary and the Christian Education building until I found the janitor, Harvey Griswold.

"Grizzly," as we called him, was a deaf mute who had Ben and me to thank for his job. We were the ones who had discovered that he could read and write and was much smarter than anyone around the church imagined. When the deacons found out he could read and respond to memos, they decided to cancel their plans for replacing him.

Grizzly was smartest of all about things that had to do with God, so I had a pretty good idea he might have something to say about angels.

I found him in the junior high room setting up chairs. I always scared him when I came upon him working late in his silent world. That was a real turnabout because he used to be the one who scared us all the time with his odd mannerisms, his wiry hair, and the grotesque, monotone sound that came out of his mouth when he got excited and forgot he couldn't talk.

I tapped him on the shoulder and he jumped back, letting go of a stack of folding chairs that fell like dominos with a crash. I started picking them up as he scolded me with his finger.

"Can you roller-skate?" I asked as I moved along with him while he pulled up one chair at a time and set it neatly in place. I suddenly realized that I had never seen him at the roller rink on skating night.

You had to remember to have Grizzly's attention when you talked to him so he could read your lips. Now he looked at me more closely and made me repeat my question. Then he shook his head "No."

"Have you ever tried?" I said as he reached for another chair.

He shook his head again.

"Why don't you come to the next church skate?" I said. I was pretty sure that all he needed was an invitation. Most people thought Grizzly was a miserly soul who preferred to keep to himself. That was only because most people left him to himself; he had no choice. Ben and I had found out that Grizzly was actually quite a sociable character hungering for new adventures.

He only shook his head again.

"Why not?" I said, forming the words carefully.

He balanced a folded chair against his leg and took out his writing pad.

"NO WAY TO GET THERE," he wrote and held it up for me.

"My parents can pick you up," I said, and he frowned.

"TOO MUCH TROUBLE."

"No," I said. "No trouble at all. Why don't you come with us? I'll talk to my parents."

He shrugged and acted disinterested, but I imagined he was overjoyed inside. Then I remembered what I really wanted to ask him—why I had gone looking for him in the first place.

"Do you believe in angels?"

He smiled broadly and wrote, "I HAVE ONE BEHOLDING THE FACE OF GOD RIGHT NOW."

"Have you ever seen an angel?"

"PROBABLY BUT DIDN'T KNOW IT."

"I know what you mean. I'm not sure, but I think I might

have been kissed by an angel and didn't know it until now."

Grizzly got a wistful look and stared off for a moment before he wrote again.

"YOU ALWAYS KISS AN ANGEL WHEN YOU FALL IN LOVE."

Something clicked when I read that statement—like it did so often when Grizzly explained things. Suddenly I realized I wasn't in love with Margaret. I had been in love, for a while, with the idea of being kissed in the bunker, but now I knew the truth. I was in love, all right. I was in love with an angel.

"Do you think that if we have our own angels in heaven who are always looking at God, that when we go to heaven, we could send one down here to check out the friends we left behind?"

It was too much for Grizzly to get all in one sentence. He motioned with his hand for me to try again.

"You have your own angels in heaven, right?"

He nodded.

"If you died and went to heaven, could you send an angel down here to—?"

Now, the second time around, he grasped my concept before I had fully stated it. His mouth went into the shape of an "Ahhh" sound and an ugly groan came out of it that completely contradicted the delight on his face.

He unfolded the chair that was leaning against his hip and sat down to think. I did the same.

"BEN," he finally wrote and held up to me. I looked at him quizzically.

"BEN'S ANGEL," he added. I smiled. He was following my thoughts. Then he finished it: "KISSED YOU?"

"Yes!"

"WHERE?"

I pointed to a place on the edge of my right lip. Then he lifted his hand slowly and, with a look of great wonder, touched the spot.

I found myself wanting to pour my heart out to him right

there. Throw him all the questions . . . all the details. Try and figure out all the ramifications. But I was obstructed by the communication barrier between us. At the same time, there was such a sense of wordless communication between us that talk seemed hardly necessary. At least it was comforting to know that in the matter of angels, I had someone who could understand.

After a moment he wrote, "NOT SURE I SEE ANGELS BUT HEAR THEM ALL THE TIME."

How could a deaf person hear angels?

"What do you hear?" I formed the words with my mouth without making a sound. It was a way that Ben and I had discovered we could talk in secret to Grizzly without anyone hearing. Often I talked to him this way even when no one was around, like right then.

"SINGING ANGELS," was what he wrote, and I remembered old rumors about unexplainable singing in the church. Maybe that was the one thing Grizzly could hear. It would make sense—that he should hear something we could not, if he could hear anything at all.

Then he wrote one more thing, going back to our original conversation.

"CAN'T SKATE."

"Sure you can," I said. "You can learn. It's easy."

Grizzly only shook his head and again held up this last written message to emphasize the fact that he would not be talked into roller skating. I had to laugh, though, because the last two entries looked like one sentence on Grizzly's pad: "SINGING ANGELS CAN'T SKATE."

He had a good laugh when I pointed it out to him and wrote: "BUT NO PROBLEM FLYING!"

5

Devil or Angel

The Back-to-School All-Church Skate Night was held where it always was held, at the Ramblin' Rose Roller Rink on the Arroyo Seca, a euphemism for a dry riverbed that ran into Los Angeles from the backside of Pasadena. At the north end of this riverbed you could see the picturesque Rose Bowl nestled in front of the San Gabriel Mountains (at least on a clear day); at the south end, just before the riverbed narrowed into a concrete wash, was the Ramblin' Rose.

The roller rink was only a block away from where the Pasadena Freeway began. In 1961, freeways were rapidly becoming the main arteries of southern California. Their subsequent hardening would necessitate numerous bypass operations, but at that time hardly any of the negative associations with these clogged thoroughfares had surfaced.

Freeways were looked upon as just one more bright hope for a more convenient future that already included automatic dryers, dishwashers, air conditioners, electric blenders, and push-button just about anything—advancements that would completely change the look and lifestyle of the modern family. Alan Shepard had made the first U.S. space flight; now Zenith brought the Space Age into the living room with Space Command TV, featuring a remote control "Space

Commander 400"—"NOTHING BETWEEN YOU AND THE SET BUT SPACE!"

This was a time of great national optimism. America had its youngest elected President and a glamorous First Lady in the White House. The era that would become known as Camelot captured the hopes of the best and the brightest and swelled our dreams for the future. The sores of civil unrest in the South had not yet festered to the national breaking point, President Kennedy had not yet been cut down on a humid Dallas afternoon, and most Americans paid no attention to the military advisors being sent to aid the tiny Far Eastern country of South Vietnam in its battle against Communist aggression from the north. At his inaugural in January of that year, John F. Kennedy had announced, "Let the word go forth from this time and place, to friend and foe alike, that the torch has been passed to a new generation of Americans." A new generation was reaching out its hand to a future full of hope and promise.

But the only thing important to me right then was that Donna Ivory was holding out her hand for me as I skated toward her during the first Couples Only skate of the night. My heart skipped when I saw her. The cutest girl in the eighth grade was waiting for me! I took her hand and we skated out onto an almost empty rink spotlighted with twirling stars.

Only a fraction of the number of people on skates actually made it out on the rink as couples, and most of these drifted in later—mostly high school and college age kids, and they always took a while to pair up. In 1961, this was as close as evangelical Christians ever got to dancing, which heightened the pressure on these pairings. Many a hope was dashed and many a dream came true during Couples Skate. The boys had to build up enough courage to ask, and, sometimes, the girls had to think about it for a while. Couples like Donna and me, who already had each other reserved, got the jump on an almost empty floor.

I liked that part about Couples Skate as much as I liked holding Donna's hand—the fact that for the first few minutes it felt as if we had the whole floor to ourselves. Even with the rolling wheels and the wind rushing past your ears and the soft music, it was almost quiet compared to the noise and congestion of All Skate with kids darting here and there and beginners trying to balance themselves like sailors on a slippery deck in a stormy sea.

But on the second Couples Skate that night I started to notice a heavy feeling, and it surprised me when I realized it was associated with Donna. I was actually getting bored skating with her. Things that had never bothered me before began to annoy me. For instance, whenever I wanted to skate faster, Donna, who was a poorer skater than I, would always pull back. Also, she never wanted to try anything different, like switching sides or locking arms or skating under another couple making a bridge. She just wanted to hold on tight and skate around and around. She never even talked much; she just smiled this pretty smile whenever I looked over at her.

I liked it when we did talk because then I would have to put my ear right up to her lips in order to hear her over the rolling wheels—so close that her delicate voice and breath buzzed and tickled my ear. Or, in order to hear me, she would have to lean in so close that I could smell the fragrance of her hair. But mostly she would just smile, shake her pretty brown hair, and say in a voice I could never hear, "I can't hear you! Tell me later." I wasn't even Grizzly, and I could read those lips.

I guess also I was beginning to realize that I had almost no contact with Donna apart from the Couples Skate. In fact, that particular night I was rather lonely because none of my usual friends were there. Not even Matt.

By the third Couples Skate, I almost didn't want to take Donna's outstretched hand. I felt like she was grabbing me and holding me back. Maybe that's why the devilish impulse to play rough came over me, just to create some excitement.

So without slowing down, I skated up to her, grabbed her hand, and jerked her up from the bench. Her body lurched forward and her feet drummed on the rubber flooring mat to try and get her balance as I pulled her toward the skating floor. She still had not righted herself as we entered the rink, so I pulled her up with a jerk, and in the process she cracked like a whip, broke away from my hand, and went flying across the floor, unable to stop until she crashed into the wall on the other side.

"Gosh, I'm sorry," I said, rushing over to her, trying to hide my amusement. "I didn't mean to let go—"

"Why did you do that?" Her face was livid with anger and embarrassment.

"I'm sorry. I just wanted to have a little fun."

"If that's your idea of fun. . . !" Just as she turned to skate away from me, I heard the familiar introduction of one of my favorite songs by Richie Valens.

"Listen," I said, skating up behind her, "it's our song."

And just in time, I began singing, "I had a girl/Donna was her name." Of course, since this was church night, there were no popular records played, but whoever played the organ kept doing versions of all the latest hits. We always thought it was a great joke on our parents that we could hear these songs we weren't supposed to know, and we would often slip notes of requests to the guy at the organ. Matt usually kept him busy with requests most of the night.

For one lap, Donna and I skated like this—with me trailing behind her and singing. I thought she might go for an exit, but she didn't. Finally she turned around and looked at me, and the smile had returned to her face. I skated up to her and saw that she was blushing. I assumed her shyness was from hearing her name and realizing that I was making a deal out of it. Like magic, the song saved me. Taking my arm, she slipped her hand into mine as if nothing had happened and we skated off dodging stars.

As we skated, I started listening to the words of the song

in my head. It's funny how you can know words to a pop song before you have even thought about them, and it wasn't until that skate that I realized this song was about a breakup. I'd always been so into the mood of the song—the music, the pathos, the name, and the fantasies of Donna in my mind— that I never paid any real attention to the lyrics. The chorus was all I really knew, and the chorus was only "Oh, Donna" a hundred times, it seemed, until it faded away.

But now I heard, "I had a girl/Donna was her name/ Since she left me/I've never been the same./'Cause I love my girl/Don-na-a-a where . . . can ya be?"

I had *a girl*, I thought. Past tense. And even as we skated together, her hand felt cold in mine. Was it over? Had it ever started? I didn't even know what it was supposed to feel like to have a girl, but if this was it, I was pretty sure I didn't want it. All we ever did was skate together, and that was starting to make me feel trapped.

I looked over at her, and she had this exceptionally soft and gooey look on her face. It made me almost want to throw her into the wall again.

Couples Skates always ended with the lights going up and the familiar "ALL SKATE SLOWLY AND CAREFULLY" announcement coming over the speakers, followed by a deluge of little skaters and growing congestion. Donna and I usually split up at that point, with a final squeeze of clammy hands, and went back to our friends. This time was no exception, and I was happy to be free of her and skating on my own. I wiped my sweaty palms on my jeans and lost myself in the crowd.

Matt must have come in late, because I had spotted him standing beside the rail during that last skate. I started scanning the blurry faces looking for him as I coasted along. Suddenly Donna came up beside me and gave me a little shove. She was with her friend Marcie Baker and a relatively new girl to our group named Donna Callaway. I'd thought the new girl was kind of homely, but on skates there was a different quality about her. She obviously knew what she was doing with eight wheels on her feet.

"Donna wants to skate with you on the next Couples Skate," said Donna Ivory. "Why don't you?"

It seemed kind of odd, but they were all smiling at me, so I went along with it.

"Okay," I said. Just as they were skating away, Matt rolled up behind me.

"What was that all about?" he asked.

"Donna wants me to skate with that new girl, Donna Callaway. Isn't that a little weird?"

"Well, at least you'll get the name right."

"You should skate with Donna Ivory," I said, knowing that he probably wouldn't. I had never seen Matt on a Couples Skate.

To my surprise, he responded, "Maybe I will." *That does it*, I thought. Margaret *was* an angel. Only an angel would be able to make Matt actually want to be with a real girl instead of just talk about them.

"What do you suppose those girls are up to?" I said, wondering why Donna would set me up with someone else.

"Leonard says you should never try and understand women. I suppose it's the same with girls. Maybe they're just practicing."

Suddenly Marcie and the two Donnas passed us at a high rate of speed. Donna Callaway went right in between Matt and me, almost throwing us both off balance. I had fallen only once in the last three skate nights, and I wasn't about to let a girl spoil my record. We were just starting to chase after them when the buzzer sounded and the announcer came on the microphone.

"CLEAR THE FLOOR PLEASE. ALL CLEAR."

"All clear" always meant they were setting up for the Speed Skate—the only time all night you actually got to skate as fast as you wanted. It was my favorite skate. You got to lean over into the wind and feel yourself fly. It was always scary on the corners because I was never sure how to turn at high speed, so I just locked my legs and leaned and hoped my skates wouldn't slip out from under me.

I also liked this skate because it was always men and boys. It wasn't a "Men Only" skate, but it turned out that way. I guess the girls didn't like going fast. And after my last boring Couples Skate with Donna, I was ready to be rid of women in general and get out there with the guys.

The three rink attendants placed yellow cones down the center of the floor to keep people from cutting across and the buzzer sounded. Then the organist started playing "The Flight of the Bumblebee" and a number of guys streaked onto the rink. Some of the little boys were the fastest. They had such a low center of gravity that balance was no problem for them. It was just full speed ahead!

Just as we were starting to jump into the action, Matt grabbed my arm. "Look! Who's that?" he said, pointing to a blond-haired figure speeding faster than anyone.

"Holy Toledo, it's Donna Callaway!" I said.

She was incredible—fast but fluid, moving with ease and grace. She even kept her feet going on the curves, one inside the other. I'd tried that a little bit on All Skate, but never while going that fast. Flying past all those men and boys with their rigid and jerky movements, she looked like a swan among ducklings.

"Wow!" said Matt. "Look at her go! Come on, let's get out there."

"Wait a minute," I said, watching my future couples partner fly by.

"What? This is the only skate of the night worth coming for. Come on. We're wasting time!"

"No, you go ahead," I said. "I gotta go pee."

"Pee later," he said a little too loudly. "Come on! What's wrong with you?"

"Go on. I'm going to sit this one out."

"Wait a minute," said Matt, dragging out the words for

emphasis. "You're not going out there because of Donna, aren't you? Too chicken to be beat by a girl?"

"I just need a rest before the next Couples Skate."

"I'll say, if you're skating with *her*," Matt said and swung himself around the railing and out onto the floor.

I couldn't take my eyes off Donna Callaway. Her curly blond ponytail flew behind her like it was holding on for dear life. She dodged in and out of the skaters around her, her legs moving in a constant pumping rhythm that seemed to keep time with the music. She was flying like a bumblebee, I thought, and if I went out there, I'd get stung.

Suddenly my legs felt like they weighed a thousand pounds, and I decided I'd take that pee I was lying to Matt about. Sitting in the stall would use up more time, so even though I didn't have to go, I took up residence on the toilet in the last stall.

What was I going to do now? The next Couples Skate would be coming up soon. How could I putter along next to that speed demon without looking like a fool? What if she wanted to go fast and ended up pulling me along like I pulled Donna? Suddenly the thought crossed my mind that Donna Ivory might have set this whole thing up on purpose, just to humiliate me for throwing her up against the rail. I should have been suspicious about her getting over her anger so quickly.

As I mulled these thoughts over in my mind with "The Flight of the Bumblebee" still reverberating through the walls, my eyes slowly focused on something on the inside of the stall door. I was glad my pants were down because I almost went to the bathroom anyway. There, scratched into the flesh-colored paint of the aluminum door, were the words "Ben B. was here."

It wasn't anything like the writing in the bunker. It was in lowercase letters except for the *B*'s, so I couldn't tell anything from the *n*. It was relatively new, however, because the door had received a fresh coat of paint since our last skate in

June. These doors were always covered with writing, and I could still see the indentations of former marks that had been painted over. Now this one had only this message and some-one's phone number who wanted a good time. It was hard to pass this off as a coincidence, not when it said "Ben *B.* was here."

Now I knew there were plenty of Bens in the world, but how many Ben B's could there be—and in Pasadena, no less? I pulled my pants up and returned to the rink a bit shaken, my concern about skating with Donna Callaway now dimin-ished by comparison.

Matt was just coming off the floor from the end of Speed Skate and greeted me with, "Don't look now, but your fly's open."

Sure enough. I guess I really was spooked.

"Matt," I said, looking both ways and zipping up, "have you been to the bathroom yet?"

"I go three times a day, whether I have to or not."

"Seriously. I mean *this* bathroom."

"No, I haven't."

"Well go check out the stall on the far left . . . the back of the door. I'm going skating."

It was All Skate time again and I welcomed a chance to lose my thoughts in the crowd. Halfway into thinking I was either imagining things or going crazy, I realized I wasn't skat-ing alone.

"You all right?" It was Becky. "You look like you just saw a ghost or something."

"I'm okay." I almost started to tell her about the writing, but I didn't want to shout about angelic graffiti over the noise of All Skate. There was too much to explain. I still hadn't told her about what we'd found in the bunker—not because I didn't want to, but because I just hadn't figured out how to tell her yet. My sister and I teased each other a lot, but I knew if I got serious, she would listen. She was good about that, especially when it had anything to do with Ben.

"I'll tell you later," I said.

"Is it about Donna?"

She would have to remind me.

"Which one?" I said, perking up.

"Oh, there's more than one now? What other Donna is there?"

"Donna Callaway."

"Oh, you mean Roller Derby Queen?"

"Wait until the next Couples Skate," I said, hiding my trepidation behind a cocky smile.

"Gosh, Jonathan," she said just before she skated off, "for an eighth grader, you really know how to pick the babes."

Rolling, rolling, rolling. The constant turning of wheels on ball bearings. The low hum of rubber on hard wood. Rolling feet, stomping amateurs, gliding experts—among them, Donna Callaway, skating backwards on the other side of the rink. Yes, backwards. I found the nearest exit and swung myself clumsily off the floor just ahead of Matt, who had been trying to catch up with me from behind.

"Okay," he said, out of breath, "I got the phone number. Now who's going to call the guy for a good time?"

"Not that! Come on, Matt, you know what I mean. Didn't you see the writing about Ben?"

"Yes," he said, turning serious. "Are you surprised that it's somebody in our group?"

"How do you know that?"

"It doesn't take a genius to know that somebody had to do it today to put today's date on it."

"Today's date? I didn't see any date."

"You're kidding," he said, his eyes going wide on me again. We both turned at the same time and stomped toward the rest room. The rubber mats around the rink were made to keep people from rolling. You couldn't skate on them, you had to tromp.

Once inside the bathroom, we had to wait for someone to vacate the end stall. We washed our hands and combed our hair a number of times while some old guy in there kept clearing his throat and blowing his nose. You can always tell old people by the way they clear their throats. It's like removing gravel from the bottom of a dumpster with a big shovel. That wasn't all he was clearing. The smell made us almost leave.

Finally a white-haired, unshaven man in a red and black checkered lumberjack coat came out of the stall. He nodded at us, winked at me, and vanished out the door.

"Pee-yooo!" said Matt, holding his nose. "I'm not going in there, that's for sure!"

I swung the door open and found it just as Matt had said. Under "Ben B. was here" there was a newly scratched 9/13/ 61.

"You're right," I said, "today's date."

"And that wasn't there before?"

"Nope."

"I think we'd better keep an eye on this wall," said Matt, trying to talk while holding his breath. "Who knows what's gonna show up next."

"Matt, this is weird. I don't like it."

"Wait a minute," he said, breathing freely again, though still making a face. "Have you ever seen that man before— the one who was just in here?"

"No."

"Don't we have the whole place reserved just for our church?"

"Yeah, but I don't know everybody in the church . . . and he could be someone's guest . . . someone's grandfather or something."

"But, Jonathan, did you see that coat he was wearing? It's 80 degrees outside!"

We stared at each other for a couple of seconds until we recognized that the same thought had entered our minds at the same time and we bolted toward the door and stood for a moment outside, scanning the crowd.

"You go left," I said, "I'll go right. If you see him, stay with him until we meet up."

When we rejoined each other, almost directly opposite the rest rooms, Matt said, "See anything?"

"Nope. Nothing. I even asked at the desk if anyone works here who fits his description."

"Or his smell!" said Matt.

"You *are* thinking what I'm thinking, aren't you?"

"That he was an angel?"

"He has to be."

"But, Jonathan, how could someone from heaven make a BM that smells so bad?"

"Ben's angel would!" I said. "No doubt about it."

Suddenly we were interrupted by Donna Callaway.

"Jonathan! Where have you been? I've been looking all over for you. The Couples Skate is almost starting."

I hadn't even noticed the lights go down and the music soften, but I did notice Donna Callaway's rosy cheeks and dancing eyes.

"Come on," she grabbed my hand, "we'll be late!"

Matt shrugged his shoulders as Donna pulled me toward the nearest entrance to the rink. It was going to be this way the whole skate, I could tell—Donna pulling me, that is.

Actually, it wasn't so bad. Once we got out on the floor, she skated at an easy pace. The first thing I noticed was that her palms were dry. The second thing was how she glided along next to me. There was no pushing and pulling like there always was with Donna Ivory. And the third thing was that it was easy to talk to her.

"Where were you for so long?"

"Looking for someone."

"I thought you'd be looking for me," she said, her eyes bright.

"I was looking for a stranger. Someone we saw in the rest room."

"Did you find him?"

"No."

"Is he dangerous or something?"

"Probably not, but you never know."

"Sounds creepy to me."

"Don't worry. He's gone now."

Donna looked convinced that I had just saved her from some menace. "Good! Let's skate!" she said, casting doubt on what it was we had been doing up until then.

She charged ahead, pulling me into a faster clip. I was surprised at how easy it was to move along with her, except for the turns. On the corners she crossed her outside foot inside the other like I had seen her do earlier, and my stationary feet felt like they had lead poured in them.

"How do you do that?" I asked, coming out of the turn after holding on to my stiff legs for dear life.

"Easy. Try it with me."

"No!" I shook my head, terrified. As we approached the next turn, I froze my feet and nearly tripped her up.

"Slow down next time and I'll try," I said. She did, and to my surprise I crossed my feet over twice.

"Hey!" I shouted. "It works!"

"Of course. You're a good skater."

By the time we had taken three or four more laps, we were crossing our feet in unison on the turns as if we were partners in a skating exhibition. The organ was playing "Moon River," and for a minute it seemed like we were skating on it. Everything was spinning past Donna's face as she glided effortlessly along the floor, and somehow I was able to skate better than I ever had, just being with her.

"I love this song, don't you?" she said.

"Yes," I said. "Where'd you learn to skate so well?"

"Right here. I take lessons every week. That older guy over there—that's Lenny. He was a two-time national champion. He thinks I could take the state this year if I concentrate."

I didn't need to read lips in order to hear Donna Callaway talking on the skating floor.

"Take the state in what—roller derby?" That was the only official skating I knew about.

"Oh, I can do that too. Want me to show you?" And she crossed her arms as if to throw me a body block.

"No thanks!" I shouted, grabbing her hand back. "I believe you. Wow, state champion. That's boss!"

"Hey, look! There's Matt and Donna," she said. "Let's go skate under them."

I hardly believed it at first, but there they were—skating together. Jealousy welled up inside me, even though I was having such a good time with Donna Callaway and actually preferred skating with her. There was no rational reason for the feeling; it was just there. I also was surprised to see Matt and Donna Ivory talking so much—more than she had ever talked with me. So much so that they didn't notice us coming.

"Comin' through!" Donna Callaway shouted, and they had to lift their arms to let us under, or split apart. They chose the former. Looking back, we both motioned them under us. We did this back and forth a few times until Lenny came over and gently told Donna we probably shouldn't do that anymore.

"You're spoiling the romantic mood," he said with a smile. Seeing Donna talking with the head attendant made me remember the mysterious character in the rest room. Maybe she knew something about him.

"Since you spend a lot of time here," I said as we separated from Matt and Donna, "you wouldn't happen to have ever seen an older guy in a red and black checkered lumberjack coat around, would you?

"Is that the man you were talking about earlier?"

"Yeah."

"No, I don't remember ever seeing anyone like that."

Couples Skate was coming to a close. The music had stopped, some couples had already left the floor, and the entrances were jammed with little kids waiting for the All Skate announcement. Matt and Donna were already off, and I caught a glimpse of Donna and Marcie leaning over the rail watching us. Donna was glaring at Donna Callaway, but she didn't notice. We just kept skating and holding hands. It had seemed like the longest Couples Skate I had ever taken, and I was sad it was over.

"Thanks for skating with me," she said, squeezing my hand and not letting go. It felt nice to be thanked. Donna Ivory never thanked me; she just expected that we would skate together. Then I remembered that she had set this whole thing up. Why? And why, since she had suggested it, was she angry with Donna Callaway?

"Thanks for calling last night, too," she said as we slowed down and started coasting to an exit. "I don't understand, though, why you wanted to know if I was coming to the skate if you weren't planning on skating with me."

"I don't know what you mean," I said, puzzled.

"Last night, when you called. You know, that was the first time any boy ever called me just to talk."

I was speechless. What was she talking about? I hadn't called her. I was about to tell her that when "ALL SKATE SLOWLY AND CAREFULLY" came on the loudspeaker and kids started pouring in from the gaps in the railing.

"Hey, I have an idea," she said, leaning in and shouting over the noise, "you want to come get an ice cream bar with me? My grandparents gave me extra money. Come on; I'll buy. The machine's over here."

Too confused to raise any objection, I followed her over to the exit near where Donna and Marcie were standing. Just before we got there, she grabbed my right arm with both hands.

"I'm sorry I have to do this, but I promised." At which, to my total surprise, she swung me around once and sent me flying toward the crowded exit. I tried to grab the railing but there were people on either side blocking it. My skates stopped dead on the rubber matting, sending me sprawling on the ground headfirst. Two skaters had to jump out of the way to avoid hitting me.

"First time on skates?" said a smart-aleck high school kid, and I picked myself up as quickly as possible, trying to dust off the knees of my new blue jeans that would not totally yield the ground-in floor dust.

I couldn't believe Donna had done this to me after she had been so nice. I went to the rail to see if I could find her. Instead, I spotted Donna Ivory and Marcie rounding the far turn, pointing in my direction and laughing. So I was right! They all had this set up to begin with!

I jumped into the moving mass of skaters and headed for the far turn as fast as I could move. Donna and Marcie must have seen me coming, though, because they swung off at the nearest exit and headed straight for the women's lounge. *Dumb, dumb*, I thought. I should have waited until they caught up with me and then gone after them. I skated around a couple more times looking for Donna Callaway or Matt but found neither, so I decided to stop and watch for them in the moving crowd.

What on earth was going on? The writing on the bathroom door . . . the phone call I supposedly made to Donna . . . getting thrown by her . . . nothing was making sense.

Suddenly I heard a feminine voice singing behind me, "Don-na-a-a where can ya be?" I turned around to find Donna Callaway standing there grinning and holding two ice cream bars.

"No hard feelings?" she said. "Here." She held out an ice cream bar. "This is from me. The throw was from Donna Ivory, I swear."

"I figured," I said, thanking her for the ice cream. "But why didn't she do her own dirty work?"

"She didn't think she was a good enough skater. Besides, I figured it was my only chance of skating with you." She blushed as she said this, and the redness of her face made the freckles on her turned-up nose stand out. She wasn't pretty, like Donna Ivory, but I decided she was cute. Really cute, with a bit of a pixie smile.

"Where is Donna, anyway?" she said. "I thought she'd be around here enjoying her triumph."

"I think she's hiding in the girls' room."

"Are you mad at me?"

"No. You really creamed me, though. Do you really skate in roller derbies?"

"No, my coach just taught me a few moves for fun. You got my best one."

I liked talking to her. She was like a friend. Donna Ivory was almost too pretty to talk to; I could never think of anything to say.

"I suppose you'll be skating the last skate with Donna," she said.

"I don't know now. I didn't know she was so mad."

"She's not mad. She just wanted to get back at you as a joke."

And her joke had backfired when I met this other Donna, but I didn't say that. Instead I said, "What kind of skating do you do, if not the roller derby kind?"

"Freestyle skating. It's a lot like ice skating. We do routines to music. You should come to one of my practices sometime."

"I'd like that."

Suddenly I heard someone calling my name over the crowd noise. It was Matt.

"Jonathan," he said, coming up behind me, quite agitated, "you need to come with me right now."

"Why?" I said. I didn't want to leave Donna right then.

"I can't tell you now. Just come with me."

"Is it in the ba—" but Matt jerked me away so fast I didn't get to say "bathroom."

"I guess I'll see you later, Donna," I said as Matt kept pulling on me. "Thanks for the ice cream bar!"

"Thanks for the skate." She gave me a puzzled look and a wave.

"What's the deal, Matt?" I said as I lost sight of her in the crowd. "Why did you jerk me away like that?"

"Because you were starting to say something about the bathroom, and believe me, you don't want to be talking to anyone here about the men's bathroom."

"Why?"

"Because your initials are in it now."

"What? Are you kidding?"

"No. Yours and Donna's."

"Which Donna?" I said. We had started out on the opposite side of the rink from the men's room and it seemed to be taking forever for us to get there.

"That's what's *really* weird. At first it was Donna Ivory, but now it's Donna Callaway. Who knows who it will be by the time we get back there. Do you know any other Donnas?"

Now I was beginning to suspect something. Matt had come in late, and after that I'd discovered the "Ben B. was here." Then we'd gone back and found the date. Now this.

"Matt, are you doing this?"

He stopped dead in his tracks when I said this, and the fright on his face was enough to at least keep me from pressing him any further—that, along with a little anger at being mistrusted.

"Okay, okay . . . sorry."

"Look," he said, stopping near a bench around the corner from the bathroom door, "you go see for yourself. I probably shouldn't be hanging around there too much anymore."

"Sounds like you've had to go to the bathroom a lot tonight," I said, still not believing him completely.

When I got in the bathroom, someone was in the end stall, so I stood in front of the mirror messing with my hair. Suddenly I felt uneasy. What if the person in there, looking at my initials right that moment, was someone who knew me? So I slipped into the other stall. I tried to look under the wall, but all I could see was a pair of roller skates. Then I looked at my own feet and realized that if the guy next door was checking me out, he would notice my pants weren't down, so I dropped them and waited. (When you're thirteen, you expect everyone to be looking under the partition because that's exactly what you would do.)

A number of questions entered my head while I sat there. How many people in this church *didn't* know me? Hardly any. My father was the choir director, for heaven's sake. How many "J.L.'s" were there in the church? How many "D.C.'s?" I decided right then and there to dump my idea of skating with Donna Callaway on the last Couples Skate.

When the coast was clear, I went over to the other stall and studied the writing. It was just as Matt had said. "J.L. + D.C.," but it wasn't a curved *C*. It had a straight vertical back line, the top and bottom of which clearly bore evidence of once being an *I*.

I came back out and sat next to Matt.

"Fly's open," he said.

Not again, I thought as I went for my zipper, only to find it was up.

"Just kidding."

"Come on, Matt, this is no time for jokes!"

"So what do you make of it?"

"I don't know," I sighed. "One thing's for sure: we've got to stay away from that bathroom or I'm gonna get charged with this."

"But what if Ben's angel adds to the message again? Don't you want to know?"

"You can look if you want. I'm not going in there anymore."

"So you don't think it's an angel doing this?" said Matt.

"I said, I don't know what to think. It could be someone playing a joke on me or trying to get me in trouble."

"Well, one thing's for sure," said Matt, looking off to the side, "you're going to be in big trouble if you don't skate the last skate with Donna Ivory. She's expecting you to skate it with her."

"How do you know?" I looked in the direction he was looking and saw Donna sitting in the spot where she usually waited for me for Couples Skate.

"She told me."

"Well, what if I don't want to?"

"You can probably kiss your girlfriend good-bye."

"That would be almost worth it, seeing as I haven't kissed her yet."

"She watched you talking to Donna Callaway and she didn't look very happy."

Donna Ivory looked over our way for an instant and then looked away when she saw we were watching her.

"I don't get it," I said. "She's the one who set me up with Donna in the first place."

"She probably didn't expect you to have such a good time."

"You weren't having such a bad time yourself. Why don't you skate the last skate with her? She talks to you more than she talks to me."

"So I guess this means you're skating with Donna Callaway," he said, changing the subject. "The writing's on the wall."

"That's the very reason why I'm *not* skating with her."

As it turned out, I didn't skate with either one of them. I had had it with Donnas for the night. Instead, I skated with my sister, who welcomed the idea because she had just been jilted by her present love interest on the last skate of the night. So Becky and I represented the lonely hearts club, and Matt ended up skating with a stone-faced Donna Ivory, whom I would not speak with again for a long time—something that would delight Ben, I thought. And as far as I could tell, Donna Callaway went home early.

The last song of the night was Bobby Vee's "Devil or Angel," which captured the evening perfectly. It would be a while before I would figure out who was what.

The one person who finished the night happily was my mother, who told me later that it made her proud to see Becky and me together on the last skate.

6

Pearly Gates

The Colorado Avenue Standard Christian Church was a typical middle- to upper-middle-class evangelical church. It was white on the outside and white on the inside, except for one family who always had a whole pew to themselves about three rows back on the left side—a row that could always be spotted by the bright colors the mother wore and the feathered hats, which always ensured a wide gap in the row behind her. That was the Pearl family, consisting of the mother, Netta, and her three children, Isabelle, Issac, and Isaiah, evenly spaced at nine, seven, and five years of age. The father had passed away before they started coming to our church. He had built a successful business before his heart attack, the sale of which had netted Netta a tidy sum that put her in a wider circle of opportunity than her more disadvantaged neighbors. She said that it was primarily because of our excellent Sunday school program for her children that she had left the First Apostolic Holy Ghost Church of God in Christ down on the Arroyo near the roller rink; but she had left her old neighborhood as well and moved into a predominantly white area of Pasadena.

In 1961, the Pearls were not called African-American or even "black." They were Negroes. And there were still vestiges of the derogatory term "nigger" hanging around then.

My uncle, who grew up in the South, still called Brazil nuts "nigger toes," and little kids still used the popular coin-toss nursery rhyme, "eenie meenie minie mo, catch a nigger by the toe."

The Pearls had been coming to our church for almost a year, and Netta had made it clear she had every intention of making the Colorado Avenue Standard Christian Church her permanent church home. She had gone through the membership class and had even been baptized. Pastor Beamering had handled the whole affair splendidly and set a great example of acceptance and love, even when it meant losing two families and living with the ongoing ire of three more who decided to stay and make life miserable for him.

That wasn't all he lost. He also lost some water in the baptistery when he baptized Netta. It actually didn't happen when Netta went down; it happened when he tried to get her up.

Netta Pearl was big—250 pounds big. Yet she wasn't necessarily what you would call fat. A bit plump perhaps, but not fat. Fat is ugly and Netta was not ugly. She was big and wide and beautiful in the way that a mother's large lap is beautiful.

Pastor Beamering had anticipated some difficulty with the baptism, and I heard my father telling my mother that Jeffery T. had even considered using the help of Assistant Pastor Ivory, but then decided that this event already had enough attention drawn to it by virtue of Netta's color without adding insult by obviously adjusting tradition to cope with her size. That proved to be a fateful decision, since Pastor Beamering lost control of Netta going down. Had she been only fat, she might have been more buoyant; but Netta Pearl was just *big*, and she sank right out of Jeffery T.'s hands, causing the water level in the baptistery to rise considerably.

When he couldn't pick her up from his normal position, facing the congregation, Pastor Beamering quickly maneuvered himself around her, putting his back to us, so he could lift with his stronger right arm. His first attempt sent a wave of water over the front side of the baptistery as he slipped from her and fell back against the wall. The second, to the relief of everyone, finally brought Netta up out of the water. All of which only served to convince her that being rescued from her underwater tomb was all a part of her real salvation. She raised her hands, jumped and shouted "Glory to God!" and sloshed out more water over the edge of the baptistery until Pastor Beamering finally managed to calm her down with a prayer. This is why it would always be remembered at the Colorado Avenue Standard Christian Church that the last row of the choir were baptized simultaneously with Netta Pearl.

And now this intimate connection between Netta and the choir was about to take on an even greater significance, for Netta Pearl's attempts to roost somewhere in our church had finally landed her smack-dab in the middle of the front row of my father's choir loft.

For almost a year, her efforts to enter some arena of the life of our church had been met with a good deal of resistance. Through all this disappointment, her countenance remained perpetually optimistic. Netta had a way of brushing off prejudice—taking it with a grain of salt and laughing back a comment that always diffused the anger. Her spirit, like her frame, was big enough to absorb anything, and now that patience was finally going to receive its reward.

My father was visibly nervous as we drove to church. Not only because it was Netta's first Sunday in the choir, but because she was starting off with the biggest bang possible—a solo.

"Don't be so concerned, dear," my mother said, "you know she has a remarkable voice."

"Oh, I know that, honey, it's just that you never quite know where she's going with it. I'm not sure Milton can follow her, and she's definitely not going to be following him."

Milton Owlsley was our church organist, and Netta Pearl was going to severely test his fastidious musical sensibilities.

"Milton is dreading this morning, and so am I. I wish

Jeffery hadn't insisted she sing in the choir without at least talking to me first."

"And what would you have done?" asked my mother. "Turn her down, like the Ladies Aid Society and the Sunday school superintendent? I think that's just awful. She's got to know that the third and fourth grade classes are doubling up due to lack of teachers—one of her children is in the class!—and then they tell her they don't need any more teachers. To tell you the truth, I'm surprised she's still around here."

"Well, sometimes I wish she wasn't," said my father.

"Walter!"

"I'm sorry . . . I didn't really mean that . . . and you're right, I wouldn't have turned her down. But I certainly wouldn't have started her off with a *solo*. I still can't believe Jeffery promised her a solo on her first Sunday!"

"He was probably trying to make up for her other disappointments, dear. What song did you decide on, by the way?"

" 'The Love of God.' "

"The one Stuart Hamlin sings?"

"Yes, and George Beverly Shea. It's the only one I could find that she knows. Ann, I told you, the woman can't read music! Jeffery gave me a 250-pound woman who takes up two chairs in choir practice and can't read music!"

"Yes, but she can sing," said my mother.

"Boy, can she ever," said Becky. "I sat in front of her once, and my ears were buzzing afterwards."

"Does she really take up two chairs?" I asked, and my father nodded his head.

"Now you two be careful," warned my mother. "Netta Pearl is simply a large woman, and a very fine person, I think."

"Mom, 'large' isn't the word," said Becky. "She's colossal!"

"She's a house," I said.

"All right, that will be enough. I think we are all in for a real treat this morning."

"I wish I could feel that way," said my father, taking a turn we didn't usually take. "I hope you're right."

"Dear," said my mother, looking suspiciously at the houses and streets we were passing, "where are you going?"

"To church, of course."

"You haven't taken this way in years."

"Haven't I?"

"My goodness, you *are* nervous."

"I'm just fine," my father said, squaring his jaw.

Despite the slight detour, we got to church when we normally did, around 9:15. Sunday school was at 9:30 and church was at 11:00. I went to the choir room first with my father. I didn't want to get to Sunday school early. It wasn't cool to be early. Besides, I didn't want to risk the fact that Donna Ivory might be there early too.

When we walked into the choir room, Netta was already there with one of the other choir members.

"Hi, Mildred . . . and, Netta, don't you look nice this morning," said my father, half swallowing his words. She had on the loudest clash of bright color I had ever seen. Netta smiled and nodded proudly.

"Walter," said Mildred, a regular in the choir, standing next to a pile of choir robes slung over a few folding chairs. "We don't have a proper size robe for Netta."

"That's all right," said my father, getting out the music folders and giving them to me so I could start passing them out on the chairs. "It doesn't have to be a perfect fit this morning. Anything close will do. We'll have Claudia take care of fitting her after the service."

Mildred gave my father a look that clearly said he had not grasped the gravity of the situation. This didn't register with him, however, because he was buried in a hymnal at the time.

"Excuse me," I heard Mildred say to Netta under her breath, and then she went over and whispered to my father, "She can't fit into any robe we have."

"Oh," he said, following Mildred's eyes over to where

Netta was sitting. "Oh," he said again when he saw with new understanding what she was wearing. "Are you sure you can't find anything?"

Mildred nodded her head slowly. "Claudia will have to make up something this week from two of the other robes or we'll have to order from the factory, if they even have such a size."

"Well, she'll have to wear . . . what she has on," said my father with a certain pain in his voice. "Can you do something about the hat, though?"

Mildred went over and broke the news to Netta, who seemed quite relieved. But my poor father was going to be in for it this morning.

Sunday school had already started when I got there. All morning long, Donna Ivory gave me what I was expecting to get, the cold shoulder. She was like a porcupine with imaginary needles that stuck me if I got within three feet of her. I hardly ever looked at her, yet I always seemed to know right where she was all the time. I could feel her icy stare on the back of my head.

The more I thought about it, though, the less concerned I became. *There's got to be more to having a girlfriend than waiting for the next church skating night*, I thought.

I also found myself looking over at Donna Callaway a lot that morning, but she wasn't terribly friendly either. It made me wonder if they were in this together, the same way they'd plotted to knock me off my skates. I decided, as I listened to the Sunday school lesson, which was about some woman in the Old Testament who drove a tent peg through a guy's head while he slept, that I didn't want to have anything to do with girls anymore. I would play with my trains and maybe invite Matt over after church.

"Matt, do you want to come over to my house this afternoon—that is, if it's all right with my parents? I don't think it will be any problem."

"I'll have to check with Leonard and Bernice," he said. "I'll let you know after church."

Although I'd been wanting to show Matt my train layout, it was a pretty big step for me to invite him over, whether he could come or not. It was the first time since Ben's death that I had asked anyone over.

———————

My father's worst fears came true that Sunday in church. The choir was the green-robed backdrop for the colorful floral display that was Netta Pearl. It was not Netta *in* the choir; it was Netta *and* the choir.

On the choral numbers, like the Call to Worship and the Prayer Response and the Doxology, she made up her own part. Though she got all the words right, the notes were her own. In spite of this, however, she never sang a wrong note— that is, a note that didn't fit. It was simply not a note that was in the music. It was a note no one else was singing—a note, indeed, that no one in the Colorado Avenue Standard Christian Church ever knew existed before Netta Pearl.

Netta had been listening to these same choral responses for almost a year, and she'd been holding all those beautiful notes inside, waiting for this moment. No, she didn't need music, she didn't need directing; she needed to be cut loose. And once freed, it was Netta's voice filling every corner where sound could go in that church.

You could look at it from another perspective, of course. My father's worry over Netta having a solo on her first Sunday was unfounded. In truth, it was irrelevant, because every piece of music the choir sang was Netta's solo anyway. And by the time she got going, her outlandish dress actually seemed appropriate.

Though it turned out to be just one more solo for her, still, when Netta Pearl sang the anthem, "The Love of God," something happened—something that took everyone beyond the walls of the church to a place outside of time and space, a place they'd never been before. Someone said it was "the Throne of God." Pastor Beamering, never one to miss the opportunity for a pun, said it was the "Pearl-y Gates" Netta took us to.

The song was not new to most of us, but the way Netta sang it made it seem like we had never heard it before. She sang every word like it was a place to park. Her wide mouth brought forth rich vowel sounds that seemed to belong to another language. Her voice was not high and angelic, like the sopranos we were used to; it was low and deep and rich, rolling over you like a vast ocean.

I noticed the words of the song for the first time that day:

The love of God is greater far
Than tongue or pen can ever tell;
It goes beyond the highest star,
And reaches to the lowest hell

Every word erupted into a picture. Tongues wagged, pens went off pages, stars shot by at warp speed, and hell burned.

In the beginning, Milton Owlsley fought with the time Netta was taking over these words. He would play a musical pattern and then have to wait for her to catch up with him. This was the type of song that needed to be stretched out, and Netta was taking it as far as it would go. It seemed like words were blooming as she sang them, with blossoms as big and bursting as the ones on the floral print of her dress.

The guilty pair, bowed down with care,
God gave His Son to win;
His erring child, He reconciled,
And pardoned from his sin

For some reason, when Netta sang these words, I understood them. Maybe she sang it slow enough so I could really think about the words, or maybe she had some spiritual gift of interpretation. The guilty pair was Adam and Eve. She didn't say that; Adam and Eve just popped into my head. Of course . . . that made sense.

Most of the congregation was transfixed—even the people who had been giving Pastor Beamering a bad time about accepting the Pearl family. Our church had never heard anything come from the depths of the soul the way "The Love of God" came from this woman.

The only people who weren't getting it were my father and Milton. My father was waving his arms, trying to direct Milton. He was not directing Netta—he was smarter than that—but he was trying to interpret Netta to Milton. It wasn't working. My father's arm-waving would have been a distraction were it not for the hold Netta had on the congregation. And it certainly wasn't helping Milton, who kept running ahead of each phrase and waiting for her to catch up.

By the third verse my father realized his directing was of no consequence and stopped. Milton realized something too, for he stopped keeping time altogether and just played the chords behind Netta's notes, moving them around her voice when she moved. That's when it all came together. That's when everyone stopped fighting and allowed Netta to paint the most beautiful picture of all.

Everyone was with her now, and Netta knew it. She approached this last verse rocking on each foot and closing her eyes to balance her giant frame so her soul could reach down to the bottom of that deep well from which she drew the bittersweet waters of generations of suffering, hope, and grace— of rejection by men and acceptance by God in a place where there was no earthly home but a heavenly mansion.

> Could we with ink the oceans fill,
> And were the skies of parchment made;
> Were every stalk on earth a quill,
> And every man a scribe by trade;
> To write the love of God above
> Would drain the ocean dry,
> Nor could the scroll contain the whole,
> Though stretched from sky to sky.

Milton had it now. Milton was off the page, and they were in sync. He opened up the organ and Netta opened her big wide arms and the choir actually swayed to the time that was outside of time as they sang behind her.

> O love of God, how rich and pure!
> How measureless and strong!
> It shall forevermore endure—
> The saints' and angels' song.

Netta finished, Milton's hands came up off the organ keys, and though applause might have been called for, there was none. Not right away. Only a reverent hush. Pastor Beamering, a veteran of the unexpected in church, though it had been a while since he'd had to consider it, slowly mounted the pulpit and stood there motionless.

It was a strange silence. Not uncomfortable, but a silence that rendered speech inoperative. There was nothing to say— nothing that could be said. It was appropriate silence. Silence with a finish. Finally, slowly and methodically, way after the natural time for applause had passed, Pastor Beamering began to clap. All alone at first, then joined by a random few, then gaining force, then thunderous and seemingly unending.

Netta Pearl found the nearest chair, which happened to be one of the oversized platform chairs, and sat down, wiping her perspiring face with a hanky as the genuine appreciation continued unabated. Then, from sheer exhaustion, it stopped and the normal sounds of humanity returned to the sanctuary. Throats cleared, noses blew, coughs were expelled, seats were retaken, bodies rearranged themselves, Bibles and hymnals were moved about, and children were whispered to or shaken by the arm.

"Open your Bibles, please, to the eighth chapter of Romans, verses 38 and 39." Pastor Beamering paused for the zip of Bibles being pulled out of the backs of pews and the feathering of a thousand pages to rise and fall. "We will continue our study on angels next week, but today, inspired by this exceptional reminder of the love of God, I want us to focus on that on which even angels long to look."

What could that be? I wondered. *What do we know that angels don't? How can we be smarter than angels?*

" 'For I am persuaded, that neither death, nor life, nor angels, nor principalities, nor powers, nor things present, nor things to come, nor height, nor depth, nor any other creature, shall be able to separate us from the love of God, which is in Christ Jesus our Lord.' May the Lord add His blessing to the reading of His holy word."

Then, without dropping his eyes to read them, he began quoting the song Netta had just finished singing.

" 'The love of God is greater far than tongue or pen can ever tell; it goes beyond the highest star, and reaches to the lowest hell.' The man who wrote these words, and the man who wrote the Scripture we just read, both knew the same thing. They knew that the greatest, the single most powerful, most sure thing in all the world is the love of God. Regardless of what happens to any of us, it is and will be our most valuable possession." He paused. "Just how high is the highest star?"

"High," came a deep voice from somewhere. Pastor Beamering halted a second, then went on.

"And how low is the lowest hell?"

"Low." The voice came again from somewhere near the pastor.

"Does any one of us know?" And this time, Jeffery T. waited for the response.

"No!" came the voice, growing in strength.

People strained to see where the odd echo to Pastor Beamering's dramatic words was coming from. It didn't take long to realize it was coming from the platform—more specifically, from Netta Pearl, who was so caught up in the extraordinary events of the morning that she forgot she was not in the First Apostolic Holy Ghost Church of God in Christ.

"I'll tell you who knows," said Pastor Beamering, spurred

on by the fact that his once-dead congregation was suddenly giving him what every pastor craves: instant feedback.

"God knows!"

"Glo-ry!" went the echo.

"No matter where you go—high or low—God has been there first."

"Yes He has!"

"He came from heaven . . ."

"Uh-huh . . ."

"And descended into the depths of hell itself . . ."

"Mercy!" The echo was coming short and quick now.

"For you and me."

"Amen!"

Netta had started answering Jeffery T.'s appeals almost in a whisper, but each successive burst grew louder until it was a verbal duet. By now, though, the poor congregation was a mixture of amusement and horror.

Pastor Beamering, knowing he had to do something, turned to his new cohort on the platform and said in a kind voice, "Netta, honey, if you keep this up, I'm never going to get my sermon in edgewise."

That broke the tension in the room with laughter and woke Netta up to the fact that she was in a Standard Christian church full of white faces. She laughed harder than anyone and quieted down after that, leaving Pastor Beamering to develop his extemporaneous sermon on the love of God. It was one of his best, recalling the days when the unexpected from Ben and me threw him into depending on something other than his notes and pre-thought words and messages.

The part of that sermon I remember the most was when he talked about the "saints' and angels' song." He said that the love of God was a song that saints could actually sing better than angels, because angels had never been sinners. Only saints knew what it meant to be a sinner saved by grace, he said, and that statement had gotten one last "Amen" from Netta—one that everyone felt, but she expressed for us. Stan-

dard Christians were not accustomed to seeing themselves as
sinners.

After the service I looked for Matt and ran into Grizzly
instead. Actually, he was looking for me, since I was his pri-
mary source of interpretation. As it turned out, there had
been some plumbing emergencies in the rest room of the old
educational wing, which kept him out of the service. His
keen visual perception of people, however, told him something was up.

"WHAT HAPPENED IN THERE TODAY?" He al-
ready had it written on his pad in anticipation of finding me.

"Netta Pearl is what happened," I said by only moving my
lips. He stared at me, unable to make the read.

"Netta Pearl," I repeated.

"WHO ATE A PEARL?" he wrote down, and then I remembered he couldn't read proper names unless he already
knew who you were talking about.

Taking his pad in my hand I wrote, "NETTA PEARL."
He brightened and nodded his head, stretching out his arms
real wide with a question mark on his face.

"Yes, the big Negro woman," I said, again by only moving
my lips. "She sang with the choir. It stopped the show."

"LIKE BEN!"

Well . . . yes, just like Ben, though I hadn't thought of it
until he wrote it down.

"HAVEN'T SEEN PEOPLE LEAVE CHURCH THIS
HAPPY SINCE BEN."

Grizzly was always one to keep the memory of Ben alive.
Most everyone else was afraid to bring it up. I never understood that. I loved talking about Ben, though sometimes I
resisted. He would always be in my life through my memories
of him, and now maybe even through his angels.

"WHAT DID SHE SING ABOUT?"

"She sang about the angels' song," I mouthed. I knew he
would like that, and he smiled when I said it.

"It's in the song," I said, and I got out the bulletin where the words were written down and showed him the last line of the chorus: "The saints' and angels' song."

"BEN'S SONG TOO," he wrote, "BEN'S A SAINT NOW—BEN AND THE ANGELS SING."

"When do you hear angels sing?" I asked. "Is it a certain time?"

"ONLY WHEN ALONE."

"When *you're* alone?"

He nodded.

"During the day? Night?"

He thought for a minute and then wrote, "COULD HAPPEN ANYTIME NO ONE HERE."

"May I listen with you sometime?"

He welcomed the idea with joy, nodding vigorously.

Just then we were interrupted by one of the deacons who informed Grizzly that another toilet in the education building was backing up and they needed him right away. So with a wave of his pad, he was gone.

I went back to looking for Matt but never found him. Instead I found Donna Callaway sitting on a bench in the narthex, waiting for her grandparents who were in line to see Pastor Beamering. It was a longer line than usual because Netta Pearl was greeting people along with the pastor.

This had come about more through the natural course of events than by any pastoral design. I knew how these things worked from observing Pastor Beamering deftly turn potential disruptions by Ben and me into events that flowed into the course of the service as if they had been planned.

Netta Pearl was still on the platform when Jeffery T. finished his sermon, since the choir had exited after her solo while she was caught up in the applause of the congregation, leaving her alone there. Pastor Beamering's usual close to a service was to start the congregation on the final hymn and then walk down the center aisle during the second or third verse so that he could give his benediction from the back of the church. This left him in the advantageous position to greet the first worshipers who wanted to speak to him or shake his hand on their way out.

So rather than leave Netta sitting alone on the platform, Pastor Beamering had taken her arm and escorted her down the aisle with him during the hymn. (Of course Netta kept singing all the way down, bringing her big voice into close proximity to those on the inside aisle and even closer to the beaming face of Pastor Beamering.) Thus, the first greeters to get to the pastor after the benediction found that Netta Pearl was there to greet them too, with a wide grin, big arms, and an even bigger heart.

"Hi," I said to Donna, sitting down next to her on the cold wooden bench.

"Oh, hi, Jonathan," she said with a little flat spot in the middle of her voice.

"Why didn't you stay for the last skate?" I asked.

"My grandparents were with me, and they were getting tired," she said, looking down. "Besides, I didn't want to watch you skate with Donna."

Her bluntness took me a little by surprise.

"I didn't skate with Donna."

"You didn't?" she said, brightening.

"No, I skated with Becky."

"Who's Becky?"

"My sister."

"Oh," she said, trying to hide her pleasure. "Donna's so pretty."

"I think you're pretty."

She bit her lip and looked over at her grandparents who had finally made it to Jeffery T. and Netta.

"Why don't you come to my practice this week?" she said, suddenly turning her whole body in my direction and looking straight at me, her ponytail bouncing behind her head.

"When do you practice?"

"Every day after school."

"Every day?"

"And two hours on Saturday."

"I have to deliver papers after school, but I might be able to come on Saturday. I'll have to talk to my parents."

"Saturday would be great! I practice in the morning at ten o'clock. Why don't you call me again this week and let me know if you can come."

Again? There was that mysterious phone call stuff again. It made me wonder, if I didn't call her, would she hear from me anyway? I thought about trying to get to the bottom of it right then and letting her know it wasn't me who called, but she was so happy and I liked where this whole thing was going, so I didn't say anything.

Just then Donna's grandparents started in our direction, and she quickly excused herself and joined them before they ever came close to the bench where we sat. She seemed embarrassed, and I wondered if it was because her grandmother was in a wheelchair. I wondered also where her parents were. Maybe they didn't go to church.

The last few people were waiting to speak with Pastor Beamering, and Matt was still nowhere in sight. I was about to go look for him when my mother came and put her arm around me and headed me toward the pastor and Netta Pearl.

"Come on, Jonathan. Let's let this woman know what a fine job she did this morning."

I started to wrestle away from her, but Jeffery T. had already spotted us.

"Jonathan!" he said, clasping his hands together and washing me all over with his pastorly glow. "I heard you came by the house this week. We've wondered where you've been. Let's not become strangers now." He thrust out his hand and flashed me his big shiny grin.

"Hi," I said while he shook my arm vigorously up and down.

"Netta," my mother said, "that was the most glorious

thing I have ever heard. I'm so happy you had a chance to share your wonderful talents with us, and I certainly hope there will be more of this." She winked at Pastor Beamering when she said this.

"Why, thank you, Mrs. Liebermann . . . and this is your boy, here? You know, we nevuh met."

"You haven't? Well, this is Jonathan."

"Hullo, Jonathan," and something in the way she said it made me swell up inside. The tone of her voice made it sound as if I were someone very important she had been waiting to meet. When I put out my hand, she totally enclosed it with both of hers. I had never touched a Negro before. I don't know what I was expecting, but I found nothing unusual about her hands except that they were big and warm and kind.

"How old are you, Jonathan?"

"Thirteen."

"Thirteen," she mused. "A year of comin' out. A year of discoverin'. What have you discovered since you been thirteen, child?"

I didn't know what to say. No one had ever demanded creative thinking from me on such short notice. She gave me no mercy. She just stood there smiling and waiting, her eyebrows perched expectantly atop the big bony ledges over her broad nose.

"I . . . uh . . . I found out angels are real."

"Splendid!" she said, and Pastor Beamering smiled an especially big smile. Of course, not knowing I had been kissed on the lips by an angel, he was probably thinking my revelation had come through his sermons. "And just how did you find this out?"

I looked up at Jeffery T.'s hovering smile.

"Through Pastor Beamering's sermons," I said, hoping not to be questioned further.

"Have you evuh met an angel, Jonathan?" she said, dashing my hopes. I did not want to explain any further. Fortunately Netta saved me by answering her own question.

"I have," she said.

"Really?" said Pastor Beamering.

"Yes suh. The night my husband died. I awoke and saw two tall men a-talkin' softly at the end of my bed. It was the very moment George died, and though his body lie next to me, when the angels left, they was three of them. It made it so much easiuh to take. It was the most peaceful feelin' I've evuh known."

"Well—" said Pastor Beamering, breaking the mood of the moment and clasping his hands as though preparing to speak.

"What a beautiful story," my mother said slowly, interrupting his attempted closure.

"Yes," said Jeffery T. "A beautiful story, indeed. Well . . . I'm ready to wrap this morning up and go get some dinner. Netta, would you care to join us? We're just going down the street to the cafeteria."

"Oh, no thank you, pastor. I have a roast waitin' in the oven."

"Thank you again for your important part in this morning's service, said Mrs. Beamering."

"Oh, mercy me, it's Him you should be thankin'. He's the one done give me this voice."

7

Up the Tower

"Now what am I going to do?" said my father as we pulled out of the church parking lot and headed down Colorado Avenue toward Beedle's Cafeteria.

"About what, dear?"

"About Netta Pearl, of course. Thanks to Jeffery, I now have one very large Negro woman who has turned my choir into nothing more than a gospel backup group. I have an organist who suddenly wants to learn to play like Booker somebody and the sports cars—"

"Booker T and the M.G.'s, Daddy," said Becky.

"—whatever they are. Where am I going to get music for this? If Netta Pearl is going to be in my choir, everything will have to be changed to accommodate her, for heaven's sake. Everything!"

We sat at a signal light in silence. We could feel the tension coming from the front seat, and Becky and I kept looking at each other, trying hard not to laugh.

"To tell you the truth, sometimes I wonder what I'm going to do with Jeffery," my father finally blurted out. "He's the one who always seems to set up these situations and then expects me to solve them. Sometimes I wish I could just wipe that silly little grin right off his face!"

"Walter! I can't believe you're talking like this."

Becky and I grinned fake smiles at each other, both of us silently wagging our bottom lips like a ventriloquist's dummy. The two of us had a running joke about Pastor Beamering that likened him to Edgar Bergen's Charlie McCarthy—the shiny face, the plastered-down hair, the hard head, and the smile that never changed.

"Well, it's true, Ann. I asked him that very thing . . . 'What are we going to do now?' . . . and he just smiled at me and said nothing. Nothing! All he did was smile at me. Honestly, I hate that . . . that—"

"Honey, cool down. We're almost to the restaurant."

Hearing my father talk about his frustration with Pastor Beamering reminded me of playing games with Matt. He would always beat me. Not only at gin, but any other games we played at the beach, for that matter, like chess or Chinese checkers—or even Ping-Pong in the youth room at church. Somehow he always managed to win. The worst was Ping-Pong. He never hit the ball hard; he'd just keep lobbing it back to me—regardless of where or how hard I hit it to him—until I finally got frustrated and smashed it off the table or into the net. I *hated* it when he did that. In the Bible that I got for graduating from the sixth grade into the junior high department, Matt actually had the nerve to write, "Since you'll never beat me at anything, vaporize!" Jeffery T.'s silent smile, like a dummy without a hand inside it, was just like Matt's lob return, and I imagined my father wanting to smash the pastor's smile down his throat right about then.

"I'm taking her out of the choir, Ann," he said as we pulled into Beedle's parking lot.

"Oh, honey, you can't do that after one week."

"Actually, it's not like that. Technically, she's never been *in* the choir. I honestly don't think she ever could sing just one part along with the other women. I *am* seriously thinking about having her only sing once a month. What do you think about that? Once a month could be Netta Pearl Sunday."

"I think we'd better go have dinner with the Beamerings and talk about this later."

My father rarely took us out to eat, but when he did, it was most likely to Beedle's Cafeteria. Beedle's was only a few blocks from the church and served an inexpensive buffet dinner that was popular with the Sunday church crowd. Once every couple months we would have Sunday dinner there, usually with the Beamerings.

I hated Beedle's. You had to wait in line for half an hour in a long, empty hallway. The food wasn't too bad once you got it, but nothing like my mother's Sunday dinner. I always thought that if you were going to go out to eat, it should be better than what you could get at home, and you shouldn't have to stand in line for it. Not so at Beedle's. Becky and I always changed the *d* to a *t* on our place mats and pretended we were hunting for beetles in the food. Once my father found a gnat in his salad. We told him it was a beetle without its shell, which we were sure he had already eaten.

"That was the crunchy part, Daddy," said Becky.

I always got halibut, not because I particularly liked fish, but because it was the best thing there. It was lightly battered and baked and looked like a giant, overweight cornflake. The best part about it was the tartar sauce Becky and I would squeeze out of little thimble-sized paper cups.

It was just as well that I hadn't found Matt after church, because I wouldn't have been able to have him over anyway. I had forgotten that we were going to Beedle's. Every time Becky or I tried to have a guest come along when we were going out, my father would get this pained look on his face, and my mother would say that it probably wouldn't be a good idea this time. If Matt had found me after church, I would have had to go through the embarrassment of un-inviting him on account of my father's face.

To add to my dismay, the Ivorys were also there that day, and Pastor Beamering was trying to get enough tables together to accommodate all three families. I breathed a sigh of relief when his attempts failed. Besides, they were too far ahead of us and were well into their meal by the time we got through the line.

The worst part about being at Beedle's Cafeteria, however, was not the food or the line; it was Pastor Beamering. His voice was as loud as it was from the pulpit. That afternoon, for instance, the entire restaurant knew all the details of his attempts to get our three families together at one seating. For a moment it seemed like one older couple sitting at a table next to the Ivorys might get up and move, but the man was hard of hearing and never got the message from his wife that the pastor of the Colorado Avenue Standard Christian Church was bearing down on them. I was rooting for the old guy all the way and was happy to see him stay put. I wanted to be as far away from Donna Ivory as possible. As it was, she kept her eyes away from me at all times.

Then there was Pastor Beamering's prayer over the meal. Believe it or not, he would actually stand up, stretch his long arms out over the three tables it took to seat our families, and bless the food *out loud!* That's when I would drop my napkin and go under the table for it.

Once through the line, you could cut back into it for seconds. After the pastoral buffet prayer, which usually had the Gospel story somewhere in it for anyone who might be listening, I surfaced with my napkin and immediately went back for my favorite part of the meal that I had forgotten to get the first time: the corn muffins. They were real tasty with lots of butter melted into them. I put two muffins on my plate and returned to my seat, only to have Peter and Joshua reach over and snatch them away. That was the other thing I didn't like about eating out with the Beamerings. The Beamering boys would always tease me. Part of this was probably because I was the youngest and they didn't have Ben to pick on anymore, but part of it was to show off for my sister's benefit.

There was a time when they used to tease her along with me. No more. My sister's sudden blooming had changed all that. Almost overnight, she went from being someone Peter and Joshua wanted to tease to someone they wanted to impress. Now they just teased me.

When I came back from my second muffin trip, Pastor Beamering was waxing on about Netta Pearl.

"Did you see the look on Mable Buecher's face when Netta started rockin' and rollin' on the second chorus? I thought she was going to roll over and die right there on the spot."

I caught Becky's eye and knew we were both thinking the same thing. If he thought "The Love of God" was rock 'n' roll, he had some big surprises coming.

"And Milton! Did you get a load of Milton? She actually had him going there. Do you know what he told me?"

"No," my father said, and I wondered if there was another version of Booker T. and the M.G.'s coming up. Sure enough. . . .

"He said he was going to start listening to Booker T. and the Emcee's—some rock group he knows about with a lot of organ in it. Can you believe that? Milton Owlsley, of all people!"

I looked around the table and it was obvious that everyone, including my parents, after being corrected by my sister, knew the pastor hadn't gotten the name of the Booker T. group quite right, but no one dared say anything to him. At moments like these I felt Ben's absence sharply. Ben would have said something. He was the only one who could. Without Ben around, Pastor Beamering got away with too much.

"You know, Walter, people weren't sure at first, but by the time she was done, they loved her. They want to hear more, Walter. They are going to hear more, aren't they?"

"Well . . . uh . . . sure. You can't have talent like that around and not use it. It's just that—"

"Good! I have a feeling this is stirring something among us. I haven't heard the church buzzing like this since Ben and Jonathan had them going. Right, Jonathan?"

"Yes, sir. By the way—"

"Well, Walter, what can you say about this morning?"

I surprised myself by trying to get a word in about the rock group, but what could anyone say after Jeffery T. had said it all?

"I'd say she had them eating out of her hands, Jeff."

"Boy, you can say that again."

Because I felt it had to be done, I wrote "IT'S BOOKER T. AND THE M.G.'S on a napkin and slipped it to Mrs. Beamering on the way out. She was the only one who could correct the pastor, but never in public. It was suddenly important to me to make sure Pastor Beamering got the name right. Maybe it was because I knew it would have been important to Ben.

"Well, that helped a lot," my father said sarcastically when we were back in the car driving home.

I noticed that I now had a nice big tartar sauce grease spot on the front of my pants, proof we'd been to Beedle's.

"You can talk to him alone tomorrow," said my mother. "He's much more cooperative when he doesn't have an audience."

"The whole restaurant is his audience," said Becky.

"Yes, Becky," said my mother. "That's all part of being a pastor."

"What, being obnoxious?"

"No, being firm and outspoken. If you can't say something nice, young lady, then don't say anything at all."

"Daddy, can I drive again today?"

"Not today, sweetheart. I have work to do for tonight's service."

"Darn."

"I wanted to have Matt over today," I said, "but we went out."

"I'd be happy to have Matt over anytime. Why not next Sunday?" said my mother.

"Okay, I'll ask him. And do you think someone could

take me to the roller rink next Saturday morning?"

"The roller rink? What for?"

"Donna Callaway has invited me to come watch her practice."

"So the Roller Derby Queen won the contest of Donnas," said my sister.

"Cut it out," I said to her. "She's not a roller derby skater."

"She practices roller skating?" said my mother. "Why?"

"She's entering competitions and stuff."

"I've never heard of such a thing, have you, dear?"

"What?" said my father, obviously somewhere else in his thoughts.

"What happened to Donna Ivory?" asked my mother.

"Nothing. I'd just like to see Donna Callaway skate, that's all. And she invited me."

"Well, I don't know about this," my mother said. "Someone would have to be with you at the roller rink. How long does she practice?"

"Two hours. You could just drop me off and come back later."

"I don't know. That sounds like a date to me, and you're not old enough to date yet. And besides, I'm not sure who this Donna Callaway is. Are they new in the church?"

"I wouldn't even be with her, Mother, I'd just be *watching* her."

"I think your father and I need to discuss this. Donna Callaway . . . do you know her parents, Walter?"

My father made no reply. His mind was still on something else—Netta Pearl, most likely.

"She always comes to everything with her grandparents," said Becky. "Her grandmother's in a wheelchair."

"Oh, so *that's* Donna Callaway. Your father and I definitely need to discuss this at another time."

"Why? What's wrong?"

"Never mind. We'll discuss it later."

I flashed my sister a gee-thanks-a-lot look, which she returned with a how-was-I-to-know? shrug.

I spent most of the afternoon up with my train set laying track in and around the completed mountains. I had already put a switch inside the mountain so that one track went in one side and two came out the other. I also had built up one of those tracks inside the mountain so it came out on top of the other. It was the high road and the low road railroad. While I worked, I thought about taking the low road and getting to Donna's practice regardless of what my parents decided.

My train layout was more exciting to work on now that I was within sight of getting all the track up and actually running the trains. It had taken almost a year to get to this point because I never had any concentrated time to work on it. I figured one good vacation period should do it—maybe Thanksgiving, or for sure by Christmas.

Often I was distracted along the way by ideas that had nothing to do with setting up the trains. My little model town had sidetracked me for months. Once I saw some ¼-inch plywood that my father was about to throw away and got the idea for raised city blocks. By cutting the plywood into rectangles with rounded corners, I was able to define the streets of my town with real curbs. I even cut notches in the plywood where I wanted driveways to be and formed ramps down from the curb level out of plaster of Paris. Then I painted the streets black and the curbs and sidewalks gray, making lines for cracks in the sidewalk. Ben would have been proud. Sometimes I imagined he was watching me from heaven. I didn't know whether people in heaven could do that or not, but it seemed like anything should be possible from up there. Sometimes I thought I heard him say, "No, Jonathan, that's a dumb idea . . ." and things like that.

In some ways I think I looked for excuses to slow down this project because I felt that completing it would be boring. There would be nothing to do but run the trains. It was much more fun to imagine and create than to actually play with the trains. None of the people who had seen my layout understood this. They couldn't understand why it was taking me so long to get my trains running. But I loved thinking about my layout, dreaming up creative ideas for it or talking to Ben about it. I loved finding odd things that would take on new significance when placed in the scale of my layout, like barrel candy that turned into real barrels when painted and stacked against the walls of a warehouse. It had been the same with the houses Ben and I worked on. The point was not to complete them but to enjoy the process.

That night church went by slowly. I had big plans for me and Donna Callaway after church. Whatever it was about her that concerned my mother had only made me more determined to see her skate and, if need be, find out about her parents myself. From my mother's tone, that seemed to be the big problem—her parents. Her parents, and now mine. We needed a place to talk away from all eyes, and I knew exactly where that would be.

All during church I fingered the little penlight flashlight that I had tucked away in my pocket. She might be frightened at first, I thought, but when she discovered how special a place it was, she would be impressed. The only problem was going to be slipping in the door without being seen. In my favor was the fact that the turnout at church was light that night, especially among our junior high group. Fewer friends to have to shake off.

Donna was sitting a few rows behind me, and at the conclusion of the service I caught her eye and pointed to the back of the church. When I got to the narthex, she was already there.

"Hi, Jonathan," she said, and her voice sounded like water dancing over smooth rocks.

"Can you come with me? I want to show you something."

"Sure . . . but . . . where are we going? My grandparents don't like to stay long on Sunday nights."

"This will only take about five minutes."

"Okay, just a minute." And she worked her way back through the exiting flow of churchgoers to find her grandparents.

"No problem," she said when she returned. "They're talking with some friends anyway. I have to be at the car in ten minutes, though."

"Good. This way," I said, and led her to an unmarked door along the back wall of the church. Glancing around to make sure there were no spying eyes, I unlocked it—thanks to Grizzly—opened the door, and pulled her into the darkness.

"Jonathan, what are we doing in here?"

I quickly got out my flashlight and lit up her startled face.

"Up there," I said, pointing the little beam at a vertical ladder that went up the back wall of a tiny room no bigger than a closet. "Can you climb that?"

"Yes. What's up there?"

"Follow me and I'll show you."

I handed her the light and started up the ladder. I didn't need to see; I knew every board in this place by heart. I sat on the landing and waited for her.

"Oh, wow, this is boss up here. How did you ever find this?"

"Exploring," I said. "Look over here," and I pointed out the little window that looked out over the church from high up on the back wall of the balcony.

"This is really swell. I can see my grandparents down there. What's with this place?"

"It used to be a bell tower, and the bell ringer would stand here and watch through the window for the service to be over so he could ring the bells right after the benediction."

" 'Every time a bell rings, an angel gets its wings,' " she said.

"What's that?"

"Oh, just a saying I know. So no one uses this place anymore?"

"No. Ben and I used to be up here a lot. It was our hideout. We used to play tricks on the church from up here, too."

"Who's Ben?"

"He was Pastor Beamering's son and my best friend. He died a couple years ago. Look over here. You can see outside."

I showed her the vent where you could look through the slats and see the front steps of the church and the sidewalk below. A quiet mist must have been falling during the service because the street and the sidewalk were wet and people were moving quickly to their cars. The faint swish of tires on Colorado Avenue attested to the gentle precipitation.

"Wow, you can see everything from up here," she said. "I can see why this would be a perfect hideout."

Then she started shining the penlight around the inner walls of the little room.

"Careful," I said, "that will show up in the window."

"What's that?" she said, stopping the light at a crumpled piece of paper tacked to the wall. She looked closer and read out loud, " 'Saturday, January 17, 1959. There is a God-shaped vacuum in the heart of Ben. There is a Ben-shaped vacuum in the heart of God.' That's beautiful. Did you write that?"

"No. Ben did. He slipped that into my hand just before he died."

"How did he die, anyway?"

"Heart failure."

"I'm so sorry. I can tell he meant a lot to you."

I was glad she wasn't shining the light in my eyes right then.

"How come you're always with your grandparents?" I risked, knowing we didn't have much time.

"I live with my grandparents."

"What happened to your parents?"

"I don't know."

"Have you always lived with your grandparents?"

"As long as I can remember."

"I can't imagine what that would be like."

"My grandparents are okay."

"No, I mean not knowing where your parents are."

"I manage."

"Don't you have any idea?" I hoped I wasn't pressing too hard.

"No," she answered in a voice I didn't quite trust.

I decided I'd gone far enough with my questioning. "I'm going to come see you skate on Saturday."

"You are?"

The change in her voice made the moment. I knew right then that nothing would keep me away from that rink, even if I had to do something bad to get there.

"Better check on your grandparents," I said, not knowing what to do with my emotions at that moment. For a second the flashlight caught her face, and her eyes seemed to reflect more light than they were given.

"Oh dear," she said, looking out the little window, "they're not there anymore. I better go."

"Here. I'll hold the light for you down the ladder. You go out first. I'll wait a while up here."

"Jonathan, why is everything so secret?"

"This is a secret place, and—" I caught myself.

"And what? It's my parents, isn't it?"

"It's my parents finding out about your parents, I guess. I'm sorry I even brought it up."

"That's okay. It used to bother me, but I'm used to it now. Anyway, I'm so excited about Saturday. No one's come just to see me before except my grandparents. My routine is getting ready for competition, too. You have no idea how happy this makes me." She threw her arms around me and gave me a big hug.

"Please don't tell anybody about this tower," I said.

"If anyone can keep a secret," she said, sounding slightly offended, "it's me."

When she reached the bottom of the ladder, she looked up at me, her face radiant in the small beam of my penlight. "Thank you, Jonathan," she said. "I love your tower! See you Saturday!" And a shaft of light lit up her bouncing ponytail as she slipped out the door.

8

Practice

"Matt," I said over the phone, "you've got to help me."

It was Monday afternoon, I had just finished delivering my papers, and I was calling him from a pay phone next to the corner market because I couldn't risk being overheard at home.

"What's the problem, Casanova?"

That comment came from the night before. Matt had been at church, but I hadn't seen him until I came down from the tower. I stayed up there as long as I could without raising suspicions. It was so wonderful to feel that secret place warmed by smiles and voices again. It had become so lonely there that I wouldn't go up, even though it was such a special place to me. Without Ben, it had become an aching place. But Donna's smile had changed all that, and I imagined Ben was smiling, too.

Without even knowing it, Donna had opened up a way for me to meet my memories again. Her face lit up that dark place in the tower much like the face of Margaret, the angel, lit up the bunker. Donna's was a younger face, with freckles and a turned-up nose, and though she was not an angel, she did have fine, curly blond angel hair.

Matt had figured something was up by the time he ran into me in the parking lot.

"Hey, where have you been?" he had said. "I've been looking all over for you."

"Oh . . . nowhere in particular. Just . . . wandering around."

"You wouldn't have wandered into a dark closet somewhere, would you? The same one I saw Donna Callaway coming out of with a big smile on her face? Was there perhaps a little kissy-face going on in there? Huh? Huh?"

In the excitement of showing Donna the tower, I had forgotten to relock the door once we were in. I remembered noticing the door open and close once while I was still up in the tower, shortly after Donna left. It must have been Matt, looking for me and finding what he thought was an empty janitorial closet. That was what most people in the church thought that door went to. So he had put two and two together and come up with Donna and me smooching in the closet. The sacrifice I had to pay to keep Matt from knowing about my secret tower was to leave his "kissy-face" allegations unchallenged. *Not that costly a sacrifice*, I thought. Not really. Thus my new moniker: Casanova.

"You've got to invite me over to your house on Saturday morning," I said over the phone, ignoring his comments.

"Okay, you're invited. What's up?"

"I've got to figure a way out of the house for a few hours. Donna Callaway has—"

"Aha!" Matt interrupted. "Why did I know this had something to do with Donna Callaway? Didn't you get enough in the closet?"

"Shut up and let me finish," I said. "Donna has invited me to watch her roller-skating practice Saturday, but my parents aren't going to let me go."

"How come?"

"I'm not sure. I think it has something to do with her living with her grandparents and not knowing where her real parents are."

"So? What else is new?"

Suddenly I realized I had come very close to describing Matt's circumstances as well. The phone felt dead and heavy in my hand for a few seconds.

"So—" he said, "go ahead. What's your plan?"

"Well, I thought maybe you could invite me over and I could pretend I was riding my bike to your house but go to the roller rink instead."

"Why do all that?"

"You have a better idea?"

"Sure. Why don't you have your parents bring you over to my house, and I'll get Bernice to take us both to the roller rink and pick us up later. We're not far from there."

"I know. That's why I was going to ride my bike and maybe go to your place later and have my mom pick me up."

"Yeah, but it's a long way over here from your place. I can't believe your parents would let you ride a bike five miles in traffic but they won't let you see a girl who doesn't have any parents. It's not her fault. Don't they know that?"

This kind of injustice was probably familiar territory for Matt.

"Well, anyway," he went on, "you don't need to do all that. This way, you don't need to lie either. You really are coming to my place. Have someone drop you off here in time for Bernice to get us to the rink."

"Wow, Matt, that's a swell idea."

"What time does she practice?"

"From ten until noon."

"So I'll invite you to come around nine. And why don't you stay for the whole day."

"Really?"

"Sure. We got to make this look normal. I wouldn't invite you over for only a couple hours. I'll talk to Bernice and call you right back."

"Give me enough time to get home."

"You're not at home?"

"No. I'm at a pay phone."

"Slick, Jonathan. Real slick."

"Hey, Matt . . . thanks. Thanks a whole lot."

"I'll call you in a few minutes," Matt said. "Bye."

I thought I got home awfully fast, but Matt hadn't waited.

"Hi, Jonathan," my mother called to me as I came in the back door and started washing the newsprint off my hands in the laundry basin next to the kitchen.

"Matt called," she went on from where she was standing skinning carrots at the kitchen sink. "He wants you to call him, and his mother got on the phone and invited you over for the day on Saturday. I figured you'd want to go, so I told her you'd love to come."

"Okay, I guess." I tried not to sound too excited, and then I got a daring idea. "I was hoping to go to the roller rink, though."

"I think it would be best for you to go to Matt's house," she said in her serious adult voice that she was silly enough to think still worked on me. I could even predict what was coming . . . *Your father and I* . . . and sure enough: "Your father and I haven't had a chance to discuss this Callaway girl anyway—"

"Mother, she's not the 'Callaway girl.' That sounds like someone in a soap commercial. Her name is Donna, and it's not her fault that she doesn't have any parents around."

The sudden silence felt like a brick wall between us. I had never spoken to my mother quite so directly before, and I was surprised at how easily it came out. I thought of trying to soften what I had said, for the sake of peace, but I was enjoying the impact too much.

My mother stood there rigidly, braced against the sink and staring out the kitchen window with a totally blank expression.

"Jonathan," she said finally in a soft, more natural voice, and then she turned to me, "you're right. We are not being fair to her. Your father and I have nothing against Donna. We don't even know her. There *are* things about someone's back-

ground, however, that are important to find out about because a family shapes a person and their beliefs. We are just
not comfortable with you spending time with her until we
know a little more about the situation."

"You know, Matt doesn't know who his parents are either," I said.

"Matthew is adopted," she said.

"Yeah, by two people who are as old as Donna's grandparents. They're probably in the same Sunday school class. Do
you know what Matt calls his parents when he's away from
them?"

"No, what?"

Suddenly I realized I might be carrying my argument a
little too far. Pretty soon she wasn't going to want me to be
with Matt either. I had to go ahead with this one, though,
since I'd set myself up.

"Leonard and Bernice."

That actually made my mother laugh and released a little
tension.

"Does he really call them 'Leonard and Bernice'?"

"Yes, but not when they're around."

We both shared a laugh and then she said, "I still think
it's good that you spend Saturday with Matthew. We can see
about Donna later. Okay?"

"Okay, Mom."

"See . . . if you just leave things to the Lord, they have a
way of working themselves out, don't they?"

"Yes. They sure do," I said, and this couldn't be working
out any better for me, I thought, but I wasn't sure what the
Lord had to do with it. I was doing a pretty good job by myself. I did know that the Lord didn't care about Donna's back-
ground, though; He cared about Donna, and that's just how
I felt, too.

My mother put her arm around me and pulled me to her.
"You're still my little baby, and I'm not ready to let go of you
just yet."

Saturday morning would not come soon enough. I tried to keep my mind on schoolwork and off Donna and the roller rink caper, but it was hard not to relish not only the thought of seeing her skate, but the overall success of my plan to get there. The only slipup that could possibly happen would be for Matt's mom to mention something to my mother about the skating rink, but Matt had such control over his mother that he probably had her properly counseled on this matter. When it came to scheming, Matt seemed to cover all the bases.

One of the things that made the week go a little faster was the fact that it was collection week for my newspaper customers, so I had that to do on top of my schoolwork and my paper route.

Dingdong! "Collecting for the *Star-News!*" I felt like a dingdong myself doing this. I hated collecting money. I didn't like interrupting people, and I didn't like the trouble some of them gave me over the $1.50 monthly charge.

Then there was the fact that half of them weren't home when I first came by, and I had to keep track of that and go back the next day, and sometimes the next day after that. If I was unable to catch them at home, they would then owe me for two months the next billing week. That was the worst, because when somebody owed for two months they almost always disputed the fact.

"Didn't I just pay you?" they would always say.

With the exception of a couple old ladies who had them but could never find them, most people never kept the receipts I gave them, so it was usually my word against theirs. I would show them in my book how I still had last month's tab, but they would say that I must have forgotten to give it to them. I would eventually get my money, but not without going through all this hassle.

Most of my customers were nice to me, though. A few even gave me a quarter tip each month, and the Watermans always gave me two dollars and told me to keep the change.

My favorite customer by far was at 332 Live Oak Street, the home of Molly Fitzpatrick. 332 Live Oak Street was where Ben Beamering's face met the back end of a Pontiac station wagon before dawn one Sunday morning when the front wheel of his bike jammed while he was helping me with my Sunday paper delivery. That accident was the beginning of the end for Ben and the beginning of my friendship with Molly.

Molly Fitzpatrick, a retired nurse, had been instrumental in helping get Ben to the hospital and, later, in properly diagnosing his ensuing problems as a heart infection. Molly had also helped me face his death, and she constantly maintained the reality of his current place with the saints and angels in heaven.

Though Molly was a Roman Catholic, we shared a strange spiritual connection. In some ways, I saw Molly's faith as being stronger and more real than a lot of folks I knew at the Colorado Avenue Standard Christian Church. There was not a trace of pretense in her. Saints, angels, miracles, blessings, curses, prayers—it was all real to her. It wasn't a question of whether you believed it or not; it was the way it was.

She was particularly fond of the saints, and her favorite book was one on the lives of the patron saints, many of whom were first-century martyrs for the cause of Christ. That same book had been on Ben's bedside table the last week of his life. He especially loved the stories of the martyrs, and when questioned about the Roman Catholic origin of these stories, he had been quick to point out that in 100 A.D. there were no Catholics or Protestants, only people who believed. That's the way I always thought about Molly. She and I were believers just like the early Christians.

Unfortunately my parents didn't see it this way and didn't like me spending much time with her, so my times with Molly were pretty much limited to collection week. I would tell my parents I was going out to collect, but one of those nights I would only collect from Molly. And I would always collect much more than $1.50. I would collect a piece of cake and a cup of her hot Irish tea and some new slant on life from Molly's book of experiences.

I knew Molly would be in her element on the topic of angels, but first I decided to find out what she thought about Donna. The tea was ready, like it always was, when I got there at about five o'clock on Friday afternoon. The late afternoon sun made the yellow walls in her kitchen look buttery.

"So what ya been doin' these days, Johnny?" she said, pouring two cups. She was the only person I liked calling me Johnny. Her accent made it roll off her tongue naturally.

"I'm going to the roller rink Saturday to watch a friend skate. I've seen her at the church skates and she's really good, but this will be different. She has a routine and everything, and she's trying to make it into competition."

"Really. I didn't know they had such a thing. What do you suppose they do?"

"I don't know. That's what I can't wait to find out. My parents don't know I'm going, though. They'd be real mad if they found out."

"There ya go again, a-flirtin' with disaster," she said with a wink of her red eyelashes. "Now what is it this time?"

"They don't want me to be around Donna because she doesn't have any parents."

"Now wait a minute here, everyone's got a mum and a dad. She's just not growin' up with 'em, eh?"

"Yeah, that's about it. She lives with her grandparents."

"Here, here, to the older generation! More power to 'em. What's she like, laddie?"

"She's okay . . . and boy can she skate!"

"Sounds like she's learned to believe she's important without the help of the two people in the world who have that as their job. That takes a lot of courage. Must be one strong little girl."

"Why can't my parents see that?"

"They will, Johnny, they will. Give them some time. Sure

you want to give them somethin' more ta be upset over by doin' this?"

"I promised Donna. You should have seen the look on her face when I told her I was coming."

"Aye. So you've made up yer mind."

"Yep."

"Well, you'll be lettin' me know how it turns out, I'm sure."

"Guess what, Molly? I've been kissed by an angel," I said, eager to move on to the next subject I wanted her opinion on.

"Her name wouldn't be Donna would it?"

"No, it was Margaret." I went on to tell her about the writing in the bunker and the bathroom of the skating rink and about my theory of Ben commissioning angels from heaven. I told her, as well, about saving Matt's life and the voice in the water.

"That was most definitely the work of an angel. I've heard many similar stories."

"But you're not sure about Margaret and the writing?"

She smiled. "It does sound like our Benjamin, but savin' lives is a little more in the line of angelic duty. Angels are very busy, you know, with very important things. The archangel Michael once took two weeks to answer the prayer of Daniel because he was busy fighting off demons in Persia. I'm not sure too many angels have time for writin' on bathroom walls, if you know what I mean. If little Benjamin did get one to do this for him, I'd be thinkin' the case was under serious review up there."

I left Molly's more sure about what I was going to do on Saturday, but also more aware of the cost should my parents find out somehow. If the plan exploded in my face, I would simply have to take the consequences.

I left, that is, and got about as far as my bike, when I turned around and went back to the front door.

Molly was expecting me. She opened the door before I

had a chance to knock and said it for me. "Collecting for the *Star-News*, right?"

I always had too much on my mind when I left Molly's to be thinking about newspaper bills.

Saturday went off with only one hitch. My dad got me to Matt's house by 9:30, but when I walked in the door, Matt informed me that Bernice had an early morning hair appointment and had already left with the car.

"Why didn't you call me?" I said.

"I didn't need to," said Matt. "We'll walk. It won't take us longer than twenty minutes to get there."

It took over thirty minutes, and we got there about a quarter past the hour.

"Oh no, it's locked," I said when we tried the front doors to the rink.

"Maybe there's a back door," said Matt.

We ended up circling the whole building, which wasn't an easy thing to do. There was a five-foot wall we had to climb and junk in the alley of a warehouse next door to work our way through. And when we finally got to the back, we found nothing but a long, unbroken wall.

"Gotta go back to the front," Matt said. "We'll just have to pound on the door."

So we went back through the junk and over the wall, and I was just about to knock when Matt said, "Wait a minute. Look at this. It looks like a doorbell." He pushed the button and we could hear a buzzer go off inside the door. We looked at each other sheepishly.

Before long a heavily tanned lady with dyed red hair slid open a window next to the door.

"Sorry, we're closed to the public," she said in a husky voice.

"We're friends of Donna Callaway," I said.

"Oh. Just a minute, then."

The smell of varnish was the first impression I had walking

in; I didn't remember noticing that at the church skates. *It must make a difference when the rink is empty*, I thought. There was, in fact, much that was different about the skating rink that morning. No music, no crowd, only the voices of Donna and her coach echoing off the floor, the lonely clap and roll of one pair of skates, and the constant hum of the soda fountain machines.

When I first looked out at Donna that day, I saw not a girl but a whirling dervish. She was spinning like a top, her arms and legs a blur of movement and her ponytail horizontal.

"Matt, look! Can you believe that?"

"I'm looking, I'm looking! No, I can't believe it. I didn't know you could do that on roller skates."

The coach, a short, muscular man in tight black pants and a black T-shirt, was holding a stopwatch and calling out to her as she spun: "Nice camel . . . now sit . . . good . . . change . . . and sit again . . . good! That's your second spin. Now skate and get set for a double salchow."

"A double what?" said Matt.

"Got me," I said.

Donna hadn't seen us come in, or if she had, she didn't pay us any mind. She was giving her coach and her work total concentration.

"Okay," said the coach as he glued his eyes on her from the center of the rink. "Now I want you to set up for a double toe walley, keeping in mind you're going to come out of it into your final spin in the center of the rink, so you should start the toe walley about—" and he skated over to the spot, "here."

"Okay. Ready?" He looked at his stopwatch. "You can do it now. We're coming up on three minutes so far. Perfect. Start your double right . . . now! Beautiful! Now spin . . . camel . . . jump . . . back into a camel . . . and out! There it is. You did it! That's a typical program. Lots of work yet on the individual parts, but that gives you the whole picture."

Weak applause came from the other end of the rink, and

Matt and I looked over to see Donna's grandparents proudly lending their encouragement. Matt and I joined them enthusiastically, and for the first time Donna looked our way.

"Okay, break time. We'll start working on the jumps next."

Matt and I were both speechless. We had just seen Donna Callaway spin, jump, twirl in midair, and somehow land without falling, then fly across the floor with her arms out as if they were lifting her beyond the realm of gravity that confined the rest of us mortals to walking on the ground.

As soon as her coach announced the break, she skated directly over to us, the wind of her movement laying the short little skirt of her one-piece outfit softly around the tops of her legs. Her face was red and radiant with a smile.

"Hi!" she said as she glided into a stop at the railing, her chest heaving rapidly. "I didn't expect you to be here. What a surprise!"

"I said I'd come."

"But my grandparents said you weren't coming. You were going over to a friend's house instead."

"How did your grandparents know that?"

"They called your house last night to see if you needed a ride. Didn't you know that?"

Must have been while I was at Molly's, I thought. *And my parents didn't even tell me.*

"Well, we're here, and I never was *not* going to be here. I wouldn't miss this for anything. That was boss! I didn't know you could do stuff like that on roller skates."

"I know. Most people don't know that. You can do everything that can be done on ice skates—some things, even better. They've had regional championships now for five years. That's what I'm practicing for. Lenny's getting me ready for the Southwest Pacific Regional Championships next June in Bakersfield. I'm so excited."

"Wow . . . June, and you're already starting?"

"Well, we've got all the jumps and spins decided. I haven't

picked my songs yet, but I have until the first of the year for that."

She broke into an even bigger smile as we stood there smiling back at her in amazement. She let out a little nervous laugh, looked down, and then looked over and waved at her grandparents. When they waved back, she pointed at Matt and me, and they smiled back and nodded.

"Well! I have to get going!" and she skated off, bouncing and dipping her shoulders as she worked up speed, and then she leaned back and glided into a turn with her arms trailing casually behind her. I had never seen anything so beautiful in my life.

"What was that white stuff all over her?" said Matt.

"I don't know, but it makes her look like an angel," I said.

"Yeah . . . move over, Margaret," he said. "Did you really kiss her in the closet?"

I looked at him and a line from somewhere popped into my head. "That's for me to know and you to find out."

"You turkey."

"Hey, I just discovered what the white stuff is," I said. "At least where it's coming from," and I went over to a break in the railing and wiped a finger across the floor. "Look." A fine white powder had built up in a line on my finger.

"What is it, do you think?" he said.

"Beats me, but look, it's all over the floor. We'll have to ask Donna."

She was at it again out on the rink, and this time her coach was working her harder. He didn't seem nice at all. Sometimes he spoke harshly to her, and I didn't understand that.

"Concentrate, Donna," I heard him say. "Dominic is going to be here soon, and I want you to be able to put this jump into a sequence. Now I know you can do this. Get your mind on it or I will have to ask your friends to leave."

"Uh-oh," I said to Matt. "Maybe we'd better back off a little."

We moved away from the rail and started walking toward

the fountain area near where Donna's grandparents were sitting. The tanned lady who had let us in the door was working in an office area behind the skate rental desk, and Matt went over and got her attention.

"You boys want something from the fountain, I reckon."

"Sure . . . what you got?"

"All I can give you right now is a soda. Everything else is shut down."

"Could we get a cherry Coke?" asked Matt, reaching into his pocket for money. "Good, we'd like two, please." I faked like I was going for my pockets, and Matt said with a grin, "It's okay. It's on Bernice."

As she started to pour the Cokes, the door buzzer went off and she left the glasses and went to the front window. She let in a slight, salt-and-pepper-haired man carrying several books. He followed her back to where we were waiting at the counter and laid his books down. I glanced at them and saw they were music books. *101 Pop Favorites* was one. *Popular Broadway Show Tunes* was another.

"I'm pourin' these here boys some Cokes. You want something?"

"Actually, do you have any coffee made?"

"Sure do. Just a second," she said. She pumped cherry syrup into our Cokes, gave them a stir with a long spoon, and then slid the glasses in front of us.

"Hi, I'm Dominic," said the man, who looked vaguely familiar to me. "And who are you?"

"I'm Jonathan, and this is my friend Matt."

"Hi, Jonathan . . . Matt. You friends of Donna's?"

We both nodded.

"She's something, isn't she?" he said, turning on his stool to where he could see her fly by.

"Yeah," I said. "We had no idea."

"Really? This is the first time you've seen her skate?"

"Yes. Except for the all-church skates."

"We didn't even know you could do this stuff on roller skates," said Matt.

"Oh yes. You can do just about anything you want to if you set your mind to it."

The lady was back with a pot of coffee.

"Thanks, Peg," the man said as she poured him a cup. "So you boys are probably from the Standard Christian Church on Colorado, right?"

"Yeah, how'd you know?"

"I know that's where Donna goes. I play the organ for all their skates."

"Of course," said Matt. "I knew I'd seen you before. Do more Top Ten songs!"

"You like that, huh?"

"Yeah. I loved it when you did 'Teenie Weenie Yellow Polka Dot Bikini' last time. That was boss."

"Well, I figured since you kids can't hear the records, I can at least give you the songs."

"Why have records anyway, when you're sittin' in the only skating rink in all of southern California with a live organ," said Peg, "next to the most popular player around?"

"Flattery will get you everywhere," Dominic said to her. "Who's the organist over there at your church now? Is it still Milton Owlsley?"

"Yes, it is," I said.

"I went to school with Milton. Funny guy. As persnickety as they come. Good church organist, though."

I thought of Booker T. "He's loosening up some," I said.

"Milton? Loosening up?"

"Well, we have a new Negro singer in our choir, actually a soloist, and she and Milton got going last Sunday. Now he wants to learn to play like Booker T. and the M.G.'s."

That made Dominic almost fall off his stool with laughter.

"Hey, Dominic!" shouted the coach from the center of the rink. "Get over here!"

"Uh-oh, duty calls," said Dominic as he got up, still

laughing. "Tell you what. If Milton wants some help with his Booker T., you have him give me a call," and he handed me a card: *Dominic Dimucci—Organist, Entertainer Extraordinaire.* He walked off laughing. "Milton Owlsley playing Booker T. Jones. This I gotta see!"

As Dominic made his way to the organ, Matt and I twisted on our stools so we could watch Donna jumping and twisting in the air.

"Wow," I said to Matt. "They bring the organist in just for Donna."

"No, not 'just for Donna,' " said Peg from behind us. "She's our best. Gonna go a long way, that girl."

We watched for a few minutes as Donna started to move with the music, and I saw right away how important the music was to the whole thing. It was the glue that held it together and gave life to each movement. There was something different about the way Donna moved her body when she skated to the music. Her moves took on a flow and became less mechanical. She seemed to be working especially hard on a particular jump that I would later learn was called an axel. It was to be the opening jump of her routine.

Time and time again she fell—more times than she made it. Her coach kept repeating, "The better you get, the more you fall. The more difficult the jump, the smaller the margin of error. To do the great jumps, you have to do everything perfectly."

I marveled at her stamina. No matter how many times she fell, she kept getting up. I imagined her body as being nothing but black and blue.

"She's very brave," I said.

"Or crazy," said Matt.

"You think this is all crazy?"

"I didn't say that."

"You suggested it, though."

"Well, she sure is punishing herself," he said. "I don't think I would do it."

"I'm not sure I would either. I wonder what makes her go?"

I looked over at her grandparents and wondered if it was them. Her grandmother was pretty feisty for an elderly woman confined to a wheelchair. I had seen her on the move in the parking lot a few times and noticed how well she could get around.

"Hey, Matt, what do you say we go meet her grand-parents."

"Sure."

We started over to where they were sitting, and her grand-father got up and pushed his wife over to meet us.

"Hi! I'm Jonathan, and this is my friend Matt."

"Yes, we've seen both of you boys at church," said Donna's grandfather, reaching out his hand. "I'm Harold Finley and this is my wife, Murietta."

"Most people just call me Granny Finley," she said, reaching out her hand to me. But I hesitated taking it. I had never met anyone in a wheelchair before, and I wasn't sure I wanted to touch her.

"It's okay," she said, still holding out her hand. "I'm like anyone else from the waist up."

I shook her hand and so did Matt, and I felt bad about hesitating.

There's certainly nothing wrong with her grip, I thought, as I checked to see that my fingers were all there. Matt, too. In fact, being Matt, he had to say something.

"Wow, you're pretty strong for—"

"For an old lady?" she finished. "You're darn tootin' I am. Have to be to operate this contraption. It's awful nice of you boys to come out here and encourage Donna. She's been talking a lot about you, Jonathan. You're Walter Liebermann's son, aren't you?"

"Yes."

"Well, what do you think of our little girl?" asked Mr. Finley.

"I think she's very talented—and brave, too," I said.

"That she is," he said.

"Brave and foolish," chimed Mrs. Finley. "It runs in the family."

Just then a faint cry shot across the hard maple floor and Mrs. Finley grabbed her husband's arm. "What was that?"

I turned to see Donna crumpled on the floor. It was not an unfamiliar position for her, but something was different this time. She wasn't getting up, and when she tried, she fell back to the floor with another soft cry.

"Harold, she's hurt," said Mrs. Finley, and off she went, rolling herself over to a gap in the railing. We all followed, and instinctively I started running out on the floor toward Donna.

"Stay out of here!" yelled the coach, waving me off sharply. "You've already caused enough trouble!"

I backed up, bewildered.

"Donna, Donna!" he said, slamming a fist into his hand. "You don't try a double when you haven't got the single down yet!"

"Peggy!" he shouted. Peg was already on her way out to them. Together they knelt at Donna's feet and started removing her skates. She winced and bit her lip when they worked on the left one. Tears glistened on her cheeks in the overhead light, and she looked over at us and shook her head and tried to smile.

The coach removed the sock from her left foot and held her ankle in his hands.

"Does this hurt?"

"No."

"Does that?"

"A little."

"Does that?"

"Ow! Yes!" and her body jerked back in pain. I looked over at Mr. and Mrs. Finley frozen at the rail.

"Now you've done it!" said the coach, and he stood up

and turned his back to her, then spun back around. "I've seen this before. This will take, at best, three months off your schedule—at worst, four or five—which would put you out of the running."

"It's okay," Donna said through her tears, with gritty determination. "I can do it."

"Honey, Lenny's a little upset," Peg said to Donna. "Don't pay him any mind right now. He don't know what he's sayin'."

"I tell you, Peg, I've seen this kind of break before. I know exactly what I'm talking about."

"Lenny," she turned to him and spoke sharply, "will you leave the diagnosin' to the doctor and help me get her up!"

The two of them lifted Donna, and she braced herself on their shoulders, walking on her good foot. Our little group had huddled at the nearest exit from the rink, so we all backed away to let them through.

Donna smiled at me and said, "Well, you got to see part of a practice at least."

"Want my chair?" said Mrs. Finley.

"I'm all right, Granny," said Donna. "Don't worry."

"Where will you take her?" asked Mr. Finley.

"St. Mary's," said the coach, and a choking blackness came over me at the sound of those words.

9

St. Mary's

"Molly?" I said on the phone from the kitchen of Matt's house as he stood there listening in on my side of the conversation. "This is Jonathan. I need your help. Remember Donna Callaway, the girl I talked to you about yesterday? Well, she broke her ankle in practice today—at least that's what her coach thinks happened."

"I know, can you believe it?"

"Well, that's why I'm calling you. They took her to St. Mary's, and I knew you would know who's the best doctor over there for this kind of thing."

"Dr. Sanderson? Orthopedics?"

"Sanderson," I said to Matt, covering the phone. "Can you help me remember that?" He got a piece of paper and wrote it down.

"No kidding. The Dodgers? Really?" I covered the phone again. "This guy is the doctor who handles all the injuries for the Dodgers."

"I was hoping you'd do that. Gee, thanks, Molly."

"No, I'm at a friend's house."

"Well, I don't have a ride right now, but my friend's mother is due home any minute." Matt shook his head in disagreement.

"No, that's okay, you leave the Lincoln in the garage. If

you can call over there, I'm sure that will be enough."

"Oh yeah, it's Callaway. C-A-L-L-A-W-A-Y. Donna Callaway."

"Oh, they left the rink about a half hour ago."

"She seemed to be in pretty good spirits, but her coach isn't doing very well, though."

"Yes. Competition is in June."

"I hope so too."

"Thank you, Molly. You're the greatest!"

"Oh yeah." I looked down at the round black and white telephone dial. "It's Sycamore 7–9729."

"Okay, bye." I hung up the phone and let out a big sigh.

"The Dodgers, huh?" said Matt. "He must be pretty good."

"Yeah, well Molly Fitzpatrick knows the best."

"How do you know her again?"

"She's a retired nurse who knows everybody over at St. Mary's. She's the one who helped out a lot with Ben. That's how we met her. He ran into the back of a Pontiac right in front of her house."

"I guess if you're gonna crash, that's a good place to do it. What was that about the Lincoln in her garage?"

"Oh, she's got a mint condition 1939 Lincoln Zephyr that never goes out on the road except for emergencies. You should have seen the ride she gave me once to see Ben in the hospital. She doesn't even have a license. When do you think your mother's going to get home?"

"If she's shopping, you can wait till the cows come home," came Leonard's voice bellowing from the next room. Matt confirmed his words with a knowing look.

"How far is it to St. Mary's from here?" I said.

Matt's dad was now in the kitchen with us. "It's about three miles," he said. "Too far to walk." He started rummaging through some papers next to the phone. "Now where does she keep that number for the taxi?"

A taxi? I had never ridden in a taxi in my life. I would

never have even thought of it. Southern California was not known for its taxis. Probably because it was so spread out that it got too expensive. But Mr. Wendorf was calling one.

The taxi was there in ten minutes, and Matt's dad gave us money for a round-trip fare, plus tip, plus enough to buy lunch. "That's just in case you end up staying there for a while, which you probably will," he said. "Call when you're ready to come back, in case Bernice is home."

"That's as nice as I've ever seen your dad," I said as we pulled away from Matt's house.

"Yeah," said Matt. "He has streaks like that. You never can tell with him."

"I've never been in a taxi before."

"You haven't? Leonard puts me in taxis a lot when Bernice is gone."

We drove rapidly through light traffic, and it seemed like I was living out a scene on "77 Sunset Strip."

"The Dodgers!" I said. "Do you know what that means?"

"It means he's good."

"It also means he's the best at getting people over their injuries the fastest. They gotta have players back in action as soon as possible. This couldn't be better for Donna, and Molly's probably calling him right now."

As we pulled up to the emergency entrance, the choking feeling returned, but I pushed it back with a new sense of duty. I had a feeling I was going to be able to help Donna. This new challenge overcame even the awful memories of Ben dying in this very same hospital.

Because of all the time I'd spent at St. Mary's, I knew just what to do. Ben and his mom had taught me all about hospitals. They made this place hop, and I was ready to do the same.

In the emergency room we immediately ran into Lenny, Peg, and Mr. and Mrs. Finley.

"Oh, it's you again," said the coach. "Haven't you caused enough trouble today?"

"Lenny, stop it," said Peg.

"Don't pay him any mind," she said to me, "he's just upset."

"Where's Donna?" I asked.

"They took her inside."

"Has she seen a doctor yet?"

"We don't know anything."

I headed right for the emergency door and barely heard, "Wait a minute, you can't do that," as the door closed behind me. There were three empty beds and one with curtains pulled around three sides of it. I walked around the curtain and found Donna sitting there with her leg up on the table.

"Jonathan!" she said. "How did you get in here?"

"I walked in. How are you doing?"

"It hurts. But I'm okay."

"Has anyone seen you yet?"

"Just a nurse."

"Good. I'll be right back."

"Don't leave. I don't like it here by myself."

"Don't worry, I'll be right back."

I walked back out into the waiting area, and Lenny and Peg rushed me as if I were the doctor.

"How is she?" Lenny said.

"She's fine. No one's seen her yet. Matt, why don't you go keep her company."

I went to the window and asked the emergency receptionist, "Is Doctor Sanderson in the hospital today?"

"Just a moment I'll check." She looked up and down a couple pages and stopped halfway down the second one. "Yes, he is on duty, but he wouldn't be down here. He's not on call for emergency today. Doctor Howard is."

"Could you tell me how I could get in touch with Doctor Sanderson?"

"Well, that would be difficult. He's most likely doing his rounds about now. He could be anywhere in the hospital."

"Would you page him for me, please?"

"I don't know . . . I have to have a reason. Who are you, and why do you want Dr. Sanderson?"

"I'm Jonathan Liebermann, and I would like Dr. Sanderson to take care of Donna Callaway, the girl in emergency right now."

"I'm sorry, that won't be possible. Only Dr. Howard will see patients in emergency today, and he's on his way over here right now."

Suddenly I heard the deep drawl of a southern accent behind me. "Jeanne, you're looking mighty pretty today." I turned around to see a tall, handsome man in a physician's coat smiling behind me. He had dark hair with touches of gray, and he winked at me through a winsome smile.

"Oh—" the receptionist lost her breath for a minute. "Doctor Sanderson! Why, thank you."

"Jeanne, have you got a Donna Callaway here?"

"Why, yes, doctor, she's . . . right inside."

"Thank you. You know, if you were any prettier, nothing would get done around here. We'd all have to just stop and look."

Dr. Sanderson turned and went through the door, and I relished my vindication long enough to smile smugly at the bewildered, blushing receptionist. *Molly Fitzpatrick strikes again!*

The little group huddled in the waiting area was very impressed with Dr. Sanderson, and even more so when he predicted a speedy recovery.

"I've treated lots of these types of injuries," he told us about an hour and a half later, after he'd set Donna's ankle. "Fortunately, it's not a complex fracture. This is the same break you get sliding into second and catching your cleats on the bag. We can probably have her back in skates in less than two months. That is, if she cooperates with our therapy program. Otherwise it will take longer."

"She'll cooperate," said Lenny.

"I'll cooperate," said Donna cheerfully as a nurse wheeled

her out of emergency in a cast up to her knee and ready to go home.

Mr. and Mrs. Finley smiled broadly, happy that Donna had been cared for so well.

"Thank you, doctor. We're so grateful to you for taking such good care of her," said Mrs. Finley.

"Thank this young man here," he said, putting a big hand on my shoulder. "He's the one responsible for getting me down here."

"We are thankful to you, Jonathan," said Mr. Finley, "mighty thankful."

I felt hot and embarrassed and couldn't think of anything to say that didn't sound stupid.

"You certainly seem to know your way around this place," said Peg. Lenny was standing around outside the conversation, a little less agitated than before, but not willing to take part in the award ceremony that was going on.

"My best friend was in here for a while," I said.

"Hey, Granny," said Donna, suddenly grabbing the wheels on her wheelchair and rocking back and forth, "I'll race you to the car!"

"You haven't got a chance!" said Mrs. Finley, whirling around and gliding toward the door. Donna tried to follow, but was prevented from doing so by the nurse.

"No you don't," she said, "not as long as I'm in charge of you. Besides, you don't have a license to operate this vehicle."

"But I ride in Granny's all the time," Donna protested, and with a quick jerk she pulled away from the nurse and followed Mrs. Finley out the door.

"Wait a minute!" yelled the nurse, running after her. "You come back here!"

Everyone laughed, even Lenny, and we all rushed outside to watch Donna rolling after her grandmother and the nurse running after Donna. Finally the nurse caught up with Donna's wheelchair and barely dragged her to a stop, like a dog owner trying to get control of a St. Bernard that had just spotted a fleeing feline. Mrs. Finley lifted her hands in victory as she crossed an imaginary finish line.

"And some folks still wonder where Donna gets it," said Mr. Finley, shaking his head.

A big surprise was waiting for me when we got back to Matt's house later that afternoon. We had used the money Mr. Wendorf gave us to get lunch at the hospital and still had enough left for another taxi ride home, even though we figured Matt's mother was probably home by then. I wanted to enjoy being in charge a little longer.

I had walked into a situation that froze everyone around me and I had been the one to act. I had been able to accomplish something positive out of all the pain I had experienced losing Ben, using knowledge and the resources I wouldn't have had otherwise. Minor consolation, maybe, but consolation nonetheless.

Such feelings were short-lived, however, because waiting for me at Matt's house was the one thing that could sap all my confidence right then. It was my parents' blue and white Ford Fairlane parked out in front of Matt's house.

"Oh no!" I said as soon as I saw it.

"What's the matter?" said Matt.

"My parents are here!"

"So?"

"Then they know. They know I went to the roller rink!"

"But you're a hero now. You saved the day for Donna."

"They don't know that!"

"Relax, Jonathan. They'll come around."

"You don't know my parents."

I sat glued to the backseat of the taxi while Matt paid the driver. "Do you have any money left over?" I said. "Can't we have him drive us somewhere else?"

"Jonathan, come on! Stop making such a big deal out of this."

"You don't understand, Matt. I once got the belt just for

talking in class. This is my first real lie."

"It's not a lie. You never said you weren't going . . . Jonathan! Would you get out of the car? We already paid this guy!"

"Okay, okay, I'm coming."

Matt's parents and my parents didn't know each other very well. Mostly because of the age difference, I think. That, coupled with the reason my parents had come—their anger over my disobedience—made for a room full of superficial smiles.

It had all been precipitated by an innocent phone call to Matt's house that afternoon to find out when they should come get me. I could just imagine Leonard's response: "Well, that depends on how long they plan on staying at the hospital."

"The *what?*" That alone would have been enough to get my folks in their car and over to the Wendorfs'. I had no idea how long they had been there, but it was clear, as soon as they saw me, that they were ready to go. There was a brief conversation, most of which had to do with how Donna was doing, as my parents feigned concern. Matt made a feeble attempt to share my hospital heroics with everyone, but no one seemed interested. The whole atmosphere was very uncomfortable, and in minutes we were out the door.

I took my last look at Matt before entering what felt like my transport vehicle to a penitentiary. It was my final look at freedom, and it angered me to see Matt standing there so casually. *How does he get away with treating his parents the way he does?* I wondered. *Hasn't he ever been in this situation before with them?* He was almost laughing at me, and I hated him right then.

The ride to our house took ten minutes. For the first five there was nothing but silence in the car. Painful silence. Then, as if on cue, we all tried to speak at exactly the same time and no one heard or understood anyone else until we all stopped and waited again through another, shorter silence.

"Dear," said my mother to my father, finally, "you said you would do this."

My father got that look he gets when he has to do something he doesn't want to do.

"Jonathan," he said in a nervous high voice, "your mother and I are very disappointed with your behavior today."

"Disappointed?" said my mother. His token sentence was the gate that opened the floodwaters of her frustration. "We are speechless. This is so unlike you, Jonathan. I never would have believed in a thousand years that our darling little boy would ever mislead us like you have done. You knew how we felt about you seeing Donna Callaway and yet you purposefully, *deliberately* disobeyed us. We are shocked, Jonathan. So much so that we haven't even been able to determine the appropriate punishment yet."

I tried to speak. I wanted to explain why I liked Donna and how important it turned out for me to be there, but there was this huge obstruction in my throat and tears in my eyes and I was sure my voice could not get around all that.

"Do you have anything to say for yourself?" said my mother.

I opened my mouth and out came a weak and cracking, "No."

"I'm just so *disappointed* in you," repeated my mother.

As we drove in the driveway, I noticed my father eyeing the rearview mirror.

"There's someone driving in our driveway behind us," he said. "Now who could that be?"

I turned around and recognized the car immediately. I had helped Donna get into that car earlier that afternoon. It was her grandparents. I didn't look very long behind me, but I thought I only saw two people in the car.

"Oh no, isn't that Donna Callaway's grandparents?" said my mother.

"I'm afraid so," said my father. "He's getting Mrs. Finley's wheelchair out right now."

"What on earth would they be coming over here for? Jonathan, do you know anything about this?"

I didn't answer. I was already out the door and headed toward the front yard to greet the Finleys.

"Jonathan!" shouted my mother, though controlled enough to keep her voice from carrying to the front yard. "You come back here this instant!"

I stopped as my mother got out of the car and came up behind me. "We are not through with our discussion, young man. I want you to march inside to your sister's room. We will finish this later."

Most kids were sent to their room. I was sent to my sister's room. My room was open to the dining room and within earshot of conversations in the living room—something my mother obviously wanted me removed from, given the nature of the impending guests.

My sister's room was separated by a hallway and two doors, both of which were shut soundly behind my mother as she left me there. But I had a plan. I immediately climbed the ladder to the attic and crawled past the boards of my train layout to a place I surmised was over the living room. I had never tried it before, but I was hoping to pick up something of the conversation below. I did even better. I found that the ceiling light in the living room cut an opening through the insulation, so by lying down across the rafters and placing my ear right near the electrical box, I could hear every word.

I heard my father say he didn't want to see these people right now. And I heard my mother say she didn't either, but they were here and they should make the best of it, and maybe this was a chance to find out about Donna's parents. That was the part I wanted to hear more than anything.

"Do we have anything we can serve them?" my father asked.

"Put some water on for tea. I think there's some Cheese Whiz and Ritz crackers we can put out. We were going to go shopping this afternoon, remember?"

"Yes, and I was going to do the yard when we got back."

"There they are," said my father when the doorbell went off. I heard a rushing of footsteps and a chorus of cheery greetings at the door. My mother excused herself immediately to the kitchen amidst the vehement protests of Mr. and Mrs. Finley to not bother with anything. They were very apologetic about their unannounced mission. Nonetheless, my mother insisted on making tea.

I knew exactly what nervousness my father was going through right then. He hated being left to entertain people he did not know or like. Small talk filled the time until I heard a tray of tinkling china being carried out with the teapot and matching teacups, eliciting the usual comments.

"Yes, this whole set belonged to my great-grandmother in England."

"Your *great*-grandmother! Well I'll be."

"What a pleasant surprise to have you drop by," said my mother as everything seemed settled in the living room. "We just heard about Donna. I'm so sorry for her. How is she?"

"Oh, she's doing quite well," said Mrs. Finley, "thanks mostly to your son, Mrs. Liebermann."

"Oh, please call me Ann."

"We'll only be a minute," reiterated Mr Finley in a kind and sincere voice, "but we had to stop by and congratulate you on raising such a fine boy. I've never seen anyone take charge like that in a hospital before, have you, Murietta?"

"No," said Mrs. Finley, and I heard the clink of a cup meeting its saucer. "What he did was remarkable for a boy his age. I've spent a lot of time in hospitals, and believe me, I know the power of the white coat and the clipboard. Your son was not intimidated in the least."

"And the doctor he was able to call in for Donna—" Mr. Finley interjected, "he's the best in southern California. Injury specialist for the Los Angeles Dodgers? My stars—"

"I kept saying to myself," said Mrs. Finley, " 'Who is this boy? Where did he come from?' "

At this point, there was a pause.

"You have heard what happened in the hospital?" said Mr. Finley. Then, "Murietta, I don't think they know."

Following was an embellished account of the proceedings of the afternoon—how I had marched right into the emergency room and found Donna alone and assigned Matt to stay with her while I attempted to get the receptionist to find Dr. Sanderson, and how he had shown up at the most opportune time, taking over the situation with his expertise. How the coach who was blaming me in the beginning ended up thanking me in the end. (That part was a little exaggerated, I thought. I didn't remember him showing me any thanks.)

I listened to all this with pleasure, except for the pain of my awkward positioning in the rafters. At least I was pleased right up until they mentioned the "retired nurse" who was my inside track on the best doctors in the hospital. I didn't need Molly's name coming up right then. I rested my head against a beam in the attic, keeping score: two strikes *for* me . . . one strike *against*. . . .

During this recounting of the hospital scene, my parents remained deathly quiet. I imagined their faces with blank smiles on them—masks for the confusing mixture of pride and anger that must have been going on inside. Then something strange happened. As I listened, for an instant I thought they were talking not about me, but about someone else. Something about the words they used and the way they said them made me think about Ben. It was the same way I used to hear people talk about him, and us, when we were together—when I had been his accomplice in crime. That's when I realized for the first time that in some ways I was becoming like Ben. It made me smile inside to think that something about Ben was continuing on in me.

What I couldn't figure out was why Donna's grandparents were at my house. What made them come over and deliver this news personally? I began to surmise that Donna might have had a hand in it. While waiting for Dr. Sanderson to look at the X-rays and prescribe the proper treatment, I had told her that my parents didn't know I was at the roller rink and that they wouldn't be happy about it if they found out.

"It's because I don't have any parents, isn't it? Isn't that why you asked me about my parents up in your tower?" she had said, and I had said it probably was, though that made no difference to me.

Donna's part in this unlikely visit seemed confirmed by the fact that, at the end of it, Mr. and Mrs. Finley themselves volunteered the topic of Donna's parents. My parents never would have brought it up. In fact, in Mrs. Finley's words, "Everyone talks to everyone else about these things except the people who are directly involved, so if your son and Donna are going to be friends, we want you to know straight from the horse's mouth, and we will be happy to answer any questions that we—"

Right then I would have heard the truth about Donna if it weren't for the Green Leaf Tree Service Company that trimmed trees for the city of Eagle Rock. Though the trees on our block were new and small, they kept them cut back severely to encourage thickness. I had seen the trucks out front when we drove up, and when the tree-eater started up, I knew that finding out about Donna was going to have to wait.

The tree-eater—that's what Ben and I called it—was shaped like a funnel. The tree trimmers fed branches in the wide end, and the churning blades inside chomped them up and spit little pieces of tree out the small end into the bed of a waiting truck. The thing made a high whining sound that dropped down to a low grind when it was fed, then slowly returned to its satisfied scream. Unfortunately, when the tree-eater was running, especially right in front of your house, it was so loud you could hardly hear yourself think. And through the attic vents it was even louder.

I descended the ladder, put my ear to the bedroom door, but still heard only the whining tree-eater. I cracked the door and could see the edge of Mrs. Finley's wheelchair backed up near the hallway. Someone must have used the bathroom and left the hall door open. I might be able to sneak down the hall and get another listen.

Whether my mother was reading my mind or trying to shut out some of the deafening noise, I don't know, but just as I got to the door a familiar arm reached out and closed it, shutting me out for the last time. Just before the door closed, however, I was able to pick up something about a place called Camarillo. That was as much as I got.

Frustrated, I lay back on my sister's bed and listened to the rise and fall of the moaning tree-eater devouring the forbidden history of Donna Callaway.

10

Go, Granny, Go

Donna's ankle healed quickly. The two months Dr. Sanderson had predicted turned out to be more than enough time, and in six weeks she was practicing again, much to her coach's delight. Part of that was because of the doctor's expertise, but most of it was because of Donna's desire. No one was more driven than Donna, unless it was her coach, Lenny LaRue.

Lenny was a fanatic about roller skating, and in 1961, if roller skating was anything more than a form of light recreation to you, you would have to have had a large measure of fanatical blood skating in your veins, because 1961 was a down time in the history of roller skating in America.

In 1900, Levan M. Richardson of Milwaukee, founder of the Richardson Skate Company, developed the modern roller skate, and by 1910 there were over 3,500 roller rinks in the United States and 8,000,000 people flying around them on skates. A large percentage of those 8,000,000 were women. In fact, roller skating was the first organized recreation in which great numbers of ordinary American women and girls participated. I know all this because, inspired by Ben's files, I started one of my own that year on roller skating.

This skating boom rolled to a crawl around 1918, however, overcome by other, more lively, suddenly affordable attractions such as radio, picture shows, automobiles, high fashion, live entertainment, and dancing—a time better known as the "Roaring Twenties." But the stock market crash of 1929 and the Great Depression that led into the 1930s gave skating another chance as it became one of the few affordable diversions most Americans could enjoy. Then, an international event altered the course of skating forever when the 1932 Winter Olympic Games in Lake Placid, New York, gained national attention for ice skating and brought a new star into the hearts of a nation—a glamorous and athletic acrobat of freestyle and grace, Sonja Henie.

Suddenly everyone wanted to skate like Sonja. But ice skating was seasonal, and there were only a few very expensive indoor rinks. So those dreaming about doing spins and jumps went to their closets, pulled out their neglected roller skates, and took to the dusty neighborhood roller rink to discover, lo and behold, it was all possible on wheels.

Thus, a new sport emerged. Roller skating for recreation suddenly became roller skating for dance, freestyle, and show. Even Fred Astaire and Ginger Rogers took to roller skates in the film "Shall We Dance?" National skating associations were formed to organize the many figure and freestyle competitions springing up in cities and towns across America, giving promising skaters a national championship to work toward. And in 1942, ten years after the Lake Placid Olympics, roller skating finally claimed its own answer to Sonja Henie in the form of a traveling review known as the Skating Vanities, featuring the exquisite skating talents of a nineteen-year-old sensation named Gloria Nord.

The Skating Vanities took their spectacular show on the road for twelve years while roller skating basked in its glory days. It was a dazzling spectacle on wheels, including musical comedy, acrobatics, speed skating, clowns on skates, and even the Rollerettes, a precision skating chorus of twenty-four women—a rolling version of New York's famous Radio City Music Hall Rockettes.

But the undisputed star of it all was the petite, blond, Hollywood-bred, dancer-turned-skater, Gloria Nord. In the words of one of her admirers, "You knew she was the star because she made her first entrance of the evening from atop a seventeen-foot ramp. As she glided down to the stage, a full complement of strings swelled to a crescendo. At the bottom, she melted into a full split and rose to find herself wrapped in the arms of her handsome skating partner. The audience was enraptured. Then the couple sped around the stage in a flashing, twirling display of lifts, turns, and dips. The audience was thrilled."

But as the 1950s came to a close, roller skating vanished almost overnight, replaced by rock 'n' roll, sock hops, and cruising the boulevard in scooped-out Chevys and Fords. Gloria Nord made her last appearance on skates in 1960, and it was as if she twirled one last time and was gone without a trace. The only thing left behind was the bump and grind of roller derby "this Saturday night at the Olympic Auditorium," or the "All Skate" and "Couples Only" down at the Ramblin' Rose. Though national and world figure and free-style competitions continued, the popularity roller skating once held, and the fact that it had been carried to the theatrical, heart-stopping level of the Skating Vanities and Gloria Nord, was remembered by only a few, among them Lenny LaRue and Donna Callaway.

Lenny remembered because he was a three-time national champion who'd once skated with the Skating Vanities. Donna remembered because Lenny made sure someone never forgot. Lenny could not bring back his glorious past, but he could instill his hope for the future in the youthfulness and natural talent of Donna Callaway. Thus, Donna was living in the middle of an anachronism—a leftover world struggling to survive in the minds of a few who remembered its glory.

In spite of Donna's grandparents and their glowing report of my gallantry at the hospital, my punishment for going to the roller rink against my parents' wishes turned out to be bad enough. Whatever happened in our living room that day seemed to make my parents even more set on thwarting any opportunity for my budding friendship with Donna to grow. I had hoped that the Finleys' visit would soften their anger somewhat, and maybe it did. Maybe what they really had in mind for me was far worse than this, but this was bad enough. For they told me that I was absolutely forbidden to ever enter the Ramblin' Rose again.

"Not even for an all-church skate?" I protested.

"No. You may go to the church skates," said my mother. "That's a different story entirely. Your father and I don't like the bad crowd this other kind of skating draws."

"What do you mean?" I said. "What other kind of skating?"

"The kind Donna is learning," said my mother. "It's no different than dancing. It's worse, in fact—the way they throw their legs around in those little skirts . . . well, it leaves little to the imagination."

"Mother, it's incredible. It's not bad. You should see what she can do!"

"No. I don't need to see anything of the kind, and I don't want you anywhere near the kind of crowd that hangs out at that roller rink when the church isn't there. The only time you may go is when godly people take over that place. Apart from that, it is no less a den of iniquity than a dance hall."

That had pretty much been the end of it, except that she warned me that any more visits to Matt's house would have the full cooperation of Mr. and Mrs. Wendorf to enforce this new policy on behalf of "your father and I."

"No problem," Matt said when I delivered the verdict to him the next day in church. "We can still go. Bernice will keep it quiet."

"You've got to be kidding," I said. "Your mom would lie for you?"

"She'll do anything I want her to."

"No, I couldn't do it anyway. It's too risky. My parents would find out one way or another. There must be a way to get them to change their minds. If they could just see Donna skate, they'd know it's not what they think."

"Why not have them take you to one of Donna's practices so they can see for themselves?" said Matt.

"Are you kidding? My mother entering that 'den of iniquity'?"

But impossible as it seemed, that was just what came to pass. And as had happened so many times before, Mrs. Beamering ended up playing an important role in bringing it about.

The six weeks of Donna's recuperation wedged a slight opening in my parents' attitude. It was a leverage brought about by the continued kindness and appreciation Mr. and Mrs. Finley lavished on me and on them. But it was Mrs. Beamering who cracked it wide open one Sunday at Beedle's Cafeteria. In a conversation about some of the debilitated members of the congregation, the subject of Mr. and Mrs. Finley came up, which then spilled over into Donna and, finally, skating. My mother was speaking in a judgmental tone about a style of dance skating that she knew next to nothing about, and Mrs. Beamering twisted her words right out from under her.

"The way they move their bodies—" said my mother.

"I know," said Mrs. Beamering, "isn't it amazing? You know, we saw the Skating Vanities in Houston the year before we came out to California, and it was one of the most spectacular things I have ever seen. Don't you think so, Jeffery?"

"Splendid!" said Pastor Beamering. "Absolutely splendid! Twirls . . . flips . . . I still can't figure out how they landed on those wheels all the time, and so smoothly!"

"Donna can skate like that," I chanced, ducking the icy stare of my mother.

"Can she?" said Mrs. Beamering. "I'd love to see that sometime. I thought that kind of skating went out with Gloria Nord. Is that how she broke her ankle?"

I dared not open my mouth again.

"Yes," said my mother, reluctantly.

"Poor child," Mrs. Beamering went on. "How serious is her injury, Ann? She'll be able to skate again, won't she?"

My mother knew the answer to that question. She was an unwitting expert on Donna's progress. The Finleys had been showering her with reports about Donna, which she received politely and never spoke of again.

I continued to keep my mouth shut during this conversation, however. Mrs. Beamering knew exactly what she was doing. She had a way of turning things around on my mother without embarrassing her. I knew Mrs. Beamering was up to something because she was questioning my mother for answers she'd already had from me. I'd had more than one conversation with Mrs. Beamering about my forbidden relationship with Donna, which she had obviously been pondering, waiting for the moment that came that afternoon at Beedle's.

"She's recovering quite well I hear," said my mother. "I'm sure she'll be skating again in no time."

"You know what, Ann? Why don't you and Becky and I go watch her practice sometime. I'd love an excuse to get away from all these men knocking around my house."

"That would be . . . lovely," said my mother as I almost choked on a dry corn muffin.

"I think it's wonderful what that little girl is accomplishing," said Mrs. Beamering, "after all she's been through."

What has she been through? I wanted desperately to ask, but dared not. This was far enough for one conversation—farther than I thought anyone would ever get with my mother on this subject.

"Do you think Martha's serious about this 'girls only' outing to the roller rink?" my father said in the car on the way home from Beedle's.

"Of course she's serious. Martha always means what she says. You should know that by now."

"I don't want to go to the roller rink with you and Mrs. Beamering," said Becky.

"Ouch!" That was Becky responding to my jabs in the backseat. I didn't want her setting back this new development.

"Do I have to go along with this 'girls' thing, Mother? . . . Ouch! Stop that, Jonathan!"

"I'll go," I volunteered.

"I'm sure you would, Jonathan," said my mother.

We rode in silence for a few blocks as we all thought about the conflict from our own perspective.

"I think it sounds like a good idea," said my father, most likely thinking about his professional relationship with Pastor Beamering.

"And why do you say that?" said my mother.

"Well . . . it would give you a chance to see firsthand what this . . . this skating business is all about."

"I know what it's all about, Walter. It's about dancing and secular music and risque costumes and the appearance of evil."

"Well then, why do you suppose the pastor's wife wants to go?"

"Walter, you know they're more liberal than we are. They come from a different part of the country."

"They come from the Bible Belt, Ann. The south is much more conservative than California. Maybe things have changed, honey. They saw the show. What was it, the Skating—?"

"Vanities, Walter. The Skating *Vanities*. And that's just what I mean. What kind of clean, wholesome group would call itself the *Vanities*? It's vain, I tell you, just like its name, and how can anything 'vain' be honoring to the Lord?"

"Good, then we're not going," said my sister. "Ouch! Will you *stop it!*"

"I didn't say that," said my mother. "I have a commitment now. I didn't say no to Martha, and once she gets going on an idea, there's no stopping her."

"Why do I have to go? Why not just you and Mrs. Bea-mering?" said Becky, holding me back at arm's length this time.

"Because she wants you to come, and I do too. We've been talking about the three of us doing something together for some time now. That part of it would be very nice. She thinks of you as her own daughter, you know, being that she wishes sometimes she had one of her own." My mother paused for a moment or two, then turned to my father again. "I don't know, Walter. Sometimes I think my constitution is lacking. Why can't I stand up to her? Martha has a way of twisting things around and suddenly I'm supporting what I am against."

"I know," said my father as we turned into our driveway. "Jeffery does the same thing to me all the time. I wouldn't have Netta Pearl in the choir if it weren't for Jeffery putting words in my mouth. I guess that's why he's a pastor."

If ever I wanted to be invisible, it was the following Sat-urday when Becky and my mother left to go see Donna prac-tice at the Ramblin' Rose. They were meeting Mrs. Bea-mering there and then going out for lunch afterward. The closest I got was Matt's house, since my mother agreed to drop me off there while they were at the rink. Matt wanted to sneak over and watch, but I didn't want to risk messing up the possibility of something good happening, which was ex-actly what came about—something beyond my wildest imag-ination.

My mother and Becky were in pretty good spirits when they left me at Matt's, but nothing could have prepared me for the complete reversal of my mother's position when they returned. First of all, they were later than expected by about two hours. Then they returned in such a giddy mood that I could have easily mistaken my mother for one of Becky's dingbatty friends. But most of all, my mother, in the period of a few hours, had gone through a metamorphosis that defied reason. The same mother who'd left in utter condemnation of the sport of skating returned such an avid supporter of it that it made me instinctively jealous of her sudden inside track on Donna's life and career.

Apparently Mrs. Finley had turned out to be the life of the party. Even my sister had had a good time. "Funny as a hoot," my mother kept saying all the way home, and she and Becky would look at each other and start laughing for no apparent reason.

"Well, this is certainly a surprise," said my father at the dinner table that night. "What on earth went on out there at the rink today?"

"Girls' day out," said my mother, sounding a little like Bernice. "And Mrs. Finley turned out to be one of the funniest people I've ever met. Martha just kept her going, too. The two of them must have gone on for at least two hours at that restaurant. I can't remember when I've laughed more in my life."

"What was so funny?" asked my father.

"Everything," said Becky. "She's got this mousey little voice and yet she's so tough. Could you pass me the string beans, Jonathan?"

"She's as tough as nails," said my mother. "What makes it so funny is that she laughs about being in a wheelchair. It makes you feel uncomfortable at first. Didn't you feel that way, Becky?"

"Yeah," said my sister. "She says all the things you're thinking and it makes you feel awful at first, and then you realize she's joking."

"That's exactly right," said my mother, sliding a piece of fried Spam onto her plate and passing the platter to me. "She tells all these jokes on herself until suddenly you find you are joining in with her. I've never felt so free around a person in a wheelchair before. Usually I'm much more nervous. And then you find out all the things she's done in that wheelchair!"

she said, looking over at Becky.

"Oh yeah," said Becky, "it's incredible. She's traveled all over the country. Gone on hikes. She rolled herself on trails up and down the Grand Canyon."

"She still swims regularly at the YWCA—at her age! Honestly, Walter, it makes you not want to complain about anything ever again. Heavens to Betsy, we've got two legs and a future, and we haven't done half the things she's done without them. And then, as old as she is, she tells you what she's not done yet. You know what she wants to do next?"

"What?"

"Jump out of an airplane!" said Becky.

"That's right," said my mother. "She wants to go parachute jumping. Can you believe that?"

"And she will, too," said my sister.

"Yes," said my mother, "she's dead serious."

"Or seriously dead, if it doesn't open," laughed my father, but no one thought it was funny.

"Becky, tell them what she said that time she cut her leg."

"Oh yeah. That was hilarious. Once she was working outside in her garden and she cut her leg pretty bad—"

"She's paralyzed from the waist down, you know," my mother inserted. "Can't feel a thing."

"Yeah, so she doesn't even know about this cut, and she doesn't discover it until she's been outside for a while, dragging herself around, and suddenly she gets to feeling kind of dizzy, and she looks down at her leg and sees this awful cut caked with blood and dirt—"

"Yuk!" I said.

"And guess what she says?"

"What?" I asked.

" 'Well would you look at that,' she says. 'That must really *hurt!*' "

We all laughed.

"You know, she and Donna had a wheelchair race at the hospital," I recalled, suddenly feeling free to mention the unmentionable, "and Donna never caught up with her."

"Speaking of Donna, Jonathan, I owe you an apology," said my mother.

This was monumental. Never before had my mother apologized to me. Once when I found a way to see Ben in the hospital against her wishes, she later admitted she was wrong to forbid me, but that wasn't exactly an apology.

"I judged this skating business before I really knew what I was talking about. You are right about Donna. She's terrific, and I hope she wins the competition. She's a lot like her grandmother—overcoming a lot of difficulties with a real flair, and my hat is off to both of them."

"What difficulties is Donna overcoming? What did happen to her parents?" I asked, and the old concerned look reappeared for a minute on my parents' faces.

"Jonathan, it's really not necessary for you to know that," said my mother. "What's important is that Donna is a wonderful girl and she needs support, and your father and I are sorry we stood in the way of what has been a very genuine caring on your part."

"I never stood in the way of anything," said my father.

"You could have stopped me," said my mother with a firm look.

"Does this mean I can go see Donna practice this week?" I asked.

"Well, not with your paper route, but certainly next Saturday. I may even go with you."

"Me too," said Becky.

Great! I thought. *How about the whole family?*

11

Under the Desk

For the next few weeks my attention was almost completely taken up with the skating aspirations of Donna Callaway. Part of that time included the Christmas holidays, meaning Donna went into extended practices every day, and almost every day I (and sometimes Matt with me) was there at the Ramblin' Rose cheering her on. I can't say I understood her aspirations, but I admired them. I admired Donna's endurance and her hard work, and I was fascinated by a world totally unlike the one I'd known up until then.

Gradually, Peg started asking me to do a few odd jobs around the place. I moved boxes, carted deliveries around, and wiped down tables in the fountain. Oh yes, and she had me touch up the inside of one of the stalls in the men's room "where some jerk named Ben had to leave his mark for posterity on our freshly painted stall." Luckily she hadn't noticed that the accompanying initials were the same as Donna's and mine. I liked doing this kind of stuff. It made me feel like I belonged there.

I think Peg gave me the jobs so I wouldn't get bored, but it was never boring being with Donna. Most of the time at the rink, of course, she couldn't be with me. So I had taken to putting on skates and joining her on the floor while she warmed up and when she took breaks from her arduous routines. Lenny had softened his tight hold on Donna's practices once he saw the value of someone giving her attention other than himself. Being able to have company on her breaks was helping her relax more, which meant she was more able to concentrate when she went back to work. Though Lenny still made me feel like an intrusion, he allowed my presence as part of his "work hard, play hard" ethic.

Donna was even trying to teach me a few simple tricks, providing herself with a little comic interlude at my expense. I could now do fairly well with the backward scissor steps and was just learning my first simple jump: taking a half turn in the air and landing backward while immediately going into the scissors—though I hadn't experienced the scissors part at the end of this jump, since so far I had landed on everything but my wheels.

"And I was hoping we could skate in the pairs competition this year," she kept teasing as she would give me a hand up.

Sometimes, while Donna skated, I explored around the rink, though there was not much room for exploring. Lenny kept as tight a control on his private affairs as he did on his skaters. His office was declared "off limits," and its location made that easy to enforce. It was like an inner sanctum—two closed doors away from the public part of the rink.

First there was the front counter from which the general public rented skates and skate time. Directly behind that were four long rows of skates racked like books in bookshelves and marked by size. Hidden behind the last row was the first door that opened into Peg's office. Peggy Lane, her name to those who knew her when she was a competition skater, was the general manager of the rink. She booked all the lessons; she handled the public; and as far as I could tell, she ran the business.

Her relationship with Lenny was an odd one that I never could quite figure out. They were best of friends, partners in business, and constant companions, but they were not married, nor did there ever appear to be any romantic involvement between them. Often Lenny would talk about having a date, and Peg didn't seem concerned at all. Whatever their relationship was, they were the kind of people who were suspect in my world, so I steered pretty clear of both of them. That seemed to be the way Lenny wanted it anyway, although Peg could be friendly in her own rough sort of way.

Lenny's office was through another door behind Peg's office, and I had never been that far in until Lenny himself, to my surprise, sent me there. Maybe I was making a nuisance of myself wandering around aimlessly, or maybe it was because Lenny was getting used to having me available, but that day he sent me into his office to get a bag of plaster of Paris for the floor. Though some of the newer rinks had plastic-coated urethane finishes on their floors, the Ramblin' Rose still had its original varnish coating that was too slick for the more involved tricks of freestyle skating. A light dusting of plaster of Paris was necessary to cut the slipperiness of the varnish enough to give the wheels the grip they needed. This was the strange white powder Matt and I had discovered the first time we came to watch Donna skate—the fine angelic dust that mysteriously settled on everyone and everything inside the rink.

Being on special assignment to Lenny's office didn't give me much time there, but it was enough to set me wondering. As soon as I entered the room, I could see why Lenny needed someone like Peg running his affairs. There were skates and parts of skates on shelves on one wall and along the floor below. Trophies were scattered in and around skate wheels, wheel trucks, and toe stoppers. The plaster of Paris in a sack in the corner had dusted the skate bags near it. A full set of barbells occupied the opposite side of the room. But it was the wall behind his desk, visible over the piles of papers on it, that drew me like a magnet.

There was a sort of wall of fame there, with pictures and memorabilia of Lenny's grand and glorious skating past haphazardly arranged. Many of the pictures were framed and signed. Some were action shots; others were posed; all of them seemed to jump off the wall at me as if these people were living again in their glory. There were large companies of people, all in elaborate costumes and all on skates, that I took to be the Skating Vanities I had heard so much about. Other shots were more candid, taken on buses or in dressing rooms with the half-dressed scurrying from the eye of the camera. In all of them, though, their young and vibrant faces exuded confidence and joy. The camera had caught them in the middle of a dream come true.

One photograph especially caught my eye. It was the most prominent picture on the wall—an exciting action shot of a youthful Lenny with a skating partner that took my breath away. Lenny was skating with his legs spread slightly, toes out, and one arm outstretched in front of him towards the audience. His other arm was straight up, balancing the horizontal body of a beautiful woman on the palm of his hand. They couldn't have held this pose for very long, but the camera had it captured forever.

I was mesmerized by this picture, so much so that I almost forgot my assignment in Lenny's office. Lenny's face had no wrinkles, and his hair had no gray. And the woman . . . what was it about her? Even the way she held her arms and her body while hovering in such a precarious place defied gravity and awarded grace. Something about her seemed vaguely familiar. I could not turn my eye away. . . .

"Jonathan, you in there?" Peg called from the door of her office. "What's taking you so long with that plaster?"

"Coming," I sang out, grabbing the heavy sack of plaster of Paris and thinking fast. "I was looking for something I could roll this out with. It's very heavy."

"I know, but you're a growing boy," she said, crossing through her office and finding me struggling with the sack. "Come on, you can do it."

It *was* heavy—much heavier than I anticipated. Inspired

by the picture I had been looking at, and somewhat curious as to just how hard it would be to do what Lenny did, I lifted the heavy sack up on my shoulder and got the palm of my hand under the bag to see if I could push it straight up from my shoulder.

"What if this were Donna?" I said, getting the sack only halfway up before it teetered and almost fell, but for my catching it with the other hand.

"We'd be going back to the hospital, kid," said Peg.

"Where have you been?" said Donna as I skated out to join her on a break. "You've got plaster in your hair."

"Really?" I said, shaking my head and watching a fine white mist float down. "I was trying to be like Lenny."

"What do you mean?"

"The picture in Lenny's office. Haven't you seen it?"

Donna looked like she'd just had white plaster thrown in her face. She twirled to a sudden stop in the middle of the rink and glared at me as I tried to stop gracefully but ended up crashing into the rail ten yards away.

"What were you doing in Lenny's office?" she said, skating over to me. "Don't you know that's off limits?"

"Well, yes," I said, shocked and surprised by the sharpness of her voice, "but he sent me there . . . to get the plaster of Paris."

"What did you see in there?" she said sternly.

"I—I saw lots of pictures."

"What kind of pictures? Who was in them?"

"Well . . . well," I stammered, totally confused by this line of questioning, "one was of Lenny holding his partner up with one hand. I tried to do it with a sack of plaster and—"

Suddenly she turned on her wheels and skated off, looking like she was going to cry. Lenny was just coming back into the rink, and Donna went into a jump followed by a camel spin in the middle of the floor and then skated over to him and barked in a curt, military manner, "Let's get to work."

Lenny looked over at me like he was wondering what I had said to put her in such a testy mood, but he didn't pursue it. He went right ahead with practice, probably happy for the opportunity to focus all this energy into her performance. As it turned out, she successfully, and quite beautifully, completed that morning, for the first time, the axel loop/double mapes combination she had been working on since coming back from her broken ankle.

At the noon break she was more like her usual self.

"You were great this morning," I said, happy to see her smile return, but still nervous about saying the wrong thing.

"Thanks," she said with a blush.

The Finleys smothered Donna with congratulations and then sent us off to the fountain area, where Peg had a couple hamburgers and two cherry Cokes waiting for us at a table. The rink was quiet except for the whirring of the refrigerators behind the empty counter. I watched as Donna sucked up her entire Coke, right down to the slurp at the bottom, without stopping.

"Thirsty, huh?"

She leaned back and let out a big sigh.

"I'm sorry, Jonathan," she smiled.

What a relief! I thought.

"Gosh, I—I'm sorry, too . . . I didn't mean to—"

"It's not your fault. It's not you, Jonathan, it's really Lenny I'm mad at for letting you into his office. I don't get him sometimes. He's up to something."

"What's the big deal with being in his office?"

Donna stared coldly at the uneaten hamburger in front of her.

"It's okay," I said hurriedly. "If you don't want to tell me—"

"No, you might as well know . . . my mother is probably in those pictures, Jonathan." She said it so matter-of-factly. "She and Lenny used to be skating partners."

I felt like I had been hit in the stomach. That was it! The

woman Lenny was holding up had to be Donna's mother. As soon as she said it, I knew. That was why she looked so familiar. Donna would hold herself just like that if she were flying in the air.

"You want to see the pictures?" I said. "It's not hard to slip in there, you know."

"No!" she said quickly and emphatically.

"Why? If she's your mother. . . ?"

"She left me when I was four."

The words hung there like they had been torn out of a book and thrown on the table.

"You haven't seen her since?"

"No."

"Doesn't she ever write you?"

"No. Nothing. Can't we talk about something else?"

Donna reached down into her glass and fished out a Maraschino cherry, bit off and ate the little red fruit, and then put the stem in her mouth and started moving her tongue around just behind her lips.

"What are you doing?" I asked, welcoming the distraction.

"Tying the stem in a knot with my tongue."

"You can do that?"

Her face went into all kinds of silly contortions that made me laugh until she finally produced the stem between her teeth, tied in the middle in a tight little knot.

"Yes," she said through her teeth.

"How did you do that?" I asked, staring at the stem but noticing more the pretty mouth around it.

"Practice," she beamed, using her favorite word and handing me the knotted stem.

"I'll cherish it forever," I said, examining it and then putting it in my pocket.

The smiles slowly fell off our faces and a heaviness returned.

"She fell," Donna said, deciding for some reason to give

me one more piece of information. I didn't get the significance at first. Who fell? Her mother? So? Everybody fell. Even the best, Lenny always said. The harder the thing attempted, the greater the chance of falling. But Donna wasn't finished yet.

"My mother fell in the World Competitions in 1952," she said, watching the ice melt in her empty Coca-Cola glass, "and she hasn't gotten up since."

She set her straw aside and drank the little bit of water that had melted in that short time, then set her glass back down in front of her, still focused on the ice as if she were melting it with her eyes.

I looked at her flat expression, and then I stared into my glass for a while. I didn't know what to say. I felt a deep pain inside me and another pain near it that I didn't understand. One was an actual physical pain, the other was deep in my heart. Finally I reached into my own glass and pulled my cherry out from under the ice.

"Here," I said, dangling the fruit by its stem over the middle of the table. "You can have mine. I don't like these."

Donna leaned in and snapped the cherry off with her teeth, leaving the stem in my hand. I looked at it curiously and then popped it in my mouth.

"You'll never get it," she said, eyes suddenly gleaming. Then she started laughing at how funny I looked trying to tie a knot in a cherry stem with my tongue for the first time. I started making all kinds of funny faces that made her laugh some more. Finally, I overdid it completely—falling back in my chair and putting my whole body into the act, which sent her tumbling uncontrollably into roaring fits.

"I give up," I said, spitting the stem across the table, where it bounced once and landed in her lap. She picked it up, put it in her mouth, and started in with that talented tongue again.

"Ta da!" she sang, pulling it out of her mouth in seconds and holding it up for me. "You want to cherish this one too?"

"All right, what's so funny over here?" said Lenny, bringing up a chair and squinting through the smoke of his cigarette. Unlike Peg, who was a chain smoker, Lenny liked to have just one smoke during his break.

"It's Jonathan," Donna said, stiffening a little at his presence. "He always makes me laugh."

"So how's your little jump coming along, Johnny?"

"Great," I said. "I've got everything down but the landing."

"Do you think he'll ever make it as a skating partner?" Donna's coach said to my coach.

"I have my doubts," she said.

I did try, but never wholeheartedly and always more to amuse Donna than to satisfy any ambitions of my own. I felt strange enough in this skating world Donna was involved in; the people I met were nothing like the people in church or my middle-class suburban neighborhood. When it came to skating, I was definitely an "all skate" person. Lenny and Peg and Donna were part of a harder, darker world.

Lenny even dressed the part; he always wore black. He must have had a closetful of black T-shirts and stretch pants because that was his uniform, whether he was skating or not. The T-shirts showed off a muscular, though not bulky, chest. Lenny was small and compact, about 5'6"; at thirteen, I was almost as tall as he was. He was built a little like a fireplug—as if God had taken a taller man and squished him down a foot. The features on his face seemed large for the rest of his body, especially his eyes; they were always red and wet and protruding slightly, making them appear ominous and buglike. His hair was his most attractive asset—thick and black with handsome streaks of grey. He always wore a gold chain around his neck, and when it popped out of his T-shirt, you could see the St. Christopher medal that dangled from it. He claimed he had worn it since the days of his own competitions.

Skaters, I learned, were often superstitious, since so much

was riding on one performance. When you thought about it, it was hardly fair. Donna, for instance, was well into her third month of practice specifically for the state competitions in Bakersfield in June, and she had six more months to go. Four days a week for nine months that would all boil down to one 3½-minute performance—a performance that could be adversely affected by nothing more than a faulty ball bearing or a bad night's sleep. Compare that to a baseball player who gets 160 games over the course of a season to prove the same thing. A ballplayer can have off days and make quite a few errors (they even keep track of them) and still end up with a good year. A skater got 3½ minutes, and one little mistake could ruin the whole thing.

Sometimes I wondered what made Donna skate, but finding out about her mother explained a lot. Even though she was angry at her mother for leaving her, she still must have admired what her mother had accomplished or she wouldn't be pursuing it herself. Perhaps she was hoping to find something of her mother in the steps and routines of her skating.

Meanwhile, Lenny was hoping to shine again through her youth. I looked at him as I thought about this and his wall of memories. Just then he exhaled, sending a plume of smoke across the table so that it stung my eyes.

"We're right on schedule," he said to Donna. "Time to start thinking about your music."

"Let's go sneak into Lenny's office," I said as soon as he left. It was a perfect opportunity. Donna's grandparents hadn't returned from lunch, Lenny and Dominic were going to work on some music at the organ, and Peg wasn't anywhere around. Probably out running an errand.

"Jonathan. . . ." She bit her lower lip and looked off at the rink, sighed, then looked back at me. "I'm not allowed to go in there; don't you understand that?"

"No. Not when there are pictures of your mother on the wall. Donna, she's so pretty," I said in my sweetest voice possible. It was suddenly the most important thing in the world to me—to get her in that room. "Come on, we could slip in there right now and no one will know. They'll think we went over to the Rocket Cafe or the market."

"I don't want to see the pictures," she said, but she was less convincing than before. We both stared off at nothing for a moment until she spoke again.

"Is she really pretty?"

"Yes! You'll go then?"

"I have to go to the rest room first. Wait for me at the front counter."

When she returned she announced that Peg was cleaning the bathrooms.

"Great. That's even better. Come on!"

"I don't like this," she said as we passed through Peg's office. Then, "What a mess!" as we entered Lenny's office.

But when she saw the wall of fame she said nothing. Having already studied it, I now studied Donna instead. She stopped and stood perfectly still, staring at the collage of memories on the other side of the messy desk where she steadied herself. She looked at me with wonder, as if to get her bearings in the present, and then back at the wall. She moved in slow motion around the desk and right up to the pictures, reaching out and touching them gently, one by one, as if a quick movement might disturb the people in them.

"Look, she's over here," Donna said softly, "and over here."

"And isn't this her?" I said, pointing to a group shot.

"Yes," she said, now smiling.

"I told you she was pretty," I said.

"She was," Donna said. "Like Lenny. Look how handsome he was."

We both ended up staring at the prominent picture in the middle, the one with Lenny lifting Donna's mother.

"How did they do that?" I asked.

"They were the best," said Donna.

"Look what I found," I said, picking up a program from a shelf under the pictures on the wall.

"Oh! It's the first program of the Vanities. I've never seen this one!"

I held it up for her. "Skating Vanities of 1942" it said on the front over a picture of a petite blonde sitting on a white table lifting up her short chiffon skirt to show off her pretty legs.

"That's Gloria Nord," said Donna.

Suddenly we heard someone entering Peg's office next door.

"Quick! Under the desk!" I whispered.

We tucked ourselves under, and I prayed whoever it was didn't need to come behind it. It was Lenny, and fortunately, whatever he was looking for was in the pile somewhere on top of his desk. When he left, we let out deep breaths and then started giggling. Even though it was safe to come out from under the desk, we stayed huddled there together and looked at the Skating Vanities program I still had in my hand.

"Look! There's her name. Esther Callaway," Donna said, her voice so close to my ear that I could feel her breath. She was pointing to a list of the Gae Foster Rollerettes: "The twenty-four pulchritudinous girls that share thirty-nine local, city, state, and national crowns."

" 'Pul-chri-tu-di-nous' " I read. "That's a mouthful!"

"Do you know what it means?" she said.

"No, but I can find out."

"Look, there she is again," said Donna, quietly worshiping her mother's glory.

It was easy to spot her mother, even in the group pictures. She had wide-set eyes, a high forehead, and a turned-up nose just like Donna's. In fact, she was young enough in these pictures that the resemblance was striking.

We found her in four pictures in the program, and we also found Lenny listed among the Roller Boys, though it was hard to tell which one he was in the only picture that included them, since they were dressed like wooden soldiers with plumed hats that made them all look exactly alike. The Roller Boys were in the back line of a formation that had the Rollerettes formed in a V in front of them. And closest to the camera, at the point of the V, was a beaming Esther Callaway.

It was right then and there, with our knees to our chins and our noses in the program of the 1942 Skating Vanities, under the messy desk of Lenny LaRue, in the inner sanctum of the Ramblin' Rose Roller Rink in Pasadena, that I fell in love for the first time in my life. And under that desk I kissed Donna Callaway's cheek, which seemed to make one hurt lessen and another one worse.

12

The Dark Talks Back

"Come on, Matt, tell me the truth," I said when I had him cornered in the lower level of the church the following Sunday. "Tell me the truth or Grizzly here is going to turn you into hamburger!"

None of the other kids in the church, Matt included, shared my friendship with Grizzly. To them, he was still the retarded janitor—the scary deaf-mute making guttural, half-human, half-animal sounds from the dark, unlit catacombs of the church. They continued to see him the way Ben and I used to see him, before we found out he was intelligent, and kind, and probably the most loyal friend anyone could ever have. Sometimes, that misconception was something I could use to my advantage. This time, it proved to be very effective in helping me extract some important information out of Matt.

I had done a lot of thinking since Donna and I snuck into Lenny's office and found her mother on the wall. Suddenly everything had gotten very complicated. No sooner did I leave the rink that afternoon than I felt confused. While I was with Donna, I had been brave and gallant. I had handled the news about her mother, reunited her with a memory, and even kissed her under the desk. But afterward, all I could think was: "Oh no . . . what have I done?"

For so long it seemed like I didn't know enough about Donna Callaway; now it seemed like I knew too much. I started feeling that a certain degree of her happiness—perhaps even her success in skating—was going to be connected to me somehow. As exciting as it had been to be close to her, there was a whole lot inside of me that wanted to turn around and run. Caring for Donna was now going to cost me something, and I wasn't sure I wanted to pay it.

I had come to this same point with Ben. I could play around with ideas forever, but acting on them was another thing entirely. I always wanted to pull back, while Ben wanted to make something big out of his actions. I believe now that part of that was because he knew intuitively that he did not have long to live. Strange thoughts for a ten-year-old, to be sure, but not necessarily a ten-year-old who knew he had a hole in his heart. And now I had a kind of hole in my heart—an emotional hole—an aching for Donna that only being with her and doing something about it would solve, and yet being with her *meant something* now. I was no longer only a cheerleader or a spectator. I was a player who wasn't sure he wanted to be put in the game. And there was no Ben around to push me through the barriers.

So as soon as I had gotten home from the rink that afternoon, I had gone up the ladder in my sister's closet and played with my trains until my father pulled the fuse on me. My parents and even my sister had tried to get me to come down, but I was blissfully entangled in switches and engines and imaginary towns and freight delivery runs that desperately needed me to run them. It wasn't until my father literally cut off the electricity to the attic that I finally came down. Still, my mother had a warm plate of food waiting for me in the oven.

That had all happened on the Thursday after Christmas. For the next two days I stayed as far away from everyone as possible, especially Donna and anything to do with skating. With the exception of my paper route, I spent most of the time in the attic with my trains. Once in a while I would think about Donna and then push the thought away. Thinking of Ben didn't help either, because I knew Ben would have had me down from the attic *doing* something, and right then I didn't want to do anything but be alone.

Saturday night my mother had tried to get through my wall of silence.

"What's wrong, Jonathan?" she said while she tucked me into bed. "Do you want to talk about it?"

"No."

"Is it Ben, honey?"

Of course it was Ben. It was always Ben in some way. It was his raw faith and what it made me do, and how it changed my life whether he was there or not—whether he was alive or dead didn't matter. Yeah, it was Ben all right.

"Do you miss him?"

Did I miss him? Actually, right then, and for the last couple days, I had wished with everything I had that he would go away. But it's kind of hard to send someone away who is already gone.

"Remember, you've got him right here," she said, laying her hand on my heart, and that was the worst thing she could have said. It was the worst because I loved him and hated him. I wished he would go away and I hated him for leaving, all at the same time.

"Good-night," she said, kissing me on the forehead.

I always had my hardest times over Ben at night. That was when the two of us used to have our best talks—lying in bed on sleepovers staring out at the dark. Some nights I didn't even want to go to bed because I knew as soon as my head hit the pillow I would be wide awake with memories.

That night, however, for some strange reason, Ben didn't seem so far away. The one time I wanted him out of my life, he seemed closer than ever. In fact, it seemed like he was right there. And then I had gotten this crazy thought that if he was right there, it would be just like it always had been. I wouldn't see him or touch him. I would just talk to the dark, and the dark would talk back.

And so I did.

"Ben?" I said out loud.

Speak, Lord, for thy servant heareth.

What? What was that? My mind must have been playing tricks on me.

"Ben!" I said it again and lifted my head off the pillow, only to see the familiar dog patterns on the curtains silhouetted by the moonlight. I rested my head back on the pillow and there it was again—that voice!

Scale the highest mountain.

I can't even be sure anymore if I actually heard this voice. I've tried to both explain and explain away that night so many times since then that what actually happened escapes me. However it happened, whether I heard the voice, whether someone else would have heard it had they been there, or whether I only heard it in my brain, doesn't really matter— didn't matter then—because the important thing was the words. They were specific words. Definite messages. And I remembered every one.

"Ben?" I said his name again, only because that was all I could think to say. The voice, or whatever it was, didn't sound like Ben's—more like a deep whisper. Ben's whisper was weak and thin, or at least that's the way I remembered his voice last, from a hospital bed.

Sing our song.

That was it. That was the end of the messages. What kind of strange thing was this? Two or three more entreaties to Ben went unanswered, and then my mother had come out to comfort me, concerned over my attempt to awaken the dead.

"Did you hear anything, Mother?"

"Only you calling."

"No other voices?"

"No, Jonathan. You were just calling for Ben in your sleep."

After she kissed me good-night for a second time, I had gotten up and written down the messages. It wasn't really necessary. There was no way I would ever forget them. But I did it anyway.

Speak, Lord, for thy servant heareth.

Scale the highest mountain.

Sing our song.

I awakened the next morning thinking back on all the encounters Matt and I had had with the supposed supernatural. Suspicious that he might have had more to do with this angelic stuff than any real angels, I had found it most convenient to dismiss these occurrences as coming from the Matt Wendorf school of practical jokes—until the events of the night before made me go back through everything in my mind one more time: the writing in the bunker, the meeting with "Margaret," the writing in the bathroom stall, the strange man in the checkered coat, and the unexplained phone call to Donna Callaway. Was any part of it real? I knew from the look on Matt's face in the rest room of the roller rink that he had been up to something. But how much?

So that Sunday morning I was determined to find Matt at church and get to the bottom of this. I ran into Grizzly first, outside the educational building.

"I have to talk to you," I told him, "in private."

He led me into the old building, down the stairs, and through the gym into a back kitchen that was only used for banquets. Matt and I knew that kitchen well. A window there looked out into a loading area below ground level, and from it you could look up a wall and see people walking along a railing that bordered a path at the edge of the parking lot. Leave it to Matt to find the one place in church where, if the wind was right, you could peek under a skirt blowing in the updraft.

I took the piece of paper with the messages out of my

pocket and smoothed it out for Grizzly on the counter.

"I heard these voices last night in the dark. Three very clear messages. What do you think?"

Grizzly studied the paper for a few minutes looking puzzled. Then he underlined the first message with his finger, *Speak, Lord, for thy servant heareth*, and looked at me questioningly.

"That's the first thing I heard."

Grizzly rubbed his chin and then got out his pad and wrote: "WHO SPOKE FIRST?"

I had to think a moment.

"I did. I called out Ben's name."

That made Grizzly's face light up.

"What? What is it?" I hated waiting for Grizzly to write. He was so slow at it.

"YOU . . . CALLED . . . ANGEL . . . ANSWER."

"Wait a minute. That's not right. That would make me the Lord and the angel would be my servant."

At that, Grizzly nodded his whole torso up and down to say that I had it precisely. Then he wrote: "MINISTERING SPIRITS."

He was right, but I had never thought about it quite that way before. Angels were actually our servants. Grizzly started writing "PASTOR BEAM—" but I impatiently grabbed the pencil from him and said, "I know what Pastor Beamering said. I was there too. What about the rest of this?"

Grizzly stared at the messages for a while and the wrinkles of puzzlement came back to his face. Then he took the pencil back.

"RIDDLES," he wrote finally. "SOMETHING YOU MUST DO."

That was when I had glimpsed through the window, out of the corner of my eye, the unmistakably white legs of Bernice Wendorf, with Matt following right behind. They were on their way from the parking lot to church, and a brilliant idea hit me. I knew a way to coerce Matt into telling me the truth, once and for all, about our experiences with angels.

"Wait here," I said with a hand on Grizzly's arm, "and scare Matt to death when I bring him back. He knows something about this."

So when I brought Matt down to the kitchen, Grizzly not only looked scary, he had found a huge meat cleaver and was waving it madly in the air. That's when I had pushed Matt up against the wall and demanded the truth.

"I'll talk! I'll talk!" he screamed, his eyes saucer-wide. "What do you want to know?"

Grizzly was playing it to the hilt. He had roughed up his hair, and he was emitting the most horrible sound out of his twisted mouth, which was drooling and foaming to such an extent that he even had me a little scared.

"I want to know if you were behind any of these so-called angelic visits we've had in the last few months." I had him pinned to the kitchen wall by both shoulders while Grizzly moved around behind me grunting and groaning. Though my face was right in front of his, Matt's eyes were not on me at all; they darted from side to side, waiting to see where the awful face behind me was going to pop up next. "I want to know the truth, starting with the writing in the bunker."

"Okay! Okay! I'll tell you everything! Just tell him to put down that . . . that meat-cutting thing!"

I waved Grizzly off and loosened my grip on Matt's shoulders. Grizzly stopped waving the cleaver and settled down, but kept on breathing like he was gargling.

"The only thing I faked was the stuff in the bathroom at the roller rink," he said, straightening his clothes and never taking his eyes off Grizzly, who had gone to rocking in a slow swoon.

"What about the bunker?"

"I don't know nothin' about the bunker. I didn't do a thing there."

"And Margaret? Did you really see Margaret the next day after I left?"

"It's just like I told you," said Matt. "Honest."

"Did you ever call Donna Callaway and pretend to be me?"

"No! I don't know anything about that. The only thing . . . in the bathroom at the roller rink—"

"Yeah?" I said, with Grizzly gurgling down my neck.

"I did everything but change the *I* to a *C*. I swear, I didn't do *that*. I wouldn't lie about that because it freaked me out. There was nobody in there but that old guy."

I stepped back and relished his misery for a while before I let him go.

"And by the way," I said, smiling, "Mr. Griswold's only faking it. He's really a nice fellow."

Matt looked at Grizzly, who broke into a smile, and back at me and never changed his expression. "I think you're both crazy!" he said and bolted out the door.

I looked at Grizzly and we both laughed. Then he found a napkin and wiped the drool off his face.

"Boy, did we have him on the ropes! What was that stuff coming out of your mouth? How did you do that?"

He opened one of the cupboards and held up a package of baking soda with a sly smile.

"Wow, that's boss! We'll have to remember that."

I jumped up and sat on one of the counters and tried to think about what all this meant. Some of the stuff had been a hoax, but not all of it. Now I knew the voices in the night were real. Matt hadn't been up to as much as I'd thought, which didn't make me very happy. I was hoping it had all been him, because then I could have dismissed the former encounters and figured out some way to explain the voices. Now there was too much to explain away, and I was being pushed again outside of my comfortable places.

While I was thinking, Grizzly had been writing, so I looked over his shoulder.

"BEN'S ANGEL IS AT IT AGAIN!"

Yes, Ben was still messing with my life, and now I had to find out why.

13

Mt. Whitney

By the time church was over that morning, it was obvious that Donna was now avoiding *me*. It came as no surprise. I hadn't been at her last two practices, including the one on Saturday, and I hadn't missed a Saturday practice since I first started going to them. On top of that, I hadn't even called her, and by the looks she gave me in church, it didn't appear that any angels had done any calling on my behalf lately, either. The nearest I got to her Sunday morning was five feet behind her in the parking lot as she walked rapidly to her car.

"Donna, stop, please! Let me talk to you."

No acknowledgment whatsoever.

"I found out what pulchritudinous means!"

For that, I at least got her to turn around and glare at me.

"It means 'endowed with physical beauty'!" I said loud enough to be heard by more than a few.

Donna just turned and walked the rest of the way to her grandparents' car without looking back.

The real blow, however, came the next day when I showed up at the rink only to have Peg announce to me through the window that Donna didn't want any guests that day. I wasn't even allowed to have a name. "Donna is not entertaining any *guests* today."

All this only made me more determined to find out what

the angelic messages meant. I knew if I was really supposed to help her, and if God and His angels and even Ben were in on this, sooner or later she would have to come around. This thing was obviously bigger than just the two of us.

There were still a couple days of Christmas vacation left, so with the rink closed to me, I knew exactly where to go next. I told my mother I was going for a bike ride and then I headed for 332 Live Oak Street.

"Johnny, come on in! It must still be your vacation," said Molly. "I know it's not collection time, so what brings you by?"

"I've been hearing from angels, Molly," I said, happy to have someone I could talk to directly about this without having to wait for them to write down their responses.

"You have, have you? And what have they been sayin' to ya?"

Once again I pulled out the piece of paper with the messages on it. Molly had to go to the next room and get her glasses.

"Mother Mary," she said as she studied the paper, "I've never heard of anything like this."

"Do you think I'm crazy?"

"No, Johnny, of course not."

"Grizzly and I figured out the first one was the angel responding to me calling for Ben."

"Who's Grizzly?"

"Oh, that's Harvey Griswold, the janitor at our church. He can't hear or talk, but he knows a lot about angels. Says he hears them sometimes in the church."

"People with problems like that know a lot about things the rest of us miss," said Molly. "I've seen it time and time again in my years at St. Mary's."

She kept studying the phrases and lifting up her glasses as if the words might change on her somehow, depending on which way she looked at them. "Well now, that last one has to be a song that angels sing, right? . . . since it says, 'Sing *our* song'?"

Of course. I hadn't even thought of that, probably because it was so obvious.

"But this other one about scaling the highest mountain . . . I wouldn't know how to take that. It could be a vague idea about doing something difficult, or it could be a particular mountain you're supposed to climb, takin' it lit'rally, I suppose. You have any difficult things waitin' to be done, Johnny?"

"Well, yes, but Ben was never vague about anything," I said. "If he's behind this, there's a trick somewhere—something you have to find out in a book, I bet."

"*Scale the highest mountain,*" Molly repeated, and shook her head.

"What's the highest mountain around here?" I asked.

"There's Mt. Wilson and Mt. Baldy. Do those mean anything to you?" said Molly.

"No, nothing. We sometimes go on family picnics to Mt. Wilson."

"Well anyway," said Molly, waving her glasses, "neither one is even close to bein' the 'highest' mountain. Do you know what the highest mountain in the world is?"

"Mt. Everest maybe? I'm not sure. I *do* know what the highest mountain in California is."

"And what would that be?"

"Mt. Whitney," I said. "I just learned that in geography the week before vacation. It's 14,494 feet high. It *was* the highest mountain in the United States until a couple years ago when Alaska became a state."

"There you go," said Molly. "If you just learned it, it would be fresh on your mind. Angels know about things like that. And it does qualify for the highest mountain—in California, did you say?"

"But what does that mean, then? Am I supposed to climb Mt. Whitney?"

"It may."

"Holy cow! How am I going to do that?"

"Either that, or as you say, laddie, there might be a bit of a trick to it."

I went home and read up on all I could find about Mt. Whitney in the *Encyclopedia Britannica*. Nothing rang a bell. Then I remembered a classmate at school who'd recently done an oral report about mountain climbing, so I called him up and found out that you could *hike* Mt. Whitney and it wasn't even that hard. There was an easy trail up the back side all the way to the top. *Hardly scaling it*, I thought. When I asked him if there was a hard way, he said, "Yes, and a number of experienced climbers have died trying."

What could scaling Mt. Whitney possibly have to do with anything anyway? I thought. Was I going to risk my life on a possible interpretation of a riddle from a voice in the dark?

I decided to call Matt and found him still mad about the day before.

"That man's a nut case. They should have put him in Camarillo years ago. You know you didn't have to do that; I would have told you the truth."

"Matt, it was just a joke, and Grizzly's not a nut case. He's very smart. You know that foam in his mouth?"

"Yeah?"

"That was baking soda. He came up with that on his own. He's not dumb."

"Just keep him away from me, all the same. He's creepy."

"What was that you just said about Camarillo? What's that?"

"It's some place where they send all the crazy people. It's a hospital, I think, for the retards. Why?"

"Oh, I just heard someone mention it the other day and wondered what it was. Hey, Matt, do you know anything about Mt. Whitney?"

"It's the tallest mountain in California, I think."

"Anything else? Anything unusual?"

"Isn't there something about it being right up next to Death Valley, the lowest spot in the country?"

"Oh yeah, I remember that. I wonder if that means anything."

"What're you talking about?"

"Never mind. It's nothing important. I'll tell you later. What are you doing tomorrow?"

"Nothing much. You want to come over and go to the rink?"

"Yeah. Only Donna might not let me in."

"Uh-oh. 'I'm Mr. Blue, wa-o-wa-ooo . . .' What happened, lover boy?"

"Donna thinks I don't like her anymore."

"Do you?"

"Oh yeah. In fact, I'm trying to help her out, but she doesn't know it yet. I'll tell you about it tomorrow. It's all about angels and stuff."

"Hey, I'm sorry about messing around with that writing in the bathroom. I only meant it for fun. I really didn't think real angels would be interested in your love life."

"Let's just call it even, okay?"

"Okay. It's a deal. See you tomorrow."

"Hey, Matt, wait a minute. You still there?"

"Yeah, I'm here."

"You *do* know it was an angel that helped me save your life last summer, don't you?"

There was a long pause on the other end of the phone. I really didn't know why I was bringing this up now, but it had been bugging me for months.

"Matt?"

"What are you talking about?" he said.

"When you almost drowned last summer . . . at Huntington Beach."

"I didn't almost drown."

Now it was my turn to pause.

"I just bumped my head, that's all."

"Matt! I pulled you out of the water! You weren't breathing! And if a voice hadn't told me right where you were, it would have been all over for you! I'm sure now it was a real angel. You didn't know that?"

"Gosh . . . no . . . I honestly thought I only bumped my head . . . Oh no! Does that mean you did *mouth to mouth?*"

"No. I didn't need to. I kicked you by accident and you spouted like a whale."

"Oh good, because I'd hate to think of you kissing me. Yuck! Gee, I guess I should say 'thanks.' "

"I think you should thank your angel. I wouldn't have had a chance of finding you if it weren't for him."

"Or *her* . . . hey, maybe it was Margaret."

"Yeah," I laughed. "Maybe it was."

It might have just been my imagination, but it seemed Matt was different after that. More friendly and interested in what I was doing. At least he didn't balk at my reporting the next day of angels in the night. In fact, after that phone conversation, Matt never joked about angels again.

That night I looked up Death Valley and nothing clicked. I didn't really think the message meant to actually scale the mountain, but I had nothing more to go on. Maybe Molly was right. Maybe it meant to do something difficult. Maybe I was already doing it. Maybe the point of the riddle was to get me out of the attic.

I also looked up Camarillo in a book on California that we had on our coffee table and found out it was just as Matt had said. There was a mental institution there, the largest one in the state. The picture was getting clearer. When Donna said her mother hadn't gotten up since she fell in 1952, maybe that was exactly what she meant. I wondered how much Donna knew. Sometimes she talked like she didn't even know if her mother was alive.

The next day Matt and I rang the buzzer at the door of

the Ramblin' Rose at 11:30 A.M. and Peg came to the ticket window again with the same announcement. "Sorry, no guests."

"Would you tell Donna that I hope she has a great practice," I said, "and if she wants to see me, I'll be over at the Rocket Cafe?"

"Sure will, but don't get your hopes up."

"So how long are we gonna hang around here?" said Matt as we walked over to the cafe.

"I don't know. I haven't thought that far."

The Rocket Cafe was directly across the street from the Ramblin' Rose and was the closest thing to a diner you could find in California. It was a bit out of place next to the desert-like Arroyo Seca and owed most of its business to the roller rink. Since that business had been faltering, so was the cafe. There were rips on some of the swiveling bar stools at the counter, and the jukebox didn't work, much to Matt's disappointment. Everyone from the rink was on a first-name basis over there, including Matt and me.

"Hey, look who's here," I said as we stood just inside the door. It was Dominic Demucci sitting alone in a booth, and when he saw us, he motioned us over.

"You boys want to join me?"

"Sure," I said, and we both slid into the ribbed burgundy seat across from him.

"Want a donut or something?" he asked as the waitress came over and brought us water and silverware.

"Maybe just some hot chocolate," said Matt.

"I'd like that too," I said. "What are you reading?" It didn't look like a normal newspaper—more like a magazine on newsprint paper.

"Oh, it's all about the local music scene—clubs and gigs and studios—things like that. Where's Donna? You two are usually inseparable."

" 'I had a girl,' " Matt sang, " 'Don-na was her name.' "

" '*Had*' is right," I said.

"Lovers' quarrel?" Dominic asked, raising his eyebrows.

" 'Wo, wo, wo, tra-ge-dy,' " Matt kept up his musical commentary.

"What is this?" said Dominic. "A walking Hit Parade?"

"I'm making up for the jukebox," said Matt. "I know all the Top Ten. Ask me anything."

"So what's the problem with you and Donna?" said Dominic, ignoring Matt's challenge.

"I missed her practice a couple times and now she thinks I don't like her anymore, I guess." Of course I didn't tell him that the last time we were together was the closest we'd ever been and that I'd gotten scared and stayed away.

"So she's giving you the cold shoulder."

"Yeah. She won't even let me in the door."

"I wouldn't worry. She'll get over it. These skaters are a stubborn lot. They have to be to keep getting up off the floor over and over again."

The waitress brought our hot chocolates, and my eye caught a book on the table next to Dominic, probably because several words on the cover jumped out at me: "crossword puzzles, riddles, word games."

"Are you good at riddles?" I asked.

"It's my business. I'm a songwriter too, you know."

"Maybe you can help us," I said. "Someone gave me a message in the form of a riddle. It's something I have to do, and I think it may have something to do with Donna's competition."

"What's the deal? Have you guys been seeing Madame Zar lately?"

"No, nothing like that," I said, and Matt started in on the chorus of "Gypsy Woman."

"Cool it, Matt," I said.

"So where did you get the riddle?" Dominic persisted.

I looked at Matt and decided I had nothing to lose.

"From an angel," Matt said, beating me to it.

"No kidding? An angel talked to you?" Dominic said to Matt.

"No. To me," I corrected.

"I've heard about this kind of thing," he said, not at all put-off like I thought he'd be. "So what's the riddle?"

" 'Scale the highest mountain,' and I'm already pretty sure the mountain is Mt. Whitney."

"Hmm," said Dominic, taking a sip of his coffee and staring out the window. It was overcast and drizzly outside. "Climbing a high mountain would be the obvious—"

"I know," I said. "I'm hoping it's not that."

"Completing some difficult task would be the less obvious."

"Yeah, that's part of it. But I think there might be a trick to it."

"Well, let's see. It *is* interesting that it uses the word 'scale.' Why not just 'climb'?"

"Maybe 'scale' is angel talk," said Matt.

"Maybe," said Dominic, "but it might mean something else. It's also a musical term, you know—like in a musical scale. Hey . . . what did you say that mountain was again?"

"Mt. Whitney," I said as Dominic started sifting through the pages of the paper he was reading.

"There it is," he said. "Just as I thought."

"What?" I said, getting excited. "What did you find?"

He folded the paper back, put it on the table, and pointed to a section called "Recording Studios."

"Whitney Sound Studios," he said. "I thought I remembered that name. I did a gig there a couple years ago. Mostly religious music. It's the only studio in L.A. with a real pipe organ in it."

"Holy cow! Matt, I bet that's it! Where is it?"

"Address and phone are right there. It's on Lankersheim in Burbank."

"Matt, do you think Bernice could take us there?"

"No, but we could take a taxi."

"I'd help you guys out, but I gotta meet Lenny in a couple minutes," said Dominic.

"That's okay. We'll get there," I said. "Thanks for helping with the riddle!"

"No problem. Good luck. Hey, don't forget this address."

He wrote it down on a napkin and gave it to me. I put it in my pocket while Matt tried to wrestle some money out of the watch pocket of his blue jeans.

"Save your money for the taxi," Dominic said with a wink. "The hot chocolate's on me. Just put in a good word for me next time you hear from that angel."

"You bet!" I said, sliding out of the booth. "And thanks!"

14

Once More
With Feeling

"I hope this is okay," I said, having second thoughts about flagging taxis near the Arroyo Seca.

"You got any better ideas?" said Matt.

I really didn't. Bernice was shopping and my father was at the church, and anyway, how could we possibly explain to anybody what we were doing?

Well, you see this angel gave me a clue about scaling the highest mountain, which we think might have something to do with Whitney Sound Studios in Burbank, so we want to go over there and see if we're on the right track, but we don't really know what to look for once we get there, or what might turn up next. We're just trying to figure out the next piece of the puzzle and go from there.

"You sure you have enough money?"

"Plenty," Matt said. "I do this all the time, remember?"

"Whitney Sound Studios," Matt said to the driver as we hopped in the backseat of a taxi that pulled up right then. I handed him the napkin with the address.

"You sure you want to go to Burbank?" said the driver, looking us over closely.

"Why?" I said.

"That's going to be eight or nine bucks," he said. "You boys got that kind of money?"

"No problem," said Matt as the driver took off down the Arroyo Parkway. Neither one of us noticed anything familiar about the red and black lumberjack coat he was wearing.

" 'Scale the highest mountain,' " I quoted the angel as we got on the Pasadena Freeway, "could turn out to be Whitney Studios. It's just like something Ben would do."

"You still think he has something to do with these angels?"

"Positive."

"So what are we going to do once we get there?" asked Matt.

"I don't know. I've been thinking about that. I doubt we can sneak in without knowing our way around."

"So why don't we just go in the front door with a reason?"

"What reason?"

"What do you do with studios?" Matt said. "You rent them, right? We're just checking it out for a recording project."

"You think they'll believe two kids are going to rent a studio?"

"Act like you know what you're doing and you can get away with almost anything."

"You're right about that," I said. "I did that in the hospital and it worked. Of course I had a little help from Molly."

"Well, if all this angel stuff you're talking about is really true, we've got some friends in higher places than Molly."

"Look, there's City Hall," I said.

"Dum, de dum dum." We both did the "Dragnet" theme at the same time.

Though it was less than half an hour away, the Los Angeles skyline might as well have been Baltimore to me. It seemed that far away from home, and my apprehension grew as the buildings grew closer together and the familiar friendly sights of residential suburbia gave way to rows of duplexes, apart-

ments, and industry. I had never been this far away from home
without my parents knowing it. We had to get back without
them finding out or my name was mud.

I watched the meter click to six dollars when we turned
onto the Hollywood Freeway, and I thought I caught a worried look on Matt's face. I was ready to say something to him
about it when the driver spoke up.

"What are you boys doing in Burbank?" He was an older
Negro man who looked like he hadn't shaved in a few days.
Stubby gray whiskers salted his black skin and a missing front
tooth made a hole in his smile.

"We're going to check out a recording studio," I said.

"Did I hear you boys say something about angels?"

"Uh . . . yeah," I said.

"The Los Angeles Angels," Matt inserted, thinking fast.

"I always liked them Angels," said the driver. "Even if
they was in the minors. I'd rather see Steve Bilko at the plate
than any of them players the Dodgers are sending up there
right now."

"Yeah," said Matt. "I saw the Angels and the Bakersfield
Saints once. Bilko hit three home runs in one game."

"Ah yes," said the driver. "The Saints and the Angels.
Those were great games. Never knew who to root for,
though. So what kind of music you boys play?"

"Uh . . . we don't play. We're just checking the studio out
for some friends of ours," I tried out our new line on him.

"Oh, I get it. You're producers."

"Yeah," said Matt, smiling at me. "That's it. We're producers."

"I like gospel music," the driver said. "Aretha Franklin
and Ethel Waters are my favorites. They're gonna be singin'
gospel music in heaven and the singers ain't gonna be white,"
and he turned around and winked at us while the taxi drifted
over one lane. Matt looked over his shoulder nervously. "Unless, of course, you think we'll all be white when we get to
heaven."

I'd never thought about it, but I had to admit, in my pictures of heaven there were no colored folks. That is, not until Netta Pearl. She was one colored person I knew would be in heaven for sure.

"Maybe when you die and go to heaven you'll be black like me," said the driver, and he turned back around and laughed loudly.

A few minutes later he pulled up to the curb. "Well, here you are, boys," he said. "Whitney Sound Studios, at your service."

The meter read $8.70, and Matt pulled a ten dollar bill out of his pocket.

"No, you keep it," said the man, pushing the money away. "You'll need it to get home. Record me some heavenly gospel music instead."

We stood on the sidewalk with our mouths open as the taxi drove away.

"Guess what?" Matt said. "This is all the money I have. How did he know that?"

We both looked up from the ten-dollar bill at the same time and saw only an empty street.

"No . . . you don't suppose—" said Matt.

"Did you notice his jacket?"

"Yeah," he said. "It was just like the coat that guy had on in the rest room at the roller rink."

"But the guy in the rest room wasn't a Negro," I said. "I'm sure of that."

"Maybe they just use the same coat," said Matt.

"Maybe . . . but a Negro angel?"

"Why not?" said Matt. "I just hope he wasn't right about us changing color in heaven."

"I'm just glad you still have your ten bucks. How were we supposed to get home?"

"Your parents would come get us," said Matt.

"*My* parents?" I said. "My parents would kill me if they knew I was out here without permission."

"I know. You've got to get your parents to relax a little bit."

"That's easy for you to say," I said, frustrated with his casualness.

The studio didn't look like anything from the outside. There was only a glass door with WHITNEY SOUND printed on it in small letters.

"If a Negro angel with a missing tooth brought us here," said Matt, "no telling what we're going to find inside."

What we found inside was a small waiting room with a desk that appeared to have someone temporarily away from it. There were notes and papers on it and a calendar book open to May, 1962. The phone was off the hook.

Two hallways opened off the room, one on either side of the desk, and when we heard the clicking of high heels echoing down one, we quickly ducked into the other. It led down blank walls to a thick open door where we could hear the muffled sound of music coming from inside. It was almost dark in the room except for the light spilling into it through a window in the door to another room—a sort of room within a room. The door to that room was closed, and there appeared to be two men in there listening intently to what we could only hear faintly.

"It's okay," whispered Matt. "I doubt they can see us. It's too dark in here."

As our eyes slowly adjusted to the dark, we inched our way along the wall inside the big room until it turned back out of view of the window. There we slid down to a sitting position and studied our situation.

The room we were in was large with a high ceiling. The walls were mostly covered with wood, except for large rectangular panels of cushiony type material every few feet. There was a piano in one corner and an organ console next to it. I pointed to the stacks of organ pipes behind and above it. It was the pipe organ Dominic had mentioned.

Microphones and music stands were scattered around the

room. Black wires stretched to each of the mike stands, coiling next to them like snakes. Everything was quiet, except for the muffled music coming from the room behind the window.

"I bet this is where people sing and in there is where they record it," I said.

"Brilliant," said Matt. "As a producer, you probably should know that."

Suddenly we heard high heels coming down the hall and stiffened. Then the music got loud for a moment as the door to the inner room was opened. That brief opening was enough to hear a few lines of a familiar song.

"Did you hear that?" I whispered. "It's Netta's song—the first one she sang in church about the love of God."

I had only heard "how rich, how pure," but that was enough to recognize it.

"And I know that voice too," I said, but I couldn't place it. When I heard the door open again to "the saints' and angels' song" I knew where I'd heard that voice before.

That voice made me think of lying in bed with a fever, listening to the radio. It was definitely a radio voice. Then I remembered that my mother would always find "The Hour of Decision" and play it for me when I was sick in bed. "The Hour of Decision" was a daily broadcast from wherever Billy Graham was doing his latest crusade, and the voice I heard spilling out through the briefly opened door was the same unmistakable, rich velvety voice I had heard at my bedside.

"Matt, that's got to be George Beverly Shea."

"Do you suppose he's in there?" said Matt.

"Let's see if we can get a better look."

The high-heeled shoes had disappeared back down the hall, so we snuck out into the room, more daring this time.

"This way," I whispered, and we followed the back wall over behind the organ console where we could get adequate cover for our spying. From there we could see three men in the room, and the one standing farthest back looked awfully familiar.

"Is it George?" said Matt.

"I think so."

"Which one is he?"

"He's the one standing up in the back, I think."

The other two men were sitting down at a big control board, facing the window. Seeing them there, facing out at us with light pouring out of the window, made it seem like they were commanding a spaceship and we were some alien enemy being hunted in the darkness. I shuddered when I thought of how vulnerable we were out there and wondered what on earth we were doing.

The music had stopped and all three were talking together when suddenly the two men at the controls stood up and headed for the door that opened into the room where we were hiding. One of them reached toward the wall and suddenly the lights went on above us. Matt and I ducked down behind the organ console and looked at each other in horror.

"You sure we can do this over?" said a voice as steps approached. *He was heading straight for the organ!*

"Yes," said the other one. "That's the beauty of three tracks."

Matt managed to crawl out under the bench before the man got there and escape behind a baffle that stood a couple feet from the wall where the organ pipes were housed. But I was caught under the bench of the organ, trying to make myself as small as I possibly could as the man sat down right above me.

"Okay. Let's fire this baby up."

I knew I had to get out of there before he turned on the organ, because I was sitting right on the pedals that played the big bass notes. Just as I heard a click on the console, I rolled out the back side of the bench and around behind the baffle. A whirring sound and a sudden rush of air filled the pipes, disguising my exit, as the wall behind me seemed to breathe in a huge gulp of air.

I was surprised not to find Matt behind the baffle, but there was a door there, slightly ajar, opening into where the organ pipes were housed. I slipped inside just as the organist hit the first note. He must have been playing a joke on the other guys because he had all the stops open and played a chord that sounded like the opening of a tragic melodrama. I must have jumped three feet when he did it.

Matt jumped too, which was unfortunate, because at the moment he jumped, he was exploring on top of a ladder that went up into the smaller pipes, and the blast of that opening chord threw him off the ladder and down fifteen feet into the big pipes below.

I knew nothing of this because the music drowned out the thud and his cry when he landed. All I could do was search for him amidst the darkness throughout the thunderous playing of "The Love of God." The pipes bellowed and shrilled. The low ones seemed to reach in and tickle my heart; I could feel them before I heard them. And more than once I jumped when a pipe went off right next to my ear.

I went up and down the ladder two or three times, completely miffed. Where could Matt have gone back there? The only light was higher up where the smaller pipes were open to the room. I couldn't see anything down below.

It wasn't until the organist released the final chord of the song that I heard a faint whimpering coming from down in the pipes, and I barely made out Matt's voice, still trying to conceal himself.

"I can't move!" he cried in a kind of shrieking whisper.

"Once more with feeling," came a voice through the loudspeaker in the room.

"No, wait!" I shouted from up in the pipes. It was their turn to be surprised.

15

A Record for Donna

My father got a big surprise, too—several, in fact. Not only because he got the call from the studio and because he had no idea that his son was in Burbank, but also because my mother and Becky were out with the car, leaving him home alone to deal with the awkward and totally unexpected visit of Lenny LaRue.

Apparently Donna's performance had fallen off so dramatically in the last few days that Lenny had stopped by on a personal mission to try to patch things up between me and his skater. It made me chuckle when I heard it—to think Lenny would be that desperate for Donna's performance. But that's why Lenny was at my house when the call came in from me; and that's why he was the only available transportation to get my father to the studio.

Now Lenny may have kept a messy office, but he somehow managed to keep the cleanest black and white '55 Corvette in southern California. And to this day, whenever I need a little imaginary entertainment, I merely picture that thirty-minute ride to Whitney Sound Studios, and the unlikely pairing of Lenny and my father, top down on a misty January day, in Lenny's '55 Corvette.

The serious questioning process didn't begin until Matt was on his way to the hospital and my father and Lenny got there. All the immediate attention was directed toward getting Matt free from the organ pipes and making him as comfortable as possible until his parents arrived.

With Matt gone, however, everyone was demanding some sort of explanation from me. It was during that explanation that the whole thing came to me—the purpose of our trip to the studio and the solution to the mystery behind the angelic messages. I hadn't realized until I started answering questions that all the information was in; it only needed to be sorted out properly. And somehow, as the questions were thrown at me, one by one, that's exactly what happened.

What were you doing here in the first place?

"We were checking out the studio."

Why on earth would you do that? Are you planning on recording something?

"Actually, yes." I was thinking right then of the taxi driver who'd told us to record some heavenly gospel music and keep our taxi fare. And I was thinking of "The Saints' and Angels' Song," which was what I was already calling "The Love of God" in my mind, once I had connected it to the third message whispered to me by an angel in the night. And I was thinking, most importantly, of Donna skating to that song—skating effortlessly and gracefully, twirling and jumping and making long sweeping turns with her arms and hands, writing the love of God with the graceful twist of a wrist on the imaginary parchment of the sky.

Strangely enough, I had seen these images in my mind while the organ blasted away next to my ears and I searched for Matt. I had wanted to stop and dwell on what I was imagining with such clarity, while at the same time feeling anxious about not finding Matt. Now I knew why I had seen those things. It was all finally making sense.

And just what are you planning to record?

Probably they were thinking they were humoring me with this question, not expecting me to have an answer ready for them—but I did.

"Netta Pearl and the choir singing 'The Saints' and Angels' Song,' " I said, convinced now that it had to be Netta. George Beverly Shea had probably recorded the song already—not to mention the one they were working on that day—but no one could sing it like Netta. Only Netta Pearl had the emotion to compete with the excitement of Donna's skating. Together, they would make heavenly gospel music dance.

What? You want to record Netta Pearl and the choir? Why on earth would you want to do that?

"So Donna can have something to hand the judges—a recording to skate to, made just for her."

I couldn't believe how I was thinking on my feet. I couldn't believe what was coming out of my mouth. I remembered Ben talking like this, but it was not like me to be so quick and so confident.

Little did I know when I revealed all this that there was something in this idea for everybody. The momentary silence that greeted me was indicative of the wheels that were turning. I only thought they were trying to figure out what to do with me.

Instead, as it turned out, Lenny was thinking about how this would get Donna and me back together and Donna back to work. And even though it certainly wouldn't be a song he would choose, the idea of making a custom recording especially for a 3½-minute routine was something that hadn't been done yet at Donna's level of competition. It would give her a definite advantage.

Then there was my father, who was upset with me, on the one hand, for sneaking away to the studio without asking; but on the other hand, here he was in the same room with two of the most revered names in Christian music, Loren Whitney and George Beverly Shea. The thought of experiencing a recording studio and having his choir recorded by the likes of the present company was a tantalizing proposition, aside from the preposterous nature of the events that had brought this odd group of individuals together.

And then there was Loren Whitney, with at least a three-hour session and a master record to cut. He had something in this, though perhaps the least at stake. That was probably why he was the one who responded first.

"Well, it looks like we've got ourselves a pretty ambitious producer here," he said. That made everyone laugh and loosened some of the tension. It also made everyone wonder if there was, in fact, something to this crazy notion I had. That's when my mother and Becky showed up, announced at the door of the control room by the high-heeled lady, who by then I had learned was named Grace.

"Walter . . . I got your note," said my mother. "Jonathan, are you all right?"

"Yes, but Matt's not. Can I go see him now?"

"Where is he?" my mother said, looking at my father, worriedly.

"Mr. and Mrs. Wendorf took him to St. Mary's. It looks like a broken leg."

"Oh dear," said my mother.

My father turned to Mr. Whitney and said, "Was there any damage to the organ?"

"None whatsoever. It's the boy we're concerned about."

"Was it a bad break?" asked my mother.

"It didn't break the skin, if that's what you mean," said Mr. Whitney.

"By the way," said my father, "this is my wife, Ann. Ann . . . Loren Whitney."

"How do you do."

"And, Ann," he could not conceal the admiration in his voice, "this is George Beverly Shea."

"Oh—" she said, taken by surprise, "Mr. Shea—what a privilege to meet you."

"Hello, Ann," said Mr. Shea in a deep voice that rendered my mother speechless for a few seconds.

"Well," said my father, clasping his hands together, "I suppose we should let you gentlemen get back to work. This whole thing has been such an intrusion upon your time and I apologize."

"Nonsense," said Mr. Whitney. "In fact, you're welcome to stay and sit in on the rest of the session. We're just doing some taping for a radio show."

My father looked interested, but my mother spoke. "We need to go see how Matt is, dear."

"Of course," said my father.

"You're welcome any time," said Mr. Whitney, shaking my father's hand. "And, Jonathan, no need to sneak in any-more." And then he handed me his business card and said with a wink, "Call me later about that recording idea. I'm sure we can work out something."

I looked at my father, who turned and shook George Beverly Shea's hand. Then Lenny shook hands all around and filed out with us.

"I'll meet you over at the hospital," he said, and I thought it was a bit odd for Lenny to be that interested in seeing Matt.

Most of the drive to the hospital was taken up with my father trying to spell out to my mother what had happened. He told the story while Becky and I sat quietly in the back. I was only brought in to complete parts he didn't know yet When he told the part about recording Donna's song, how-ever, I noticed that he didn't present it as an entirely ridicu-lous idea—indeed, he made it sound almost as if it were a logical reason for us to be there, though certainly not an ex-cuse for not letting them know where I was.

As we pulled into the hospital parking lot, an all-too-fa-miliar heaviness pressed in on my chest. I had Donna's brief hospital visit to combat memories of Ben, but I still could not make this feeling go away. Besides, I knew Matt's injury was worse than Donna's because my parents had called the hos-pital before leaving the studios to find out that he was being admitted and would be there at least overnight. He had a mul-tiple fracture; he had broken his leg in three places.

"I don't want to go in," I said at the last minute as everyone started getting out of the car. My mother looked at my father with an aren't-you-glad-you-weren't-hard-on-him look and turned around and patted my hand.

"It's okay, honey. This is nothing like Ben. Ben had problems long before his accident. You know that now. It's just a break; and breaks heal."

"It's a bad break."

"It will heal just the same."

As obnoxious as Matt could be sometimes, I was starting to like him, and liking someone who was about to spend the night in the hospital was just a little too familiar.

"No. I'll wait here. You guys go ahead."

My mother flashed my father a worried look and said, "Why don't you and Becky go see how Matt is. I'll stay here with him."

My father looked like he wanted to protest, but my mother had a look of resolve on her face that kept him from saying anything.

"Tell me about this recording idea," she said as soon as they were out of sight, surprising me with her interest. At first I thought she was only doing this because she was trying to get my mind off my fear of St. Mary's Hospital, but the more we talked, the more she convinced me she was genuinely interested.

I told her all about recording Netta Pearl—everything except the angels, that is—and as I talked, she grew more excited.

"I think it could be a wonderful idea, Jonathan," she said, "something the whole church could get behind."

"You really think so?"

"Yes I do. It's a great opportunity for the Gospel, too. Pastor Beamering would like that. Donna would be skating as a testimony to the love of God."

It was almost as if she was convincing herself, too. Maybe she was seeing this as a way all her objections to skating could be overcome—as if Donna's skating could be sanctified through this song and the purpose behind it.

I hadn't even thought of the effect Donna's performance might have on an audience. Up to that point I had been too busy solving angelic riddles to see any broader ramifications. Now my mother was opening the door to a bigger purpose.

I liked being with my mother right then. She had turned sideways in the seat to talk to me, leaning her head back against the window with one arm resting on the top of the seat, and I thought she looked very pretty. I wanted to ask her why she couldn't be like this more often, but I didn't.

"Does Donna know about this idea?" she asked.

"No. Do you think she'll like it?"

"I think she'll like the fact that you came up with it and that you've risked life and limb to pursue it."

"I risked Matt's limb," I corrected her, and we both smiled.

"I don't know," I said, "she doesn't want to see me right now. The last two times I showed up at the rink, Peg told me she was not 'entertaining any guests today.' "

"That won't last long," she said. "In fact—"

"What?" I said, following her moving gaze to the lane leading to the hospital and whatever it was that caught her eye right then. What it was made me excited, scared, and embarrassed all at the same time. It was an immaculate black and white '55 Corvette with Lenny's silver-streaked hair waving in the wind from the driver's seat, and a familiar blond ponytail bobbing around next to him.

"Why are they here?" I said.

"To see Matt and probably to see you."

"Not me."

"And why not?"

Now I was really confused. I was enjoying being with my mother right then, but not sure what to do about running into Donna with her around. That's when my mother surprised me the most.

"I'll go on in," she said. "You come with them." And she left me.

I wanted to run after her and give her a big hug, but I didn't want to lose track of the Corvette. Lenny was heading for the other side of the hospital, and I had to run as fast as I could without slipping on the wet pavement. I rounded the far side of emergency just in time to see them already walking toward the back entrance.

"Donna!" I called out.

They both stopped and turned around, and when they saw it was me, Lenny said something to Donna and went on through the door, leaving her standing there waiting for me. I tried to slow down and look cool, but it was no use; I was entirely out of breath.

"What . . . are you . . . doing here?" I said, grabbing for air.

"Lenny told me what happened."

"Oh."

"I hope Matt's okay," she said.

"Me too."

"Lenny also told me about the song. I actually think he likes the idea."

"Really?"

She was looking all over except when she spoke; then she looked right at me.

"Do you like it?" I said.

"Oh yes! I like it a lot. I've always liked that song, and with Netta Pearl singing it—I know I could skate to that. But you don't think it's really possible, do you? I mean . . . the choir and everything?"

"It's starting to look that way. Even my mother seems to be excited about it. I bet the whole church would get behind it. You'd be skating for everybody."

"Wow, I never thought about it like that, but I guess you're right."

There was an awkward silence when I wanted to apologize but I didn't know how to say it, or I was too proud, so I didn't say anything. Neither did she. All I was hoping for was some kind of sign that everything was okay, and her excitement seemed to telegraph that.

"Let's go find Matt," she said, but I hesitated, immobilized by the old fear again.

"Come on!" She smiled and grabbed my hand, pulling me into the hospital in much the same way that Margaret had pulled Matt and me into the dark of the Bolsa Chica bunker.

16

Milton Plays Motown; Netta Goes Downtown

"No! Never!" said Matt when I started telling him how things were shaping up for the recording of Donna's song. It was three days after the accident and he was home and uncomfortable in a cast all the way up to his hip. "I never want to hear that song again!"

"But, Matt, you and I have to be the producers. Mr. Whitney said so."

And he had, too. My father was the one who made the initial call to inquire about the estimated costs of such a project and to pursue the idea further. He and Jeffery T. had decided to go at least that far with it. When my dad found out that it wasn't nearly as expensive as they had feared, the level of talk and anticipation had jumped considerably, and word was already spreading around the church that Netta Pearl and the choir were going to become recording artists.

"Well, you'll have to just produce it without me!" Matt insisted.

"Matt, it wasn't the song that broke your leg."

"I don't care," he said. "Haven't you ever barfed up vegetable soup because it was the last thing you had to eat before you got sick and you know you'll never be able to eat vegetable soup again? It's kind of like that."

"I know what you mean," I said. "That happened to me once with macaroni and cheese, but I got over it. You'll get over it. The session won't be for a couple of weeks yet."

"A couple weeks won't be enough. I'll never get over 'The Love of God,' " he said. "So it's really going to happen, huh?"

"It sure looks like it," I said. "And that part about us being producers is for real, Matt. Mr. Whitney made a big deal about it when my father talked to him. It was his only condition for giving us a good price. You and I had to be the producers. So you see, you have to do it."

"So what are producers supposed to do anyway?" he asked.

"Tell him what we like and what we don't like about what's happening."

"That doesn't sound tough. I do that all the time. How do you know so much about this?"

"I've already talked to Mr. Whitney a couple of times and that's what he told me. He said not to worry about it; we'd know just what to do."

"Sounds like you and this Whitney guy are real tight."

"I'm taking the deposit over right after this and picking a date for the studio."

"Well pick one far enough away so I can forget that song for a while."

"It has to be as soon as possible. Donna needs the recording to build her routine around."

Things were moving fast. The day before had been Netta Pearl Sunday, and though my father had tried to keep the news quiet until plans were a little more finalized, it was impossible.

"You wouldn't believe the things people were asking me yesterday after church," I said as Matt tried to get in a more comfortable position on his bed.

"Like what?"

" 'Does Netta Pearl really have a recording contract with Motown Records? Is she singing a duet with George Beverly Shea or Aretha Franklin? Is Billy Graham really going to be there for the recording? Who's directing, your father or Cliff Barrows?' Honestly—the things people come up with."

"What does Milton think about it?" Matt asked.

"Milton is in seventh heaven. He's sure the single is going to go gold. Pastor Beamering is wondering if he'll get to preach at the competitions, and Netta is already planning what she's going to wear to the studio."

"It's only a recording," said Matt. "No one's going to *see* her sing!"

"Yeah, but try telling her that. Besides, it's 'Hollywood,' or at least the next town over. That's close enough for Netta."

"I thought it was expensive to record. Who's going to pay for all this? Donna's grandparents don't seem the type to have a lot of money."

"The choir has already taken up a collection that will cover most of the recording session. It's seventy-five dollars an hour for a choir, and Mr. Whitney thinks it will take about three hours, including setup and takedown."

"Now you're starting to sound like a producer."

"Oh yeah, there's also this businessman in the church who's going to pay for the pressing of five hundred singles because he knows he can sell at least that many in the church alone."

"Wow!" said Matt. "A lot has happened in a few days."

"So you're in on it—even if you do hate the song?"

"Yeah, I'm in. Here," he said, handing me a pen, "sign my cast."

So I signed it "Get well fast. Jonathan. P.S. There are easier ways to play an organ!"

It didn't take long for the whole church to get caught up in the recording idea and even the skating competitions. There was already talk about taking a busload of choir mem-

bers to Bakersfield to see Donna perform, and once the recording was out, they had to make that two buses because of
all the families and friends. By the time we did the recording,
the businessman who was financing the pressing had to in-
crease his order to take into account relatives and friends of
church members who'd already signed up for copies of the
single.

Donna was a little taken aback by all the attention, but
Lenny knew how to handle that. He had been through star-
dom before. He knew how fickle an audience could be and
how foolish a fad could become if you didn't keep focused
on your original intent. He'd watched roller skating go from
the Skating Vanities to Roller Derby, so he knew you didn't
get too excited about anything other than your performance
and your own personal goals.

"To compete well in the competitions," I heard him say
over and over to Donna during those final months of practice,
"to know you went up there and skated your best, to walk
away with your head up, that's what you're looking for. Nothing more, but nothing less than your best. *Your* best. No one
else's. Regardless of what the judges say, you want to know
in your heart you skated the best you possibly could."

We set the recording date for the last Saturday in January.
That gave Matt some time to get to where he could at least
move around on crutches. It also gave Lenny, my father, and
Milton Owlsley time to reconstruct the arrangement of the
song to fit the 3½-minute requirement. That meant a Saturday session with Donna and Netta Pearl at the Ramblin'
Rose to try and work it all out. It took some doing, in that
the song, the way they sang it in church, was over five minutes
long.

"We'll have to cut it down," Lenny said, and everyone
agreed except Netta.

"Couldn't I just sing it faster?"

"You'd have to sing it like Alvin and the Chipmunks," said
Dominic, who was sitting in on this session more because of

his curiosity over watching Milton play Motown than anything.

"You know, Milt, I gotta hand it to you," he said afterward, "you make a pretty good Booker T." That made Milton's buttons almost pop off his shirt.

We ended up cutting out the second verse. Two verses and two choruses took exactly three minutes to sing, which left half a minute for the introduction and a key change transition between the second verse and the last chorus. That was the climax of the song and everyone's favorite part. Netta would repeat the last line, "Though stretched from sky to sky" (except when she sang it, it was more like "sta-retched"), while Milton transposed it up one key, and for a split second there was a gaping hole that Netta's big voice would rush in and fill with, "The love of God, how rich and pure. . . ." That was right when Donna planned on landing with her arms outstretched from the biggest jump of her routine, and the music would catch her.

As the day of the recording session finally approached, it seemed half the congregation wanted to come, but the number of people had to be limited to what we could fit into the small control room. That turned out to be Donna, Donna's grandparents, my mother and father, Lenny, Pastor and Mrs. Beamering, Mr. and Mrs. Wendorf, and Matt and I.

"What about the sister of the producer?" argued Becky, and I had relished the rare power to refuse my sister.

"Well, after all the nasty things you've done to me," I strung her out . . ."you can come."

Loren Whitney had an engineer to help him, and though he had co-workers who were perfectly capable of running this session without him, he took this project personally. He was a very kind and accommodating man who seemed to have taken a special liking to Matt and me and treated us like adults. More than that, he treated us, just as he had promised, like producers. I had been thinking that his insistence on our being the producers was just a way of being nice to us, but that was clearly not the case. Even though he ran the session, he consulted with us often, and he never made a decision without our okay. A number of times during the session he said to Lenny or my father or Milton or Netta Pearl, "Well, what do Matt and Jonathan think?" This was nothing short of an irritation to all of them.

Donna also was brought into the actual recording, since having a general idea of certain moves she wanted to perform at particular junctures in the song allowed us to embellish portions of it appropriately. This usually amounted to Netta stretching out a note, or coming in late on another one to allow for a twirl or a jump to be completed.

What should have taken an hour, however, ended up taking two, and most of that was due to having too many people voicing their opinions. My father had an awful time of it out in the studio, having to deal with forty-five opinions from the choir and occasional outbursts from Pastor Beamering or Lenny actually running out into the studio to try and influence the recording.

"No one will go into the studio unless I say so," said Mr. Whitney after the second infraction. "Is that clear?"

But the worst place of all was the control room itself. It was too crowded to begin with, and then people kept offering their unsolicited remarks and observations. Jeffery T. wanted to make sure certain words came across with sufficient clarity to convey the message of the song. Bernice and my mother took exception to some of Netta's more breathy sections which they thought were too "jazzy." Lenny kept trying to make the music more uptown, Milton Owlsley wanted it more Motown, and Netta Pearl simply wanted to go all the way downtown with it.

I watched Mr. Whitney grow more and more exasperated, until at exactly the hour mark, he announced that everyone must clear the control room except for the producers and the skater. Matt and Donna and I sat quietly while the adults filed out red-faced. There was some laughter when the door closed behind them, but mostly we got down to work.

The real turning point came when Netta got so nervous after a couple more attempts at the song and the interruptions of varying opinions that she broke out in heavy perspiration and almost fainted.

"She's just too uptight," I said in the now-quiet control room as forty-eight people stood with taut nerves on the other side of the glass. "They need a break."

"Good idea," said Mr. Whitney. "Come back to it fresh. Matthew, you tell them. Here, just press this button and talk into the microphone."

"All right, you guys," Matt's voice made its effect on the other side of the glass, "we're going to take a fifteen-minute break. There's stuff to drink out in the waiting room. Everybody relax. You're doing great. Donna can't wait to skate to this!"

"Matthew, where did you learn to be so natural at the microphone?" asked Mr. Whitney.

"We have a special radio elective at our school. One of the shop teachers used to be a DJ. We have our own broadcast booth and our own station that covers three blocks."

"I didn't know that," I said.

"Yep," he said. "I'm going to be a DJ someday."

"Well, Matthew, you have the talk-back microphone from here on out," said Mr. Whitney. "Look at them out there. They're loosening up already."

"And I have an idea how we can loosen up Netta Pearl even more," said Donna. "There's nothing wrong with Netta that a few minutes with Granny Finley wouldn't cure."

"Perfect!" I said.

So Donna went and got her grandmother while we rolled back the tape and got the machines ready for another try. Then we watched Granny Finley roll right up to where Netta had nearly collapsed in a chair. She patted Netta's face with tissue and started talking to her, and in seconds Netta Pearl was laughing so hard she was bouncing up and down and crying all at the same time. And the effect of this lightheartedness passed on to the rest of the choir. You could see the heightened animation through the window, as if Granny Finley somehow pumped everyone full of happy juice. Suddenly, everyone remembered this singing along with Netta was once fun to do.

That gave me the next idea.

"I think the problem with everyone out there is they don't have an audience. Netta needs an audience to perform to. She's lost without it. Why don't we leave Granny Finley out there?"

"Better than that," said Donna. "What about everyone else waiting in the reception room? Would there be room in the studio for them? They could be the audience."

"If they'll behave themselves," said Mr. Whitney.

"I think they will now," I said.

"Great, then," Mr. Whitney said. "Donna, why don't you go invite them back in; and, Jonathan, you come help me set up some chairs. Matthew, the controls are all yours. Just don't press that red button over there. That will start the tape rolling."

Matt sat proudly at the console with his leg up on a chair while Mr. Whitney and I started setting up chairs in the studio.

Suddenly Matt's voice came over the microphone: " 'I'm just a lonely boy/Lonely and blue/I'm all alone/With nothin' to do.' "

Mr. Whitney smiled and waved him off.

Matt came right back with, "That's number seven this week, kids, 'Lonely Boy' by Paul Anka. And number six and holding for yet another week in our Top Ten countdown is 'Rama Lama Ding Dong' by The Edsels, followed by our leading gainer, from out of nowhere, 'The Love of God' by Netta Pearl and the Colorado Avenue Standard Christian Church Sanctuary Choir from Pasadena!"

That made everybody laugh even more, and cheer too.

"You're good, kid," said Mr. Whitney as he and Donna and I came back into the control room. "You've got a future in this.

"Okay," he went on, "let's run this down one more time. I have a good feeling about this one."

Happy to be back in on the action, Pastor Beamering waved his arms at us through the window.

"Oh no, what is it now?" said Mr. Whitney.

Matt punched the talk-back button. "Yes?"

"I'd like to lead us all in prayer," Pastor said in a faint voice that was faint only to us because he was not near a microphone. Jeffery T. Beamering never had a faint voice in his life.

"Why didn't he think of that sooner?" Mr. Whitney said on our side of the glass.

Matt clicked on the button and looked at Mr. Whitney for the answer.

"Go right ahead," said Mr. Whitney, pushing the volume up on the microphone nearest Pastor Beamering, which unfortunately happened to be right in front of Netta Pearl.

"Dear heavenly Father," he began, his voice stronger now in the control room, "we thank Thee for this opportunity to use these voices and this studio to glorify thy name—"

"YES, LORD!" boomed Netta Pearl, nearly sending us through the roof.

Mr. Whitney quickly fumbled for the volume control on Netta's microphone while Donna and I fell on the floor with laughter, followed by Matt's scream because I knocked against his leg when I landed.

"Sshhhh!" Mr. Whitney said over everyone's giggling. "They might hear us out there. Wow. Do you think the Lord heard that one?"

"I'm wondering if I will ever hear anything else again," I said.

" . . . and lead us not into temptation . . ." Pastor Beamering had them into the Lord's Prayer now. Then he finished up by praying for Donna, that she would skate her best to the glory of God, and for the proclamation through everyone of God's great and glorious love.

"In Jesus' name, Amen."

"Amen!" said Netta Pearl, her voice back down to a low roar.

"Play ball!" said Mr. Whitney, and he started the tape.

The presence of an audience to sing to changed everything. Netta glowed. The choir sang out at twice the volume (we knew that because Mr. Whitney had to pull their recording volume down to keep the dial from going into the red). Even Milton stretched out and found that magical spot with Netta that they had discovered that first Sunday.

Somehow, everyone stopped trying to make it happen and let it happen instead, and the result pleased everyone. They got it the first time; everyone knew it; and there was great joy and celebration.

"Mercy, is that me?" said Netta Pearl as we played back the recording through the studio monitors.

"Glo–ry!" she said in a hushed whisper, and people listened humbly, overtaken by the quality and the depth of their own voices.

They all said it was Pastor Beamering's prayer that did it.

17

Route 99

North of Los Angeles 109 miles sits the rural community of Bakersfield. It is situated in the southernmost part of the Central Valley, which stretches 500 miles to the north and lies between the golden hills of the Coast Range to the west and the purple Sierra Nevadas to the east. This fertile valley forms the largest and most important farming area west of the Rocky Mountains and produces almost every kind of crop imaginable. The upper portion of the valley, north of San Francisco Bay, is known as the Sacramento Valley. The larger, southern part is called the San Joaquin Valley. Each is named for the river that cuts through its valley floor and flows to the Sacramento Delta.

This is the heartland of California, and it resembles the Midwest in both lifestyle and terrain more than it does the mountains and the beaches, those things people normally associate with California. This is John Steinbeck country, dotted with small towns, dusty roads, shanty homes of migrant workers, and row upon row of orchards, vineyards, and farmland flourishing in the fertile soil.

Bakersfield is the gateway to the San Joaquin Valley from the south. To get there from Pasadena you must travel the "Grapevine," the popular name for that portion of California Route 99 that crosses the San Gabriel Mountains north of the

Los Angeles basin—the route we traveled that June day in 1962 to attend the roller-skating competitions in Bakersfield.

Air conditioning was not standard in cars then, and once we hit the valley, which opened before us like a broad plain, my father regretted not attaching the water cooler. We always took the water cooler on our annual trip to visit relatives in Texas, but that was through the desert in August. My father didn't think it was going to be that hot in the Central Valley in June, but it was. Like a furnace.

"The temperature must have gone up twenty degrees over the Grapevine," he said as we came down off the mountain and hit the first long stretch of road in the valley. Our windows went down immediately, and Becky and I stuck our faces into the hot, dry wind.

"No, no," said my father. "Hands and arms inside the car. That goes for heads too."

"What's that smell?" Becky said.

"Fruit trees," said my mother. "There are miles and miles of orchards here, and all kinds of crops."

The San Joaquin Valley was known for its almonds, apricots, cherries, figs, grapes, nectarines, olives, oranges, peaches, plums, and walnuts, and the hot sun beating down on all those fruits and nuts created a rich aroma that rushed to meet you.

"That's not only crops I'm smelling," said Becky.

"And a few stockyards too," said my father.

"How much longer to Bakersfield?" I said just as we came up on a sign that read Bakersfield 30, Fresno 138, San Francisco 323.

"Looks like about half an hour," said my father.

"We're way ahead of the buses," I said, studying the straight, steamy road that wiggled in the heat behind us before it started winding back up into the mountains from which we had just come. "They're nowhere in sight."

"Donna's still back there, isn't she?"

"Yep," I said. "Comin' right along."

I had been keeping an eye on the Finleys' '39 Plymouth. Sometimes older cars overheated in the mountain passes, but they didn't seem to be having any trouble. Mr. Finley did drive quite a bit slower than my father, however, which meant we were traveling slower than we would have if we weren't traveling in a caravan.

"Do you see Lenny up ahead?" I asked.

"I haven't seen him since the other side of the mountain," said my father.

"With that car, he's probably already been there for half an hour," I said. "Do you have the directions to the Civic Auditorium, Mother?"

"Yes, Jonathan. I've told you three times now, I have them right here."

"Relax, little brother," said Becky. "Everything's going to be all right."

"I'm not worried," I said, "just excited."

"Well you've been keeping your eyes glued to Donna's car since we left Pasadena," she said. "It's a wonder you're not carsick from looking backwards all the time."

The last four and a half months had been relatively uneventful. Once Donna had a song, her practicing took on a much more focused direction. She spent the first month after the recording session deciding exactly what she was going to attempt to do and the next three learning how to do it, piece by piece. It wasn't until the last four weeks, however, that she actually started putting the whole thing together.

A good program consisted of elements you did well, along with elements you stretched to perform. A skater might perform flawlessly, said Lenny, but if the skater's program was below his or her perceived abilities, it would not be judged as highly as a routine that included more difficult elements, even though they might not be perfectly executed. In other words, the judges wanted to see you reach. The best scores came when skaters attempted something slightly beyond their grasp and seized it.

So Donna's program was constantly in a state of flux right up to the day of her performance. That also meant she never skated her routine twice in exactly the same manner. What she attempted on a particular day—in a particular second, even—depended on her mental confidence and her physical strength at the time. The slightest thing could alter it.

Donna's physical strength and stamina continually amazed me. Watching someone skate freestyle in a performance or competition is deceptive. The audience sees only the finished product, and the practiced style and grace make it look easy. But I'd had the privilege of watching Donna learn, of knowing what went into creating that style and grace, seeing the bruises come and go on her legs, and hearing her grunt and groan in practice as she put her body through incredible paces. I saw the gritty face before the smile went on.

There had been no more angelic visitations since I'd received the messages that landed us at Whitney Sound, proving what I now believe to be the case: that their purpose was to get me over the barriers that had kept me from being involved with people I cared about. The angels were like Ben, poking and prodding me until I found myself doing Ben-type things, saying Ben-type things. And I still hold that they performed these functions in my life because, in fact, they were sent by Ben.

I did try and hear angels with Grizzly once. We even stayed overnight in the church one Friday night, and though no voices awakened us, I felt like I'd had a kind of angelic visit in just being alone in the sanctuary with the moon shining through the stained-glass window overhead and Grizzly moaning hymns out of the hymnbook as I sang along. Many people would have thought the sound of his voice grotesque, and I would have been one of them if I didn't know him. But that night there was truly something beautiful and clear and honest about his sounds. They expressed a love for God more beautifully than words could.

I also believe, to this day, that Ben had a hand in getting Donna and me together; that he had picked out my next friend—someone to replace him. Someone with his tenacity, his frankness, his faith, and his obtuse relationship to society and what most people regarded as being cool. What a surprise to discover his choice was a girl!

And now we were finally on the long-awaited trip to Bakersfield to see her skate. Even Matt, who had gotten bored with Donna's practices and hardly come to the rink at all during the past couple months, was coming too. I told him the producers had to be there, so Leonard and Bernice were bringing him, somewhere in the caravan behind us.

Everything had been leading up to this, and I had a feeling that something more than just the competition was going to take place.

This was the first year the Southwest Pacific Regional Championship was being held in Bakersfield rather than Los Angeles. Roller skating had atrophied to where it was too small for L.A. The Pan Pacific Auditorium had swallowed it up the last few years, and the city never even stopped to notice. Not to mention the expense. The entire event lasted for a whole week, and, depending on your classification, there could be a few days between qualifying and the finals, if, in fact, you were fortunate enough to get that far. That meant a few nights' lodging and meals for out-of-town contestants, and in L.A. that was pretty steep for the budgets of most skaters and their families.

By contrast, in Bakersfield the regional championship was a big deal. And this being the first year there made it even bigger. The city was rolling out the red carpet. Bands were going to play, the mayor and a number of councilmen were going to attend; there was going to be more press coverage over this than the championship had had in years.

It was definitely a big event for the Colorado Avenue, Standard Christian Church. Rolling behind us were two buses full of choir members and their families, along with a number of people, like us, who were driving their own cars so they could have the freedom of staying or returning, depending on the outcome. The buses were only coming for the day, for Donna's qualifying skate. If she went on to the finals, she would skate again sometime during the next two or three days. Most people, of course, didn't have the time or money to put into that kind of commitment. My father, for instance, was not real happy about not knowing exactly how long we were going to be staying. He liked to plan his trips months in advance and keep to a certain predictable schedule. He was prepared to stay for one night if necessary, but no longer than that. Becky and I were hoping for at least one night in a motel.

"This trip was not in my budget for this year," he had said. "If the finals are later than that, we'll have to go home and come back up for it."

There had been some consideration as to when to bring the buses. Everyone would prefer to see the finals, but then again, if Donna didn't make it that far, they would miss her entirely.

"Of course she'll make it to the finals. Our Donna? She's the best!" That was pretty much the sentiment around the church, but Lenny made it clear to my father that even the best can have their bad days. If they wanted to be sure their trip up to Bakersfield would be rewarded by seeing Donna skate to their recording of "The Love of God," they had better plan on coming to the qualifications. Let people decide individually what they wanted to do after that.

"Besides," Lenny said, "Donna needs the support to qualify. It's much harder to qualify than to win. If you make it to the finals, you have already won in a way. The pressure to qualify is much greater."

And so it was decided—which meant that Donna's qualifying skate would undoubtedly be accompanied by the biggest entourage in the history of the regional championships. And if the mayor of Bakersfield wasn't impressive enough, we had the mayor of Pasadena himself, Mayor Seth Wilson, in our caravan, still driving the 1958 Edsel convertible that had made him Ben's lasting friend and, as a result, a member of our church. He and his wife passed us twice on Route 99, once on the uphill grade and once on the straightaway into Bakersfield on the other side of the mountains—the reason for these two passes being a stop to put their top down once they hit the heat of the valley floor.

"Dad, you're going too fast again," I said. "I can hardly see them."

"Well, Mayor Wilson just passed us and waved us on," he answered. "Now he'll think I'm some kind of old fogy."

"Let him think what he thinks, dear," said my mother. "We can't lose the skater."

As I looked back at the wavy impression the front of the Finleys' Plymouth made through a mirage, I thought of the cherished box I had seen on Donna's lap as I closed her in the backseat of their car before we left the parking lot of the church. It was a package she had received in the mail—a total surprise—only three days earlier. She'd probably held it on her lap all the way up Route 99.

Frustrated over not being able to get anything more out of anyone about Donna's mother, I had finally asked Donna herself if she knew anything about Camarillo.

"Who told you about that?" she had snapped.

"No one. I figured it out."

"Jonathan, I'll tell you everything I know. My mother's alive, I think, but what state she is in, I do not know. I have not heard from her in nine years. I don't even know if she knows I exist. Granny says that when I'm old enough she will tell me the whole story. Apparently I'm not old enough yet, because I haven't been told. In the meantime, anything that would remind me of her has been removed or forbidden, like the pictures in Lenny's office."

That's why the box sat in Donna's lap right now, and the note was probably still inside, right where it was when she first opened the box three days ago.

Once the recording was completed and the routine worked out, the only other item to be decided was what outfit Donna would wear for the competitions. For a while, when she was going to skate to "La Paloma" by Billy Vaughn and His Orchestra—the song Lenny wanted her to skate to until Netta Pearl and the Colorado Avenue Standard Christian Church Sanctuary Choir came on the scene—she was going to wear a Spanish-style costume with a matador's cape. "The Love of God" called for a more traditional approach, however, and when Donna would start to question what she should wear, Lenny would say he had it all taken care of, not to worry. Well, that speech had gone on right up until a week ago, and Donna, in a panic, had tried to get her grandmother to help her make an outfit.

"I have to know I have something," she told me. "If whatever Lenny has in mind doesn't pan out, I won't have anything."

It was unlike Lenny to push things that late, and also unlike him not to have an alternative plan. That's why Donna was so confused.

"He must be absolutely sure or he wouldn't do this. It's just not like him," she kept repeating.

"But what if I don't like it or it doesn't fit?" I heard her say to him. "What will I do then?"

"You'll like it," he kept saying. "Trust me."

Well, she didn't really trust him. She couldn't with something this important. And she didn't get any help from Granny Finley either. Oh, Granny hemmed and hawed about doing this or that, but there was always something in the way—some excuse that kept her from getting to it.

"I honestly think they're in cahoots," Donna told me.

Out of frustration, she had finally designed her own outfit and was halfway through making it when the package arrived. She was so excited she couldn't tell me about it over the phone. Since it was summertime now and I was out of school, I rode my bike to her house. It took me over an hour to get there, and she was waiting for me on the front porch with the box on her lap.

"Open it," she said.

I looked at my hands all wet with dirty perspiration from the handlebar grips on my bike that were covered with three years of newsprint. I showed them to her and she ran inside and got me a towel, which I used to wipe everything I could find on my body to wipe. It was almost 80 degrees and I had just ridden over five miles uphill.

"Open it!" She had no patience.

I removed the top of the box and there was a note lying on tissue paper.

"Read it," she said, eyes sparkling. "Read it to me. I want to hear what it sounds like out loud." So I read.

Dear Baby,

Here's the outfit I wore in my first performance. I would have been about your age then. It is still my favorite. I made it as simple and comfortable as possible. I sure hope it fits. The fur collar comes up the back and wraps around your throat, but unfortunately I have lost some of the snaps. The collar is kind of special to me. It can be snipped off and worn without it, but maybe you can fix it. If you don't like the suit, just give it to the Goodwill, but please keep the collar and save it for me.

Good luck. I'm real proud of you.

Love, Mama

Donna could only look at me with eyes shining and her legs pulled up under her chin.

"Read that last part again," she said. "That part about keeping the collar."

" 'Please keep the collar and save it for me,' " I read.

"You know what that means? That means I'm going to see her again sometime . . . sometime soon, maybe!"

It was the greatest gift she could have received. And Lenny was right. It fit. It fit like it was made for her. Granny helped her fix the snaps, and she had done a dress rehearsal in it the day before.

It took your breath away just to watch her glide through the air in this outfit. It was white with sequins and rhinestones in front and a short satin skirt gathered slightly. In the back there was a deep plunge lined with white feathery fur that came up to the tops of her shoulders and then wrapped around her throat like a furry ribbon. It was that final touch that set it off. The furry band seemed to make her eyes sparkle and her hair dance.

This had, of course, raised a whole set of new questions. Lenny obviously had some kind of contact with Donna's mother, enough to be confident that the outfit would arrive by the time she needed it. How much did he know, and what was his relationship with Donna's mother anyway? Was he, in fact, Donna's father? That question crossed my mind, though I never told Donna. If he wasn't her father, he certainly fulfilled that role for her in many ways.

It would also help to explain the attention he gave her—attention that was out of proportion to the significance of the event. The competitions were important within the circle of amateur skating, but not as important as Lenny made them. Anyone could go to Bakersfield as long as they were associated with a club. There was no prize money except at the world level. It was simply a passion for some people and an enjoyment for others. But to Lenny it seemed to be much more than that.

" 'Welcome to Bakersfield'!" my father read triumphantly as we passed the sign, " 'Gateway to the San Joaquin Valley.' Get out the directions, dear. Tell me what to do."

"Well, nothing until we get into the center of town."

I had an important box with me, too—a surprise for Donna that she didn't know about yet. My mother had helped me with it. It was a small delicate wrist corsage made of tiny fragrant orchids.

My mother and I had gone to the florist the day before to get flowers to give to Donna after she finished skating, and I had spotted the corsage in a refrigerated display case. It was in a box with a cellophane window just like the box the model Edsel came in that I had gotten Ben for his birthday right after I first met him. Knowing what I knew about Donna's outfit, I could imagine how terrific this would look on her wrist. We wondered about it getting in the way of her skating, but the saleslady assured us she could tie the flowers down well and make the elastic especially tight.

"She could direct a Beethoven symphony with this on when I'm done with it," the lady said, and so we took it.

I reached down under the seat where the box was riding and looked at it again.

"Better keep it out of the sun," my mother said, noticing it in my lap. "Why don't I keep it with me and you can get it from me when you're ready?"

I handed it to her and imagined Donna's excitement. Maybe this would be her second best gift.

The Civic Auditorium was in an older part of town that didn't look anything like southern California. Nothing in Bakersfield did, as a matter of fact. Everything was flat, and there were few trees or tall buildings. The older part seemed a little like the Old West with buildings that had facades for faces. The auditorium itself was nondescript. Back in Pasadena it would have been a supermarket.

We pulled into a gravel and dirt parking lot that was already filling up with cars. I spotted Lenny's Corvette well up the line, but he was nowhere in sight.

We waited for Donna, and a small crowd of our caravan started to form, then Donna and the Finleys, and finally the buses about ten minutes after that. Just before the buses arrived, Lenny showed up with Donna's official packet.

"We don't have as much time as I thought," he said. "They've moved you up two hours, Donna. You're skating at one o'clock now. That's only two hours away. Jonathan, here are the tickets. You see that everyone gets one. I'm going to take Donna in and get her familiar with the floor."

It was eleven o'clock in the morning and we were already wiping the perspiration from our faces and foreheads.

"Don't worry, folks," Lenny said. "It's air conditioned inside." That was welcome news to everyone.

The buses pulled in on a cloud of dust I could taste.

"Mercy, where are we?" said Netta, first one through the door. "This sure ain't Hollywood, honey."

She was in a bright pink and green floral outfit with new white shoes that she looked down at disgustedly as she stepped off the bus into the dirt.

"Where's the red carpet? Who was it said Bakersfield was puttin' out the red carpet for us? I could use one of them right now."

Netta's bus emptied out in a very jovial mood. I could hear singing from the back, and I asked if that had been going on all the way up.

"No, just the last hour," someone said.

"If this place ain't air conditioned, I'm gettin' back on the bus," said Netta, fanning herself with the program I was handing out with the tickets.

"Don't worry," said Granny Finley. "They wouldn't be able to skate if it wasn't."

That made everyone want to go inside as soon as possible.

The inside of the Bakersfield Civic Auditorium looked pretty much like a school gymnasium to me. The large floor was marked for basketball, and the backstops were pulled up to the high ceiling. There were about fifteen rows of bleachers on either side and a grandstand of red theater seats at one end. The other end was the officials' platform, backed by a ceiling-to-floor curtain with the emblems and initials of the Roller Skating Rink Operators Association of America (R.S.R.O.A.) and the United States Federation of Amateur Roller Skaters (U.S.F.A.R.), the two organizations that sponsored this competition.

The Southwest Pacific Regional Championship was attended by clubs from Arizona, Nevada, and California. Winners from here went on to the nationals and then the world competitions. Donna, entering as a freestyle skater, would be skating in the Freshman Girls Singles group at one o'clock. Since there was always the possibility that competition times might be changed, as they had already done with Donna, it was a little chancy coming up on the same day as the qualifications. Most coaches brought their teams up the night before and gave them time to get acclimated. Lenny had a different philosophy.

"Coming up early only makes you more nervous. All your patterns are altered. You stay awake half the night because nothing is familiar. Better to spend the night in your own bed, drive in, and skate. If you qualify, then you will probably have a couple of days to adjust, but by then you already have a successful skate under your belt to ward off the jitters."

So having Donna arrive only two hours before her qualifications was actually within the parameters of Lenny's overall plan. Lenny's other skaters, whose qualifications were the next day, were not coming up until then.

Our contingent equaled almost half the crowd that was already assembled inside, though more people were filing in all the time. Most of our group were already wandering around inside when the Wendorfs drove up.

"She's on in an hour and a half," I said as I met them getting out of their air-conditioned Thunderbird.

"Whew, it's a furnace out here," said Leonard. "I told you it would be like this."

"Don't worry, it's cool inside."

"Good thing," he said, "because we would have turned around right now."

"Oh, Leonard, come on now," said Bernice. "We're here for Donna and the choir. Speaking of Donna, there she is right now."

I turned around to see Donna heading toward the parking lot. She waved at us and smiled as she went to the Plymouth and unlocked the door.

"Well she certainly looks calm for a girl who's going to be on the ever-lovin' spot in a few minutes," said Mr. Wendorf.

No sooner had he said this than we were shaken by a bloodcurdling shriek from Donna. By the time I got to her, she was slumped in the backseat of her grandparents' car with one hand over her face and the other holding a wavy piece of round plastic with a large hole in it. It was the recording of "The Love of God" by Netta Pearl and the Colorado Avenue Standard Christian Church Sanctuary Choir, all curled up and melted by the San Joaquin sun through the back window of a '39 Plymouth.

18

For the Love of God

"Surely someone here has another record with them," said Mrs. Wendorf.

"Doesn't Lenny have one?" I said.

Donna just kept shaking her head and crying. "He sent me out here to get mine because his was not in his briefcase."

"I'll go get him," I said.

"No, I'll go," said Matt, holding me back and moving out as fast as his healing leg would allow.

"I just knew something like this was going to happen," Donna said, staring hopelessly at the curled-up disk of vinyl in her lap. "Things were going too well."

"Now now, honey, don't give up," said Mrs. Wendorf. "There are a lot of folks here. Something will turn up."

And something about what she said started the wheels turning in my head. She was right. There *were* a lot of folks there—a lot of just the right folks, too.

Matt returned with Lenny who, when he saw the ruined record, threw his hands up in the air and began pacing back and forth in exasperation. Then he pointed to me.

"Go round everybody up. There's got to be another record in this group somewhere."

"Where shall I tell them to come?"

"We'll have to meet outside. There are no rooms available."

"Come on, Matt," I said, and we rushed off together.

There was one tree near the parking lot of the Bakersfield Civic Auditorium and everyone squeezed to get under its shade, wondering what this was all about. Some sat down on the sparse grass and the rest stood around the edges of the shade. Lenny got everyone's attention.

"Folks, we have some bad news. Unfortunately the only copy of the recording we have with us is now a melted piece of plastic. Does anyone here have a copy with them?"

There was a long silence. Then someone spoke.

"I'd be glad to go home and get mine."

"There's no time," said Lenny. "Donna skates in an hour."

"Couldn't they give her a new time, later in the afternoon?" asked Mrs. Beamering.

"I can make an appeal, but it's highly unlikely anything will happen. These judges have no reason to be flexible. Besides, in the time it would take someone to go back to Pasadena, they'll be into another event."

"What normally happens in a case like this?" asked my father.

"They have a backup recording that they play, and the contestant has to do their best to improvise, or perhaps borrow someone else's record."

There was another long, sad pause. Donna was sniffling while Granny Finley held her hand.

"Wait a minute—" I blurted out. Eyes turned to me, and I suddenly realized I had succeeded in something I had not intended: I had everyone's attention. My own private thoughts were about to intrude upon this meeting with what was becoming obvious to me, but not necessarily anyone else. Lenny was glaring at me, probably wishing, right then, that I had never come into his life. Probably thinking how much easier it would have been for him if I hadn't. He would be at these competitions right now with a predictable song and with a few skaters and their immediate families, not a caravan of buses and cars and these strange religious fanatics.

"Well?" he said. "We're waiting."

"We may not have the record," I said, "but we have everyone here . . . everyone who made that record . . . don't we? Why can't we just do the song?"

Murmurs welled up in the group as Lenny thought out loud, "A live performance . . . while Donna skates. . . ."

"I like this boy!" said Netta Pearl. "I'm game! Show me to the microphone!"

"They have an organ," chimed Milton. "I saw the console on the platform." And the murmurs rose higher in approval.

"Not so fast now," said Lenny. "You're right, Milton, they do have an organ. In fact, Dominic has been hired to play it for the dance competitions. But the problem is the judges. I can tell you right now, they'll never go for it."

"What if we just did it before they have a chance to decide whether they like the idea or not?" said Mrs. Beamering to a chorus of affirming comments.

"Donna would be disqualified," said Lenny. "No question."

"Sounds like it all rests with the judges," said another voice from the choir.

"Let's pray for the judges right now," said my father. "Pastor, would you lead us?" And all heads went down.

"Wait a minute," said Lenny and heads came back up. "You pray for them if you want; I'll go *talk* to them. In the meantime, you should be ready to sing, just in case. Sit together in the bleachers as close to the platform as you can. Milton, find Dominic and have him get the organ ready. I know he's here somewhere. The only way this *might* work is if we present the idea to the judges right before Donna skates."

He glanced at his watch. "It's twelve o'clock. I'm supposed to be turning in Donna's music right now. I'll alert them to the problem and try for a possible time slot tonight or tomorrow. If that fails, and I'm confident it will, Donna will present this 'live music' idea to the judges right before she skates. You'll have to be ready on the spot in case they go for it, but I'm pretty confident they won't." And he stepped over the legs of a few choir members sitting on the grass and headed back to the auditorium at a brisk walk. He appeared to be eager to get out of the way of our impending prayer.

"Ain't never seen a man so confident about all the wrong things," said Netta as we watched him go.

"I'm confident that the Lord has us here for a reason," said Pastor Beamering. "Let's pray." And then he led us all in a prayer, punctuated every few phrases by the "amens" of Netta Pearl—a prayer that pushed over, pulled down, and bound up judges, thrones, kingdoms, authorities, powers, dominions, rulers in heavenly places, and the devil's strongholds from here to eternity. I opened my eyes when he was done and checked to see if the Civic Auditorium was still standing.

Next, my father took over.

"All right, how many altos do we have? Altos? Line up, please. We don't have much time. Sopranos over here. Tenors? . . . Marv, thank goodness you're here. . . . Basses? . . . Come on, people," and he clapped his hands. "I know it's hot, but we need to go over this at least a couple times. The sooner we get it, the sooner we can get back inside where it's cool."

The print flowers on Netta's dress were already starting to wilt, Milton ran off to try and find Dominic, and Donna came over and grabbed my arm. Her face was bright again with hope and excitement.

"Jonathan, I can't believe this is happening! All these people! Jonathan, thank you. You are very brave." She kissed me on the cheek and turned and headed back to the auditorium.

The choir went through "The Love of God" a couple times with Netta until my father was satisfied that they remembered it. By the end of the second time through, a small audience had formed and applauded the parking lot performance. Then we all went inside.

At the opposite end from where the judges sat was an area, just outside the rink wall, which served as a sort of "on-deck circle" for the skaters. Only the next three skaters and their coaches were allowed in there, but Matt and I sat near it on the edge of the bleachers where we could see and hear what was going on. Seven girls were skating in the Freshman Girls Singles competition, and Donna was number three.

At a quarter to one she came out sparkling in her mother's outfit. She had one new addition: a tiara in her hair made of silk flower petals that reminded me of the corsage. I looked down the bleachers to where my mother was sitting in what was now the sanctuary choir section, and she must have thought of it at the same time because she stood up and pointed at the box in her hand. I ran around behind the grandstand and brought it back to Donna.

She loved it so much she almost came apart. She put it on her wrist and twirled with it overhead and told me it was the most beautiful thing she had ever seen. Then Lenny saw it and he came apart too.

"No, absolutely not," and he glared at me and then back at Donna. "How could you possibly think of skating with something like that on your arm?"

Donna kept giving him the most pleading looks, but it was no use.

"Take it off!" he demanded in a voice so mean that she looked like she was going to cry.

I felt awful. I wished I had never given it to her. What a terrible time this was turning out to be for her. I began to wonder how she was going to be able to skate at all with her emotions as torn as they were right then.

A few minutes later they called for the warm-up, and all seven girls went out onto the floor to loosen up for four and a half minutes, during which time you could tell a lot about them. Donna and one other girl both had natural grace. The others appeared to be jerky in their movements. You could probably decide the finalists just by watching them warm up. This seemed to relax Donna a little and give her some confidence.

Finally, after they were all off the floor and the first three contestants were ready, a voice came over the loudspeaker: "And now for our first contestant in the Freshman Girls Singles competition, we have from Las Vegas, Nevada, Miss Percy Engleman!"

Percy came out to light applause and bowed in the center of the rink. She struck her opening pose as the first strains of "Moon River" came over the speakers. She skated well, but very mechanically, with little connection to the music. She could probably have skated just as well to any piece of music and done the three jumps and one twirl she attempted. She skated off to a polite round of applause.

Next was a girl from Sacramento. I didn't get her name, but the song was "Moon River" again. I was thinking only of Donna coming up next and wondering what she was thinking. At one point she bowed her head and prayed, and when she did, I prayed too. I opened my eyes a minute later to see her looking right at me.

"Thank you," she said.

"You'll do great!" I said.

She was taking deep breaths now and her chest would fill up and then collapse suddenly as she dropped her shoulders and let the air out with a sharp heave. The Sacramento girl finished and Lenny started giving Donna her last-minute instructions. He was speaking softly, up close to her, so I couldn't hear much. She listened with a stern face, unmoving.

"What's he saying?" said Matt.

"I think he's telling her what to tell the judges about the record and the choir and everything."

"Sure hope this works," said Matt.

"Me too."

"Contestant number three, from Pasadena, California, Miss Donna Callaway."

There was thunderous applause, relatively speaking, from Donna's supporters as she skated directly to the judges' table at the other end of the rink. They were on the ground floor with a red, white, and blue bunting covering the front of their table. Behind them on a riser was the announcer, the organ console, and the person playing the records.

"If I had his job, I'd do something about song selection," said Matt. "If I hear 'Moon River' one more time I'm gonna puke."

"Yeah, well in his job you gotta play what they give you. Lenny was right. Donna wanted to do 'Moon River' in the beginning, and he said everyone would be doing it."

"If I had that guy's job I'd pop something on like 'Duke of Earl' just to see what happens. That would mess them up, huh?"

It sure would, and from the looks of it, Donna was about to be messed up by that very thing—skating to a song she had not planned for. You could read the writing on the wall from the other side of the rink. Since she started talking to them, the judges' heads hadn't gone any direction but side to side. Side to side. Side to side. Donna turned around and skated back to Lenny, who met her at the rail right in front of us.

"I can't do it," she said, on the verge of tears again, but maintaining a regal posture.

"Yes you can, Donna. What's the song?"

"The theme from 'Exodus.' "

"That's fine. Now listen to me. Skate your routine from start to finish."

"But I can't," Donna protested. "I have to skate to the music. If I can't follow the music, I can't skate."

"Yes you can, Donna. Ignore the music. Just stick to your routine."

"Let me skate to the song with the choir and Netta like we talked about. I don't care about qualifying anymore. I just want to do my routine to this song—for the audience and for everyone who came up here."

"Donna," Lenny put his hands on her shoulders and addressed her nose to nose, "now listen to me. Pay no attention to the music. Remember what I told you: they're looking for content and performance. On any normal day you're better than any of these girls here. You watched them warm up. If you skate well, you'll qualify, and by the final we'll have 500 records here, and the Mormon Tabernacle Choir if you want!"

"I don't want the Mormon Tabernacle Choir. I want Netta Pearl and the Colorado Avenue Stand—"

"I know, I know," interrupted Lenny. "I was just kidding. Donna, just skate. You'll do the song for the finals."

Donna managed a tough little smile and turned to skate toward the middle of the rink. She wiped under her eyes, heaved her shoulders one more time, and took up her sculptured opening position. When the theme from "Exodus" began, she went immediately into a dramatic twirl which went beautifully with the opening cymbal crescendo of the music, but that was not in her routine. Nor was anything else she did from that point on. I looked over at Lenny and he already had an angry look on his face, even though Donna had started out so well.

"No," I heard him say under his breath. "Stick to the routine." But Donna had other ideas, and for the opening minute they worked surprisingly well. She came out of her twirl with a smooth flourish at the cymbal crash that brought spontaneous applause from an audience eager to acknowledge any kind of success amidst an obvious challenge. They did not know what was wrong, but they knew Donna was fighting something—that she was good, but something was in her way.

Her first jump was right on target as well, and that too met with applause that seemed to give us hope. So far she was in another league from the first two skaters. But that euphoria was short-lived. Her second jump didn't connect at all with the music, and that seemed to visibly deflate her. Donna had practiced so long and hard with music that she was married to it. She could not separate a routine from the music that drove it. It was the only way she could skate. She had to express what she heard, and when she did not know what was coming, she fell apart. She did the best she could with what she remembered of the hit version of "Exodus," but the third jump was so far out of sync that it landed her in a heap on the floor.

For a while the music played on to a hushed crowd.

"Get up," I heard Lenny say, and I thought of Donna's mother—locked in some place for crazy people, still on the floor after all these years.

"Get up," I said under my breath. "Get up, Donna!"

But Donna didn't move.

"Is she hurt?" said Matt.

She wasn't crying or grabbing on to any part of her body like you would expect if she had injured herself. She was simply slumped over like a rag doll, like a puppet without strings, as if someone or something had sucked the life out of her and she had folded on the spot, all of her limbs going every which way.

I knew Donna was not hurt, at least not physically. Lenny knew too, and I'm sure that's why he did not run out immediately to try and help her. If she was not going to get up, nothing he could do or say would change that. She would have to decide this on her own. It was not a matter of broken bones. It was something more important than that. It was a broken spirit.

Suddenly I knew what I had to do. It was very simple really, though not that simple to do. It was deathly quiet now. The DJ had lifted the needle off of Ferrante & Teicher's version of "Exodus," and I realized that if Donna couldn't get up, I had to get up for her. Perhaps, in some small way, I could convey some courage by standing with her. When I did, the old grandstands squeaked and echoed through the silent hall and all eyes turned in my direction. I stood there for what seemed like a long time, but that was only because that simple act started a chain reaction of events that still move by the walls of my memory in slow motion as if time has stopped to savor each one of them.

The first thing was that my lonely squeak was joined by others in the hall—a few random creakings that gradually swelled into a huge chorus of rattling grandstands as the entire crowd got to its feet. I noticed that my mother, Mayor Wilson, and Mrs. Beamering were among the first to stand.

Then I heard the familiar booming voice of Pastor Beamering. He started quoting Scripture, of all things, and that voice, which at other times in public places had been such an embarrassment to me, seemed at this time the most appropriate thing that could happen.

" 'Wherefore seeing we also are compassed about with so great a cloud of witnesses,' " he began, " 'let us lay aside every weight, and the sin which doth so easily beset us, and let us run with patience the race that is set before us.' "

His voice boomed like it was amplified. It seemed to fall from the middle of the ceiling. It fell on Donna and awakened her spirit enough to get her sitting up.

" 'Looking unto Jesus,' " Pastor Beamering continued, quoting that familiar benediction, " 'the author and finisher of our faith; who for the joy that was set before him endured the cross, despising the shame, and is set down at the right hand of the throne of God.' "

That made me immediately think about angels. Whenever Pastor Beamering referred to the throne of God, I always imagined angels around that throne, and I wondered if angels were around Donna right then.

Another hush fell on the crowd when he finished. Everyone in the hall was standing except Donna, the three judges, and Granny Finley, or so I thought. I thought of Granny Finley right then because she was the next one to break the silence.

"Esther!" came that familiar voice barking out of the still-
ness. "Esther," she repeated, "get up!"

I strained, with the rest of the crowd, to try and see where
the voice was coming from. I found an empty wheelchair before I found Granny, for she had gotten two strong men from
the church to lift her up out of it and take her right up to the
railing of the rink where her voice and her vision could address her granddaughter.

And yet it was not her granddaughter she was speaking to.
Her gaze was not at Donna, but somewhere across to the opposite side of the rink.

"Esther?" I said under my breath.

"Who's Esther?" said Matt.

"Esther," I repeated. "Esther Callaway! Matt, it's Donna's
mother! She must be here!"

Matt didn't know the story so he did not understand the
significance; he just looked puzzled.

For the next few minutes everyone forgot about Donna
and followed Granny Finley's gaze to the other side of the
rink where a blond woman sat in a wheelchair, locked in the
grip of Granny's stare. Suddenly it was not Donna we were
pulling for, but Donna's mother, because she was trying, with
every ounce of her strength, to get up out of her wheelchair.
The crowd was focused on her as if they knew. Did they? Did
they know it was this woman that Donna was skating for? Did
they know she was the one who had not been able to get up
for nine years?

Esther Callaway's arms shook as she pushed the dead
weight of her body up out of the chair. Her jaw was set in
determination, and the rest of her face distorted itself through
the strain of her efforts. She got her arms straight, but her
lower body flew out in front of her, uncontrolled. Her legs
were not paralyzed like Granny Finley's; they had merely become useless through a mental paralysis—a way of thinking
that had held her captive for so long.

Two spectators helped steady her, but she brushed them

off, somehow managing to get her balance long enough to take two short, faltering steps to the railing, where she grabbed on and straightened herself with a great air of dignity and a determined grace. There she stood, at the rail, alone, shaking and looking straight at Donna.

"Glow-ry!" said Netta Pearl under her breath but loud enough to be heard in the hall. She didn't know the story either, but she knew a healing when she saw one.

Donna and her mother were now locked in each other's gaze, reunited after so many years in front of all these witnesses. Though in their eyes, the witnesses fell away right then. For an instant it seemed there was just the two of them in the whole world.

I saw Donna's lips move slowly, as if she were awaking from a trance. "Mama" was what I'm sure she said, though there was no sound. Esther Callaway held her own against the rail and finally spoke through the tears in her voice.

"Baby," she said, and immediately I thought of her note to Donna that began the same way. She must have called her this in her mind all along.

"Get up!"

Though the tears were welling up in Donna's eyes—tears of joy I was sure—at those words they went away, and a bright, confident smile swept across her face. Suddenly those magical words reminded her of where she was and what she was doing—indeed, of what she was yet to do.

Slowly, Donna stood up, and those who were there will confirm this: there was something odd about the way she did this. If you were to describe it as Donna getting up under her own power, you could not fully account for the strange way in which her body rose up off the floor. But if you explained it as Donna being lifted up by some invisible power, you would have it perfectly in your imagination—the way it looked to the undiscerning eye. Netta Pearl later said she saw them—two tall angels gently lifting Donna up by her arms— saw it as plainly as she saw the angels leave with her husband that night God took him home. And Donna herself will swear to it: that someone got a hold of her under her arms, lifted her up, and placed her on her wheels.

And as she rose, music started to fall from the rafters of the building, because that's where the organ speakers were housed.

"It's Milton!" said Matt. "He's at the organ."

"Way to go Milton!" I said.

The announcer ran over to the organ to try and do something about this unauthorized intrusion, but Dominic stopped him. The poor gentleman then turned around to get back to his beloved microphone, only to find a very large Negro woman in a flowery dress gripping it with both hands, leaving him no choice but to stand there helplessly.

The choir, of course, was already up with everyone else in the auditorium, but my father got a chair and stood up on it so he could get their attention. He had that look in his eye that he gets when he is about to lead a performance. It's a look that brings the best out of him and out of everyone else.

The whole building was suddenly caught up in excitement and anticipation. Donna was going to skate. The organ was playing. Netta Pearl was going to sing. The choir was going to back her up. Nothing was going to stop any of them now, and had the judges tried, they would have been overruled by the entire assembly still on their feet and waiting.

Milton hadn't started the official introduction to the song yet; he was ad-libbing something that sounded a little like "The Love of God" but wasn't quite it, like he always did in church when he was filling in between things.

Through all of this the announcer stood stone-faced, and the judges kept shaking their heads as if their necks were only jointed to move sideways. They pushed themselves away from the table and crossed their arms in front of their bodies as if to wash their hands of whatever was going to happen next, making it perfectly clear that nothing, after Donna's fall, would have any bearing on the official results of this competition.

Finally, Donna skated out toward the center of the rink, ready to take up her starting position once more. But suddenly she stopped short of it, as if she had forgotten something. Milton kept improvising and the audience dangled on a precipice of emotion. Then she turned and skated over to Lenny with her arm out in front of her, pointing to her wrist.

"My corsage, please," I heard her say proudly.

Lenny had no choice but to get it for her. And why not? The judges didn't matter anymore. Rules were out the window. Winning and losing were irrelevant. Donna was ready to skate, and she could skate it any way she wanted.

And did she skate! She skated up one side of the rink and down the other. She skated with a strength and a grace that exceeded anything I had ever seen her do. She skated into the darkest unknown of her abandoned childhood, throwing her body down, down, down, until she was a tiny ball spinning in a fetal position . . . and suddenly, when Netta sang the words, "The love of God . . . ," she spun out of that darkness as if she had a gleaming ball of light in her hands which she flung out against the wall of that homely auditorium where it cascaded down like glittering fireworks that became the sequins of her dress as she caught them and landed effortlessly from a double spin on those trained, muscular legs.

She skated into the deep psychological depression of a woman who for nine years had forgotten how to get up . . . at least until today. Yes, she skated for her mother, and her mother reveled in her every move—every nuance of perfection. And while strong arms held her grandmother up like Moses against the Amalekites, she skated for the lifeless legs of Murietta Finley, and the heart of Murietta Finley skated within her.

And as I watched her, she seemed to skate for me too—right into the Ben-shaped vacuum in my life, and with one wave of her outstretched hands she cleared it of the cobwebs of anger and bitterness that had built up there and replaced the emptiness with a sense of purpose and gratitude—with the knowledge that I had helped her come to this moment just as Ben had helped me, so many times, out of my comfortable loneliness. It was then that I realized I didn't need Ben anymore—didn't need to miss Ben anymore. I had Ben, in that all the things he had been for me, I was now learning to be for myself, and for someone else besides me. Ben was here. He would always be here—I knew that now—challenging me and testing me and making sure I did not hide.

And I suppose if anyone else there that day were telling this story, they would tell you where it was that Donna skated to in their own life, because that was the way it was. Every lonely, awful place in your life that day became a place that Donna found. She found it, skated into it without even asking, and came back out victorious. We all saw ourselves somewhere in what she accomplished, because her victory was our victory.

The irony of all this was that Donna was disqualified by the judges for falling on the prescribed number. It hardly mattered. Not to Donna, not to Esther Callaway, not to Granny Finley, not to Netta or Milton, not to Pastor Beamering or my father, not to the choir, not to me, and not to the crowd who stayed on their feet for minutes, cheering her performance. Bouquets of flowers rained down from the grandstands—flowers intended for the winners but they went to Donna instead.

Even Lenny was pleased, because Donna had accomplished what he always told her to strive for: to skate the best she knew how. And he knew, just like everyone knew, including the judges, that Donna could never skate any better than she skated that day. It was said that no one could.

And besides, Lenny had to like it. She kept to her routine. The only thing she changed was the very end. She was supposed to end kneeling. Instead, she ended with a spin that seemed to go on forever. And though her body was turning like an eggbeater, her arm, which she held straight up, seemed to move in slow motion, almost as if it were not attached. And on her wrist, turning softly as her head and shoulders fell back away from it, was the beautiful white orchid corsage I had given her, perfectly intact.

JOHN FISCHER was born in Pasadena, California, in 1947. He attended Lake Avenue Congregational Church through high school and loved going to the all-church skates at the Moonlight Rollerway. He graduated from Wheaton College in Wheaton, Illinois, and has lived in the San Francisco Bay area and in Newbury, Massachusetts.

Besides being an author, he has published eleven albums of original songs in the genre now known as contemporary Christian music. Many of his songs, such as "Love Him in the Morning," and "Have You Seen Jesus My Lord?" are now camp and youth group favorites.

John speaks and sings nationally at churches, retreats, and colleges, and his insightful columns in *Contemporary Christian Music* magazine have been a favorite monthly feature since 1980.

He now resides in Dana Point, California, with his wife, Marti, and their two children, Christopher and Anne, who, of course, are avid Rollerbladers.

Acknowledgments

Three books on roller skating were valuable and fascinating resources to me for this story. *Winning Roller Skating*, by Randy Dayney (Chicago: Contemporary Books, Inc., 1976); *The Complete Book of Roller Skating*, by Ann-Victoria Phillips (New York: Workman Publishing, 1979); and most importantly, *The Wonderful World of Roller Skating*, by David Roggensack (New York: Everest House, 1980) from which I gleaned the quote in Chapter 10.

I am indebted to Bob LaBriola of the Fountain Valley Skating Center in Fountain Valley, California, for educating me on skating championships circa 1961, and for enduring the interruptions of a number of phone calls for follow-up details. I was also thrilled to find an actual program of the original 1942 Skating Vanities, starring Gloria Nord, at Sports Books in Los Angeles, and I have it now cherished perpetually in plastic wrap. Attempts to find the attractive Ms. Nord herself came up empty, even though she resided in nearby Newport Beach as recently as 1980. From the looks of her picture at 60, in David Roggensack's book, she would be a young 72 at this printing.

I would like to thank Clark Gassman and Bill Cole who served as resources for what the recording business was like in Los Angeles in 1961, and, yes, thanks to Loren Whitney himself, obviously an expert on the placement of the sixteen-foot organ pipes in his own studio—a studio which has since been sold. Thanks again to Dr. J. Jones Stewart for medical advice, and a special thanks to Gay Magistro for a letter to Anne, our daughter, which I borrowed almost word-forword to create a very special note accompanying Donna's skating outfit.

Finally, thanks are in order to Kathy Cunningham for reading the manuscript, to Judith Markham for editing it, and to my children, Christopher and Anne, who were probably my most ruthless critics, being closest to the ages of the most important characters in this story. I am also indebted to Noel Stookey, whose exuberant support of *Saint Ben* has helped keep me fanning the fires of fiction. And most of all, to my wife, my deepest acknowledgments. Let the world know, all my best ideas are yours, Marti.

One final note to those who may be '60s music buffs. I must confess to stretching one piece of history for the purposes of my story. Booker T. and the M.G.'s were not famous until 1962 when their first hit, "Green Onions," went to number three on the charts. The Mar-Keys, who later became the M.G.'s when they hooked up with Booker T., would have probably been more familiar to Matthew and Jonathan when this story takes place in late 1961 when they had their own number three hit, "Last Night." It's conceivable that Booker T. and the Mar-Keys might have teamed up by late '61 and gotten some air-play and recognition as Booker T. and the M.G.'s, but not likely. That's something that probably only Booker T. Jones and Casey Kasem know for sure.